Catherine Tinley has loved reading and writing since childhood, and has a particular fondness for love, romance and happy endings. She lives in Ireland with her husband, children, dog and kitten, and can be reached at catherinetinley.com, as well as through Facebook and on Twitter @CatherineTinley.

MISS ROSE AND THE VEXING VISCOUNT

Catherine Tinley

MILLS & BOON

First published in Great Britain 2023
by Mills & Boon, an imprint of HarperCollins*Publishers* Ltd,
1 London Bridge Street, London, SE1 9GF

www.harpercollins.co.uk

HarperCollins*Publishers*, Macken House, 39/40 Mayor Street Upper, Dublin 1, D01 C9W8, Ireland

Miss Rose and the Vexing Viscount © 2023 Catherine Tinley

ISBN: 978-0-263-30541-8

10/23

This book is produced from independently certified FSC™ paper to ensure responsible forest management.
For more information visit: www.harpercollins.co.uk/green.

Printed and Bound in the UK using 100% Renewable Electricity at CPI Group (UK) Ltd, Croydon, CR0 4YY

For my amazing mammy, Sheila, who will
dance merrily alongside us for a little longer.

Prologue

Run! Maria hurried on as quickly as her ungainly gait would allow. Anxiously glancing over her shoulder, at every moment she expected *them* to appear, to find her. If they even *saw* her again they would surely recognise her…and then she and her unborn child could be in as much danger as her beloved—

No! Thoughts of him could overwhelm her.

Grief. Agony. Loss.

She must be strong now, for his child.

Cursing again the misfortune that had brought her enemies to the same inn as the stagecoach she had been travelling in, Maria scuttled out of the inn yard and out into the narrow village street, desperately hoping they would have no reason to return immediately to their carriage.

Thankfully she had recognised the crest on their well-sprung coach through the small window and had immediately risen, cloak, bonnet, and reticule in hand, making it out through the side door just as they were entering from the yard. Stupidly she had glanced back just as they were entering and for an instant her eyes had met the cold blue gaze of the woman, although thankfully her gaze had seemed to pass over Maria with disinterest.

But I was seen.

In a minute, or two, or ten, the woman might suddenly realise whom she had laid eyes upon, and might wonder why she was here, alone, and dressed as she was. If the woman realised what was occurring then Maria might be in real danger.

This misfortune was, she realised, not so much coincidence as lack of foresight on her part. It was the Great North Road, after all, and this the last stop before Edinburgh. Most of the carriages stopped here, whether a well-sprung private conveyance like the one belonging to her foes, or the common stagecoach. It had always been possible that she might see someone who knew her at one of these stops. The true calamity was the coincidence that had brought precisely the people who meant her harm to this very inn today.

Making her way through the village, Maria now found herself amid fields and hedgerows. Having no idea where the twisting road led, she continued on regardless, anxious to put as much distance as possible between herself and her enemies.

Were they pursuing her? Had they somehow discovered the truth? Or had fate simply made them choose to travel at the same time as her? They would likely be going to the house in Newtown, she realised. A house she had never seen, but had once hoped to visit, perhaps even to make her home. She shuddered. How abruptly her dreams had been shattered, rudely stolen by those who hid their evil behind a veneer of civilisation.

The stagecoach passengers would even now be enjoying a quick bite and a visit to the retiring room. Twenty minutes, the driver had said. If they were not back in the coach on time it would leave without them. Knowing she could not have hidden from her enemies in such a small inn and yard for even ten minutes, Maria had realised instantly that she would have to abandon her stagecoach journey and try to find another way to reach the city.

Ahead was a crossroads. Linton, the painted sign declared, other destinations also highlighted. Gifford. Lennoxlove. Haddington, whence she had come.

Lennoxlove.

She thought for a moment.

Lennox. Love. Maria Lennox.

Trying it out in her mind, she nodded…

It is as good a name as any.

Scurrying past the sign, she took the narrower road. The quieter one. Somewhere here she would find shelter. An abandoned cottage, perhaps, or a barn. A place to hide for a night or two, until she was certain the danger had passed.

On she went, her ears constantly alert for any sounds of pursuit. Hopefully they had not taken her under their lofty notice. Well, why would they? The voice of reason within offered her some reassurance. Dressed in dowdy clothes, clutching a serving maid's cloak and an old bonnet… No, she would have meant nothing to them…a random woman at a coaching inn. And yet terror consumed her still. For if they recognised her, they might surely deduce what had happened.

For months she had remained hidden, until word had come that her location might be known, that those who meant her harm might be on their way. She could have sought refuge with the people who loved her yet, although to do so might have brought them, too, to harm. And so, rightly or wrongly, she had pursued this course—let go her faithful servant, told no one her intentions, and bought a ticket for the stagecoach to Scotland.

He had always loved it here, had spoken many times of them making their home here. And of course they had travelled to Scotland once before… She shook her head. Would her romantical notions prove to be her downfall?

Abruptly, she stopped stock still in the centre of the road.

My trunk!

Picturing it strapped onto the roof of the stagecoach, she realised that she had no chance of getting it back. Why, even now the brief comfort break at the inn would be ending, the driver calling to all his passengers to retake their places. Would they look for her, even briefly? No, probably not. And when the coach made it to Edinburgh, its final destination, no doubt the coachman and his boy would sell off her things, and discard items of no value.

No value.

The miniatures—including the ones of Mama and Papa, gone. Her hidden papers, gone. The letters he had sent her, gone. All but one. She touched her reticule, reassured by the crackle of parchment inside. The last letter. The one that had bade her run, run far away. And she had done so. Instinctively she had run to Scotland, trying to reach the city where he had been so happy as a child. Before everything changed.

Fumbling, she checked inside her silk reticule once more. Her earrings, a gift from her grandmother, were still there, contained within a tiny wooden box. Swiftly she checked for the other item, then expelled a breath. The folded velvet cloth was safe, its contents protected. This was a treasure too precious for her trunk. A treasure so distinctive, so unusual, that it could bring doom upon her. A treasure she must not lose.

'You are my true treasure,' she murmured, placing her hand over her swollen belly. 'You are everything to me now, for there is no one else.' Her love was gone, and she had even turned away from her family. For answer, a sudden pain gripped her. As it slowly built to a crescendo, she gasped in fear. It was too soon! By her best estimate, she was a little more than seven months along.

'No!' As soon as the surge of pain eased, she forced

herself to walk again. The babe would need warmth and shelter. She could not give birth to her first and only child out here, in the middle of nowhere! The February air was cold, and she could see her breath. There would be frost tonight.

She managed to trudge another mile, as the sun goldened to the west and the pains came and went. Oh, she had been niggling for days—false labour, they called it—but had thought nothing of it, her pregnancy not being far enough advanced to think it might be her time. Fear and worry had stilled the progress of the painful surges each time they had come. But no more. This baby—likely to be large and healthy, judging by the comments other women had made about her seven-month belly—had decided it was time to be born, and nothing was going to stop it.

She paused. To her right was an impressive entranceway, large gates open and a well-tended driveway beckoning her in. A crest worked into the wrought iron caught her eye. It was an eagle, wings spread wide as if to offer protection. Abruptly, she made her decision. Here there would be cottages and barns, byres and woodsheds. Here she might be able to bear her child in safety.

Gravel crunched beneath her feet as she trudged along the drive. Dimly she could see a large mansion ahead, solidly built in red sandstone, multiple windows warm with candlelight, serving to emphasise her sense of being alone, cold, and abandoned. Dusk was now fading to darkness, and she could not see where to put her feet. Another pain took her and she moaned, stopping to rock gently from side to side.

'Who is there?' The voice was sharp and she blinked as a lantern was thrust in her face.

It was too much. The sudden shock, after all she had endured, brought faintness, swift and absolute. The world went black.

Chapter One

*Belvedere School for Young Ladies,
Elgin, Scotland, February 1812*

'Is that everything?'

Rose nodded as Agnes, the maid-of-all-work at Belvedere School, closed the lid on her trunk, slamming it with a finality that made her jump. 'Thank you, Agnes,' she murmured softly. 'I shall miss you.'

'Aye, get away with you, miss! When you are about to finally go out in the world, to mingle with your own kind and go where you will! Why should you miss me, or this place? What an adventure!'

Adventure?

The very notion of leaving Belvedere, the school that had been her home for nigh on eleven years, was causing a horrible sick feeling in Rose's stomach. 'Izzy might think it so. I should much rather stay here, where everything is familiar.'

'Miss Isobel has a taste for adventure, and that is the truth!' Agnes cocked her head to one side, reflecting. 'You are all three different. Isobel meets a challenge head-on, Annabelle will stay calm and manage it, while *you*, Miss Rosabella—'

'I am likely to be found cowering in a corner waiting for my sisters to solve the problem!'

Agnes shook her head. 'No. You are the one who will think of people's feelings as you work it out. If Annabelle is the mind and Isobel the might, then you are the heart.'

Tears pricked Rose's eyes. 'What a beautiful thing to say!' Impulsively, she hugged Agnes. 'Thank you, Agnes!'

Donning her gloves and bonnet and picking up the reticule she had made for herself in sewing class just last year, she took a final look around the bedchamber that had been hers and her sisters' since they had come here as young girls. Three narrow beds. A shared garderobe. The dormer window with its patch of sky.

I might never see this place again.

Swallowing hard, she descended to the parlour, where her sisters waited.

London

'*Three* sisters? *Three* of them? And you accepted?' Lord James Arthur Henry Drummond, the Viscount Ashbourne, gentleman about town and darling of the *ton*, could scarce believe what he was hearing.

'My brother does not often request a favour from me. I thought—' His aunt's expression was abruptly crestfallen at his reaction. 'Why, do you think I ought not to have agreed?'

James shrugged. 'The decision is yours, Aunt.' He gestured about him, at the beautifully appointed drawing room in his Mayfair home. 'As Dowager Viscountess you are mistress of Ashbourne House and you are of course free to entertain any guests you choose. It is only—'

'Yes?'

There was an anxious crease in her forehead.

Lord, she has not thought this through at all!

'Not one but *three* giggling girls, all to be launched at once, Aunt? You know how often we have despaired at the antics of the maidens in the marriage mart! They flirt, and dissemble, and have not a single interesting thing to say! And yet here you are, having agreed to take on *three* of them. I—' He shook his head. 'I cannot understand it! Have they no mother of their own to launch them in society?'

'Orphans!' she declared sadly. 'My brother is their guardian, but as he rightly points out, he is not a suitable person to sponsor their season. As you know he is a bachelor, and never leaves Scotland. Why, you have never even met him!' She sighed. 'Indeed I have only seen Ian twice in the last…' She thought for a moment. 'Lord, has it been twelve years since I saw him in Edinburgh?'

'Indeed, I had almost forgotten you had a brother, I must admit, Aunt. When you married my uncle *we* became your family. Me, and my parents, and my uncle.'

She patted his hand affectionately. 'And I could not have asked for better.' She shook her head. 'My husband is gone now, and your parents too. Now I have only you…and my brother. And he so rarely asks anything of me that I feel obligated to do this for him. It is my duty.'

Duty.

They both knew the importance of family loyalty, of protecting and preserving the links and the honour that came with one's family name. James's aunt had become Lady Ashbourne when she had married his father's older brother, but she would always, he supposed, feel loyalty to her maiden name, and to her only blood kin.

'I do understand that, Aunt. But does he expect you to find husbands for all three of them? In *one season*?' At her hesitant nod, he made an exasperated sound. 'But most families launch their girls in turn, not allowing the second her debut until the eldest is betrothed.' A new thought occurred to him. 'Their dowries?'

She grimaced. 'No more than respectable. But he assures me of their great beauty and charming demeanour!'

'And you believe him?'

Her eyes widened. 'It is true that sometimes people may exaggerate a little…'

'A little? We have both exclaimed at the so-called beauties who turn out to be little more than passably attractive. And those who are indeed fair of face…' His voice tailed off, knowing she would understand him.

'Are too often spoiled, and pert, and throw tantrums at the smallest inconvenience. I know, I know…' She put a hand to her head. 'But what am I to do? It is all arranged. He expects them to travel to London by the end of the month.'

'Can you not write back and tell him you have changed your mind?'

'No. It is too late. I cannot let him down.' She squared her shoulders. 'I shall just have to make the best of it. It is only for one season, after all.'

James stifled a sigh. Since inheriting the title on his uncle's death two years ago he had enjoyed a peaceful existence. His aunt kept house for him, and he was free to pursue his own interests with a minimum of inconvenience. Having lost both his parents and his uncle in the same carriage accident that awful night, he had come into his responsibilities unexpectedly, and abruptly.

His blood ran cold as he recalled that night—the sensation a familiar one. His aunt had been unwell and had missed the party, while he himself had been out carousing with his friends when word came. Suddenly sober, he had been taken to a scene of utter devastation. The carriage had overturned and rolled into a lake, and the sight of the bodies of three of the people he loved the most had never left him.

That night had changed him for ever—had turned him from carefree and reckless to being prudent and cautious. Life was precious, and might be shorter than anyone knew. It was important to enjoy one's activities, yes, but not to make decisions in haste or without consideration. Unfortunately he suspected his aunt had made this particular decision in an ill-considered manner—driven by a sense of duty to her brother.

She should have discussed it with me.

He was certain he might have dissuaded her—while of course respecting her right to entertain as she saw fit in Ashbourne House.

He sighed inwardly. Due to his aunt's rash decision to sponsor not one but *three* debutantes, he now understood that for this season his peace was to be disturbed. Not only that, but he would doubtless be called upon to support his kind-hearted aunt through whatever mischief and mayhem these girls would bring.

Well, he thought grimly, *if they think to run my beloved aunt ragged, they will soon learn that I shall have something to say about it!*

Elgin, Scotland

Rose sat in Mr Marnoch's office, as she had regularly these past few years, and reflected on the fact that things were undeniably different this time. Their guardian, a lawyer in his middle years with a kind smile and a jocular manner, was altogether more serious than usual today. His demeanour was sober, his smile absent. Exchanging glances with Izzy and Anna, Rose understood they both felt it too.

'Welcome, girls, welcome! And so this day is finally upon us!' He looked from one to the other. 'Tell me, which of you is which?'

They told him, reminding him that they tended to wear certain colours in order to help others tell them apart. To Rose, Anna's face was entirely different to Izzy's, and to Rose's own, but they were undeniably identical triplets. Only the staff and students in Belvedere had learned to distinguish between them. Everyone else seemed to see them as a single entity rather than individuals. Today Anna was wearing her usual cool blue, bringing out her azure eyes and reflecting her self-contained, calm demeanour. Izzy's muslin was in white, with jonquil-and-green flowers embroidered riotously at the hem and bodice by her own hand.

As for Rose, she was in her usual pink. Both she and Anna occasionally ventured into lavender and lilac shades, but Rose had never forgotten hearing that the ribbon the midwife had tied around her wrist at birth had been pink, and which had inspired Mama to name her Rosabella. The wrist-ribbons—the midwife's habit at any birth involving more than one baby—had not only served to help them know for certain their birth order, but had also been the reasoning behind the girls' chosen colours.

'You are all beautiful,' Mama had said, many times. 'My three miracles! I was determined you would all have that beauty in your names.'

Hence, *Belle*. Annabelle, Isobel, and Rosabella. Or Anna, Izzy, and Rose for short.

'As you are aware, your mother…' Mr Marnoch began, and Rose sat up straighter. He was one of the few people who had known Mama, and Rose always hungered for any information he might share with them. 'Mrs Lennox made me your guardian over ten years ago once she knew her days were numbered, and I must say it has been a privilege to watch you grow from girls into young women.'

The silence stretched, Rose aware that Anna and Izzy were just as rapt as she was.

'Yesterday you turned twenty-one, and you have left Belvedere School for the last time. Your mother cared for you deeply, as I well know, for she clerked for me for almost five years. She left no clear instructions, but as your guardian I have arranged for you to travel to London, to be presented at Court and to enjoy the delights of the season. You will be sponsored by my widowed sister, Lady Ashbourne. She married a viscount, you know.' He was unable to hide the pride from his voice at his sister's advantageous marriage, but inwardly, Rose was devastated.

To leave Scotland! To go somewhere new and frightening and...and different?

'We had not been aware of this possibility, Mr Marnoch.' Anna's tone was neutral. 'We had talked of finding positions near here. In Elgin itself, or possibly in Inverness.'

'Positions? You thought you might *work*?' Anna might as well have suggested a career on the stage, judging by the horror in his expression. 'Never! You are young ladies—daughters of a lady! You are not of the class who should work!'

'But Mama worked!' Izzy's tone was mutinous. 'She worked for you!'

'Your mama's circumstances were such that—but she was of gentle birth.' Mr Marnoch was firm in his assertion.

'Well then,' asked Anna, practical as ever, 'if we do not work, how are we to survive? Belvedere was our home. We had food and shelter and safety there. And despite being "young ladies", we are not rich, I think, and so it makes sense that we should each follow a profession. We have talked about it at length.'

They had, and Rose, whose talent was for instructing the younger girls at Belvedere, had dreamed of being a teacher. Indeed, she had already raised the matter with Miss Logie, the Belvedere headmistress, who had seemed interested in employing her, but who had warned that they needed permission from their guardian before any of them could take up work.

'As to that…' Mr Marnoch flushed slightly, and Rose abruptly had the sense he was dissembling. *But why?* 'You each have a small dowry—no more than respectable, I'm afraid. Plus I am sending my sister an allowance for you to be dressed appropriately in London. You would like that, would you not?'

Anna shrugged. 'We have not been raised to value the fripperies of fashion, but instead to value good sense, and understanding, and kindness to others.'

'Although wearing new dresses might be entertaining!' Izzy added, mischief dancing in her eyes. 'I think a trip to London would be delightful!'

I must speak up, or this will all happen without my voice being heard.

Gathering her courage, Rose offered tentatively, 'I should much prefer to stay here.'

Mr Marnoch paused, looking from one to the other, then shook his head. 'Your mother was a singular woman,' he declared finally, 'with a strong mind of her own. It is hardly surprising that you are like her in this regard, by which I mean that you have decided opinions. The difficulty is that you seem to be at odds on this matter.'

It was true. Izzy seemed eager to travel all the way to London, to mingle with strangers and be out in society. Did that not involve being presented before the Queen herself? The notion gave Rose the shudders. In truth, she would be content never to leave Belvedere School, spending her life amid her students and her beloved books. Belvedere was safe. London was decidedly not.

Stealing a glance at Anna, Rose saw a thoughtful expression on her face. Anna always led from her head rather than her heart. No doubt she would be coolly considering the advantages and disadvantages of Mr Marnoch's scheme.

I may well be outnumbered here.

Their guardian was not done. Nodding to himself, he opened a drawer under his desk and withdrew three folded papers. 'Very well. If the usual inducements will not work, I shall provide you with an added incentive.'

Taking the three papers, he shuffled them about, all the while keeping his eyes on Rose and her sisters. 'I had anticipated this possibility, and I admit to a certain curiosity on my own part...'

He set the papers on the edge of his desk, one in front of each of them. It was clear he had allocated them randomly to each of the girls.

'Your mother appointed me your guardian until you turn twenty-five, or until you marry. She has left in my keeping a sealed package with strict instructions not to open it until my guardianship ends. There is some mystery there, and given your quick minds, I wonder if you might enjoy trying to find some answers in London. While she was extremely reticent, I do know that she was English, and she let slip once that she had had her own season, many years ago. That means she was of the *ton*, the highest-ranking part of English society.'

'And what of our father?' Izzy's eyes were alight with curiosity.

Mr Marnoch shrugged. 'She told me nothing of him, save that he was deceased. Do you remember him at all?'

Desperately, Rose searched her memories, as they had all done on many occasions.

Nothing.

Despite the fact they were exactly the same age, Anna's memories from years ago were clearest. They could all remember glimpses of the place they had lived before they had come to Elgin at the age of five, and they all remembered Mama of course, having been ten when she died of a slow wasting disease. Rose swallowed against the sudden lump in her throat.

'We do not remember him at all,' Anna responded soberly. 'Did he—did he ever correspond with Mama after we moved here?'

He shrugged. 'I do not believe so. She described herself as a widow from the first, so I believe he was already deceased by then. You do know she came here when you were five years old, and of course I became your guardian when you were ten.'

There was a pause, as they all remembered that terrible time. Losing Mama. Mr Marnoch's kindly helplessness. Moving from the little rented cottage beside Mr Marnoch's law offices to the school just outside the town. Belvedere. It had become home to them.

He nodded to the papers. 'You will, I hope, forgive me for a little…theatricality in this matter, but I am somewhat constrained. I must honour your mother's request not to share whatever is in the package in my safe, but I also see that you are young women now, and it would only be natural for you to wish for more information about your origins.' He took a breath, then added, in a more formal tone, 'Here are three quests, one for each of you. You do not have to accept them, of course.'

Izzy had not even waited for him to finish. She had picked up the piece of paper in front of her, read it quickly, and now exclaimed, 'I am to discover the name of our father? But how? How am I to do this?'

Mr Marnoch shrugged. 'Honestly, I have no idea. I

have written down all I know on the matter. The rest is up to you.'

Anna was reading her own paper. Frowning, she folded it carefully, then stowed it away in her reticule. 'This is a challenging task—attempting to discover the circumstances behind Mama's coming to Elgin.'

With a shaking hand, Rose picked up the paper in front of her. She read the words in Mr Marnoch's neat hand.

Your quest is to discover who your mother was. Her family, her background. What was her name before it was Lennox? She had a London season, and you triplets look a little like her, although her eyes were hazel, not blue.

Yes! Instantly, she recalled Mama's eyes. Hazel, with flecks of green. A wave of longing rippled through her. *Mama!* Could she find answers, if she went to London? It would take courage on her part to leave behind the town she knew and postpone her plans to teach.

But I might discover who she was...who I am.

Her sisters were eyeing her—Anna with quiet calm, Izzy with barely held excitement.

They would prefer not to overrule me.

She needed to make her own decision.

Can I do this thing? Go far away from my home, perhaps never to return?

Her mama had been so strong. A young woman herself, she had managed to make a life for herself in

Elgin, with three five-year-olds. Then, just a few short years later, looking her long slow death straight in the eye, she had ensured her daughters were protected, persuading Mr Marnoch to become their guardian. Compared to the trials Mama had faced, a trip to London was nothing.

It is the least I can do for her, to perhaps learn her real name and honour her memory.

Rose's eyes met Mr Marnoch's, and she nodded. 'I am to attempt to discover who Mama was. Very well. I shall do this if my sisters also wish to travel to London.' Her voice trembled a little. 'I do not know if I can succeed, but I shall do my best. May I ask for assistance from Anna and Izzy?'

Anna squeezed her hand, while Izzy's eyes were now blazing with joy. They both knew that Rose was the most reticent, so if she was willing to go it meant they could all agree.

'Of course!' Mr Marnoch replied. 'I mean for you to work together on all three quests. Equally, I firmly believe you will have more chance of success if each of you has a different focus.'

'That makes sense,' mused Anna. 'Logic suggests giving each of us a specific task, yet we always work best together.'

'I cannot wait to get started,' declared Izzy, her eyes shining. 'When do we leave for London?'

'There is no need to delay, I think. My sister has already written to say she is expecting you. Would next

Thursday suit for you to set off? I can retain your room in the inn for a few more nights.'

'Perfect!' Rose could *feel* Izzy's enthusiasm, yet could not match it, for all she felt was nervousness and trepidation. Yet while she was much less confident of success, she knew that her quest held great meaning, and was quietly determined to do all she could to learn more of her mama.

London awaited, big and unknown and…and *terrifying*. For Rose, though, now there was a reason to go there.

My sisters will be with me, and we can achieve this. For Mama.

Chapter Two

London

It was late when the private carriage finally pulled up outside Ashbourne House. Darkness lay upon the buildings like a pall, blocking out the freshness and openness Rose was accustomed to. In Scotland even at night they had the stars, or a magnificent sky blanketed in clouds, or even the cool rain. Here it was *warm*, even in early March, and the air was stultifying with smoke, noxious smells, and the closeness of so many buildings. Even Edinburgh had not felt oppressive like this.

They had all tried to sleep after their last rest stop, some hours ago. It had taken more than two weeks of coach travel to get here, at what had been described as an easy pace, and Rose had become wearily accustomed to the jostling carriage, the discomfort of short breaks, and the novelty of staying in a different inn each night. Mr Marnoch—bless him—had organised everything as best he could, and the journey had passed relatively smoothly. Izzy had apparently had a brief run-in with a gentleman in Grantham whom she had described as arrogant and boorish, but thankfully their encounter had been brief, and unwitnessed by anyone else—including Izzy's sisters. Rose sighed. Izzy often seemed to find herself in such encounters.

Like Rose, Izzy had not slept during this last part of the journey, and Rose briefly wondered if her sister was experiencing the same nervous anxiety as she. One glance at Izzy's shining eyes and eager expression, illuminated by the lanterns either side of the mansion's door, was enough to disabuse her of the idea.

'Wake up, Anna! We have arrived!' She shook Anna's shoulder, then turned back to the window. 'What an elegant house!'

Anna yawned, stretched, then sat up straight. 'Make sure you have your reticules, girls. Bonnets on!'

Quickly, as the coachman opened the door and let down the steps, they busied themselves with bonnets and reticules, and shook out their matching red cloaks.

'I do hope Lady Ashbourne is agreeable!' Rose murmured as they stepped down from the carriage. Of all her anxieties, this seemed most pressing at present. Ahead of them she saw the door opening, a tall footman in full livery emerging to stand rigidly to one side awaiting their entry.

How formal!

'If she is anything like her brother she will be more

than agreeable,' Anna replied calmly, settling Rose's nerves as only she could.

Of course!

Mr Marnoch was a darling, and his sister was likely to be just as warm-hearted.

Following her sisters inside, Rose had an impression of elegance, wealth, and opulence—and they were still only in the entrance hallway. The Ashbourne town-house was a long way from the simple comforts of Belvedere, or indeed the familiar chaos of Mr Marnoch's office. Here were sparkling floor-tiles, gleaming side tables, walls adorned with paintings set within decorative plaster surrounds, and a magnificent staircase. Rose's eyes darted everywhere—left, right, above, and below, in a futile attempt to take in all the details.

Relinquishing their bonnets and cloaks to a uniformed house maid, the girls followed the footman upstairs as requested. In Belvedere, the parlour had been on the ground floor, and it was there they had been used to meeting Mr Marnoch when he came for his regular visits. They had also been in the habit of calling to see him regularly in his offices, and his two clerks knew them well. Rose sighed inwardly. Mr Balmore and Mr Redburn seemed a thousand miles away.

Naturally she had been told the London aristocracy tended to receive guests in public rooms upstairs on the first floor, away from the sights and odours of street level. It all just seemed entirely foreign to her. The footman paused outside a tall set of doors with gilded handles and checked their names and even their birth order, his expression remaining impassive throughout. Opening the door, he announced them.

'Miss Lennox, Miss Isobel Lennox, Miss Rosabella Lennox!'

Of course! Anna, the eldest by twenty minutes, would have the honour of being 'Miss Lennox', with Izzy and Rose relegated to 'younger sisters' in his announcement.

Lord, such formality!

Their hostess—a handsome woman on the shady side of forty—was already rising to greet them, her polite smile fading as the three of them made their curtseys. Blinking, she looked from one to the other and back again, her expression one of utter astonishment. 'But—I do not understand… Twins—no, three of them—like peas in a pod!' Her right hand had fluttered to her chest. 'Ian must have forgotten to mention…' Shaking herself, she began again. 'You must forgive me, my dears! I had not known to expect the three of you to look like a triptych of mirrors!' Stepping forwards, she held out a hand. 'Which of you is Miss Lennox?'

'I am Annabelle.' Anna stepped forward, taking her hand and curtseying briefly again. 'I tend to wear blue. This is my sister Isobel—'

Izzy grinned at her. 'I wear greens and yellows, most of the time!'

'And Rose—Rosabella—is the youngest, having been born half an hour after Izzy, according to our mama.'

Rose took Lady Ashbourne's hand, sending her a shy smile as she curtseyed.

'And do you usually wear pink, my dear?'

'I do.'

'Rose-pink! Then I expect I shall learn your name first,' Lady Ashbourne declared. 'Well! Triplets!' Crossing the room, she rang one of two bell-pulls on the wall. 'We shall have tea, and I shall attempt to recover from the shock. Do sit down, girls!'

They sat, and had tea and cakes for supper, and answered Lady Ashbourne's questions as best they could. No, they knew little of their family background, on either side. Yes, their journey had been interesting, and reasonably comfortable. No, they had never visited London before.

'Your brother, Mr Marnoch, has been an excellent guardian to us,' Anna offered. 'We have appreciated his kindness and generosity these ten years and more.'

'Aye, Ian is a good man,' she replied, sounding distinctly Scottish in that moment. 'As a confirmed bachelor it saddened me to think he would never be a father. I knew he had taken on the guardianship of three orphans a number of years ago, but I had thought he sent you all away to school.'

'Oh, no!' Izzy made haste to enlighten her. 'He sent us to Belvedere School for Young Ladies, which is just on the outskirts of Elgin. We saw him very frequently.'

'Belvedere?' She nodded, her eyes taking on a distant look. 'I do recall an old mansion by that name, from my childhood in Elgin. So they turned it into a school, eh?'

'It has been a fine home for us since our mama died,' Anna stated firmly. 'The teachers are sensible and warm, and we received, I think, a reasonable education—although…' She frowned. 'We never expected a London season, and I do not think our teachers have thought of preparing us for one. I fear we may let you down, my lady. If you would prefer, we do not have to be out in company.'

Rose felt compelled to speak, as being out in company was the last thing she would choose. Surely Lady Ashbourne could help them find out about Mama from the comfort of her ornate and luxurious home? 'Indeed, yes. We shall be perfectly content enjoying a quiet time here in the capital, if you should prefer it.'

'Well!' Lady Ashbourne looked rather flummoxed. 'I never thought to see the day when young ladies would offer *not* to have a season!'

'My sisters…' Izzy offered, 'may speak for themselves. But I for one would love to dance at a ball, and go to the theatre, and wear pretty dresses!'

'As you should, my dear!' Lady Ashbourne held a hand up. 'Wait…you are Isobel, yes?'

'I am. You will learn that I am the outspoken one, while Rose is timid, and Anna is always practical.'

Timid? I am not timid!

A few years ago Rose would have disputed the matter hotly. She was not timid, only *careful*. Careful, and reserved, and given to silence—sometimes even when she had something to say. She could be as brave as anyone, given the right circumstances. Just not… foolhardy. And being brave tended to necessitate quite a bit of inner encouragement before acting. Sending Izzy a cross glance, she resolved to speak up, if only to prove Izzy wrong in her assertion of Rose's timidity.

'As to that,' she offered softly, 'such opportunities sound…interesting. But I also recognise that our education in Belvedere, though excellent, may not exactly have prepared us to enter the heart of the *ton*.'

'Indeed? Well, I do hope you have had an adequate education. What did they teach you at Belvedere?'

Now this was solid ground for Rose. 'Our knowledge of Greek and Latin is excellent, and we can speak French, Spanish, Italian, and German creditably well. We have done well in algebra, and the globe, as well as logic. We can also all sing and play reasonably well. And Izzy is an excellent artist.'

'I see.' Lady Ashbourne looked a little bewildered. 'I see.'

Anna joined in. 'We also had lessons in deportment, in household management, and embroidery. We can all set a neat stitch. However…'

Izzy continued their report, her eyes dancing. 'However, our knowledge of those named in Mr Debrett's book is cursory, for the names meant nothing to us. And our dancing lessons focused more on Scottish country dances rather than whatever is currently popular in London.'

'I see,' Lady Ashbourne repeated, and there was

now a decided frown furrowing her brow. 'It sounds to me as though you received an education more fitting for young *gentlemen* than young *ladies*.'

'Really?' Anna looked as confused as Rose felt. 'How so?'

'The female talents are there, no doubt.' She ticked them off on her fingers. 'Household management. Embroidery. Deportment. Music. But as for the rest...let me advise you, girls. It would not do to appear too bookish, or too learned. Gentlemen may find it off-putting. Some ladies too.'

The girls looked at one another, sharing a sense of surprise. Anna was first to recover. 'We are ready to be guided by you, Lady Ashbourne. And as I said before, we need not go out in society if you think it inappropriate.'

'Thank you... Anna. Let me think on it. But for now, you must surely be exhausted, and ready for your beds.'

Ringing the bell again, she informed the housemaid that the young ladies were ready to retire and asked her to fetch the housekeeper. A few moments later Mrs Coleby, the housekeeper—a coolly efficient woman in her middle years—was briskly assigning them each a personal maid to see to their needs.

As the three housemaids bobbed curtseys to the triplets, Rose had to clamp her mouth shut to prevent her jaw from dropping. She could scarce believe it. Never had she expected a lady's maid to serve her. It felt wrong, somehow. Agnes had, over the years, become a friend to them. These girls, lined up in identical uniforms and with identical neutral expressions, looked rather forbidding.

Bidding their hostess goodnight they followed the housekeeper to the second floor where, she informed them coolly, the family bedrooms were located.

'Miss Lennox.' Opening a door she inclined her head, indicating that Anna was to enter the first chamber to the left.

Oh, no! We are to have separate rooms!

Helplessly, Rose watched as Anna entered with her maid, who closed the door.

'Miss Isobel.' Izzy disappeared into the second room, her lady's maid at her heels, and Rose was left with the housekeeper and her own maid.

'Miss Rosabella.' Swallowing hard, Rose thanked her and ventured inside. The room was opulent and sumptuous, with a large four-poster bed, a fireplace, and elegant furniture in the French style. The windows were covered with satin brocade curtains in a golden yellow shade, to match the coverlet and the pale gold walls.

Yellow? This should have been Isobel's room!

The maid, curtseying, offered to assist Rose to undress. 'I have already unpacked for you, miss.'

The nightgown laid out on the bed was familiar. Rose had made it herself, out of a length of soft muslin they had bought at the haberdashery in Elgin a few months ago. Her sisters had matching night-rails, the embroidered details the only difference between them. 'Thank you.' Awkwardly she allowed the girl, a stranger to her, to undo her buttons, loosen her corset, and help her into her nightgown. This was a task she and her sisters had done for each other all their lives—or from whenever it was they could first manage buttons and bows.

'Please sit, miss.' The girl stood by the table and gilded chair, and Rose did as she was bid. Sitting passively as the maid removed her hairpins and brushed out her long hair, she eyed her own reflection. The image was, naturally, deeply familiar to her—not just as her own reflection, but as the features of both sisters. Fair hair. Blue eyes. Straight nose. Good teeth. For the first time, it occurred to her to wonder if she was attractive. People always looked at them, for they were always together, and seeing three identical young ladies always seemed to make people gape, no matter how well they knew them. Only within Belvedere had they been known as individuals. Even Mr Marnoch still could not always tell them apart.

Belle or Bella or Miss Lennox. That was how others had addressed them, when unsure which of the triplets they were speaking to. Very rarely had Rose heard her own name spoken, apart from the lips of her own sisters or the girls in Belvedere.

And never before in her life had she slept in a bedchamber by herself.

The maid left, taking Rose's day dress and boots with her—for cleaning, she stated—and Rose finally allowed her shoulders to drop. Pacing about, she discovered her trunk in the corner of the room—empty, as the maid had indicated. Opening the garderobe door she saw her own meagre clothing. Three dresses, two petticoats. Gloves, a spare bonnet, two pairs of slippers for indoor wear. Her serviceable red cloak and plain straw bonnet were downstairs, and now the maid had taken the clothes she had been wearing today.

What must she think of us?

Whether she meant in her own mind to refer to Lady Ashbourne or the lady's maid, she was uncertain. One thing was sure though. This life would be wildly different to everything she had known before. And she did not like it.

The sooner I get back to Elgin the better!

Somehow, in order to survive the terrible newness of everything, Rose had convinced herself that her old life in Elgin awaited, and all she would have to do to get it back would be to return there. The notion was comforting.

Acting on impulse, and feeling rather intrepid, she opened the door. Were Anna and Izzy already in bed? Or might their maids still be with them? Listening, she could not hear a sound and so, greatly daring, she tiptoed out to the landing. A deep carpet went down the centre of the upper hallway, its way marked by side tables displaying china vases, marble busts, and elegant candelabra at intervals.

So many candles alight at once.

Rose did not dare to even *think* of the cost of such extravagance.

The chambers were large, and so it took almost twenty steps to reach Izzy's door. Pausing, she leaned to listen, but the doors were solid and she could hear nothing within. Suddenly a motion ahead of her caught her eye and she lifted her head, freezing as she came eye to eye with someone mounting the stairs.

It was a man. Young, handsome, and well-formed, he wore the knee breeches, waistcoat, and jacket that were *de rigueur* for evening wear for the wealthy and the aristocracy. Mr Marnoch had used to wear similar garb at Christmastide when he would invite them to his home along with a teacher-chaperone for an annual feast. This gentleman, though, did not have dear Mr Marnoch's paunch, nor his kindly, lined face. This gentleman looked like the images Rose had seen in books of art at Belvedere. He was a Michelangelo. A Leonardo. A Raphael.

Her heart was pounding so loudly she felt it might explode from her chest at any moment. Her breathing was shallow, her body frozen with shock, and surprise, and something else she could not name. Something she had never felt before. He was—he was—*beautiful*.

And Rose was standing there, wearing nothing but her night-rail, staring at him! With a muffled shriek she fled, making for the safety of her chamber. Covering the distance in a fraction of the time it had taken to get to Izzy's room, she dived inside and closed her door, leaning against it with her eyes closed, her breathing fast and her heart racing. She could not, however, shake the image from her mind.

Unbidden, the details had seemingly etched them-selves on her inner vision. His hair, dark and thick. His eyes, wide with surprise as he had swiftly perused her from head to bare toes, his hand frozen at his neck where he had been in the process of loosening his cra-vat when she had first laid eyes on him.

Who was he? Some relative of Lady Ashbourne perhaps? Her son? No, for he looked to be somewhere between twenty-five and thirty, and Lady Ashbourne could not be more than five and forty.

Oh, why was I not more cautious?

Truly, she had needed a dose of Anna's practical-ity just now, rather than succumbing to a moment of madness that was more like Izzy!

She swallowed, acknowledging the truth. It had been weakness, not bravery, that had led her to leave the sanctuary of her chamber. In that sense she was all Rose. Quite simply, she had been frightened to be alone. No doubt her sisters were also feeling the strangeness of a solo chamber. Unlike her though, they had been strong-willed enough to stay put.

Berating herself all the while, she methodically blew out all the candles in her bedchamber—so many candles!—save the one on her nightstand. Climbing into bed, she knew that, despite her exhaustion, sleep would be slow in coming tonight. Not only was she in a strange chamber, and missing the reassuring sounds of Anna's and Izzy's breathing, but she had just had an unexpected encounter with a man while in a state of undress! The only men at Belvedere had been the two manservants, who had never ventured near the upper floors where the bedchambers were situated unless to mend something—and only then with specific arrangements in place organised by the senior teachers.

Yet it was more than that. Her mind wandered back to the image of him, hand poised at his cravat, and his gaze connecting with hers. The unknown gentleman and the effect of his eyes on her had deeply disconcerted her. Never before had she seen a work of art that was living, and breathing, and looking at her in *such* a way. The memories once again caused her pulse to race and her breathing to quicken. What on earth was happening to her?

And I am only just arrived in London.

Somehow, she knew that after tonight, she would never be the same again.

James continued on to his bedchamber, suppressing a chuckle. So his aunt's visitors had arrived, then? It had been entirely unexpected to see a vision of loveliness in his own home as he had climbed the stairs seeking his bed. Indeed his heart was thumping in a most inconvenient manner, even now.

While remaining determined to protect his aunt from any trouble or strife, he knew that, with this girl at least, he now had the upper hand. That shriek had told him encountering a strange gentleman whilst in a state of undress had disturbed and shocked her.

Good!

Naturally, he was not unused to private connections

with enterprising ladies—generally willing widows or bored wives who had already done their duty by their husbands. Country house parties were renowned for such encounters. Once the heir and ideally a spare were secured, there were all too many wives seeking bed sport with gentlemen such as himself—unmarried and rather jaded. Last season, he had had carefully managed encounters with three such ladies, and fully intended to at least match it this year.

Caution was now his watchword. Never had there been tittle-tattle about him or any adventures he may have had, for he chose his partners with care, prudence governing everything he did. Not for him the risks of disease from attending the pleasure-houses of London. He had even learned how to take certain... *precautions* to reduce the risk of impregnating one of his merry widows or bored aristocratic wives.

One thing was certain however. Unmarried virgins held no interest for him, being absolutely out of bounds. There was the forlorn hope that he might find one who could manage to hold his attention for the couple of years it might take to secure his own line. At this moment, he could not imagine ever marrying—and yet he must. Someday he would make an advantageous marriage—one in keeping with his title and wealth. He would choose a bride using cold, hard logic, allowing nothing to distract him.

Only son to a younger son, as a child James had never been expected to ascend to the title. But as the years passed and his aunt remained childless, he had gradually realised that the responsibilities of being head of the family might land with him one day. With his dear uncle in good health, James had run rather wild at Oxford, knowing any responsibility would be far in the future—or so he had thought. The death of his uncle had been entirely unexpected, and what was worse, James's parents had perished in the same carriage accident.

That had left Lady Ashbourne, James's childless, widowed aunt, all alone. Despite being on the wrong side of forty, nevertheless James's aunt had not fully given up on the hope of having a child of her own, until the very day her husband had died. Sadly it was not to be.

Now the responsibility had fallen to him, and he took it seriously. Someday he would have to find a wife good enough to grace this house as its lady.

He sighed. *Unlikely.* These past few seasons had given him an abhorrence of the marriage mart in general, and Almack's in particular. Even before his parents' death he had avoided Almack's and the marriage mart, preferring the gaming hells and alehouses of London. Now he made his bow at balls and soirées, but knew himself to be decidedly *not* on the hunt for a wife.

Yet he knew that one day he would have to force himself to make his choice. Making such a vital decision with all its ramifications seemed impossible, for his inner sense of caution screamed at him every time a risk or flaw was identified in any plan of his.

Plenty of time for such endeavours as marriage.

His thoughts drifted back to the young lady he had just seen, and his loins tightened at the memory: unbound golden tresses, a beautiful face, and that nightgown! It had managed simultaneously to be both entirely modest and yet completely alluring. She had been covered from neck to ankle yet even in candlelight he had seen the entire outline of her delectable form.

She would have no idea, but the thin muslin nightrail had left little to the imagination. Or, more accurately, it required him to use only a small amount of imagination. The perfect amount indeed, to be tantalising. Had she been naked she would have been much less bewitching.

Still, one question had been answered. At least one of the Lennox sisters was not in the category of plain and dull. Instead she was in the other: beautiful and likely spoiled.

Chapter Three

Rose descended to the breakfast room, her maid as her guide and her mind foggy with lack of sleep. Really, she ought to have slept like a dead thing, given the trials of the long distance they had travelled yesterday. Having become accustomed to the oblivion of exhaustion during the fortnight of inns and roads since they had left Elgin, she had been proven right in her expectation that last night, sleep would prove elusive.

She had missed her sisters…and the unknown gentleman had severely disturbed her. Half-remembered dreams—strange, heated things—had caused her to awaken multiple times in the night, and it had been a relief when the maid had come to help her rise, wash, dress, and prepare for breakfast.

Had there been disapproval in the maid's expression when she had laid out one of Rose's other dresses? Like all their clothing it was plain and unadorned, save a little line of embroidered flowers along the hem in her own rose-pink. London fashions, Rose surmised, might be entirely different to those of rural Scotland.

Lady Ashbourne had the same notion, it seemed. 'Now then, girls,' she declared briskly as soon as Izzy, the last to descend, had taken her seat. 'Help yourself to breakfast, for today we are going *shopping*!'

Izzy grinned. 'How exciting! I adore seeking out new ribbons and trims to revive an old bonnet or dress. Perhaps we might even buy some fabric—all three of us are adept seamstresses, my lady.'

Their hostess chuckled. 'Not in a hundred years would I allow you to make your own clothes while you are under my roof.' She shuddered. 'The very notion! No, my brother has sent adequate funds for each of you to have a wardrobe suitable for your coming out.'

'But—' Anna looked flabbergasted. 'That would be an absolute fortune! We have heard that a court dress alone may cost hundreds of pounds. And there are *three* of us!'

'And what of it? He has chosen to be generous. I say you should make the most of it.'

Rose shook her head. 'It would not be right, for we know our mama was not wealthy. Mr Marnoch allowed her to clerk for him when we lived in Elgin. She also had some money I think from her previous employment, but there is no way she earned enough to cover the cost of three wardrobes!'

Lady Ashbourne rolled her eyes. 'Girls, girls…if you are going to have such Quakerish notions you will never *take*. You must understand, as is now very clear to me, that since the day and hour he agreed to become your guardian, my brother has clearly seen you as his *daughters*, not his wards. Oh, he and I exchange letters only occasionally, and he did used to mention you, but I confess I had no idea he would wish you to come and visit London, until he wrote to me recently. In that letter he spoke of you in the most flattering terms, making it clear to me that he is proud of you all and holds you in great affection. And with regard to your season, the sentiment in his letter was clear. You are to be launched as young ladies of the *ton*. Your dowries are no more than respectable—my brother is, after all, a lawyer, not a wealthy landowner—but he was unambiguous on this point. I am to ensure you are all "appropriately turned out". Now, I wish to hear no more about it!'

Chastened, they applied themselves to breakfast—opting for honeyed porridge, rolls, and delicious chocolate rather than the kippers and beef presently being enjoyed by their hostess. As she masticated Lady Ashbourne provided a bewildering list of places she intended to take them—mantua-makers and milliners as well as bazaars and bootmakers.

'And you will make quite the impact, I think.' She gave a satisfied chuckle. 'Now, who will rival you? Let me think! Lady Renton is to launch that shy daughter of hers this season. And everyone is expecting Miss Chorley to be this year's diamond, despite the fact her father's family were in *trade*. How I should love to defeat them all! Well!'

She grinned, and Rose, like her sisters, could not help smiling back. Lady Ashbourne was so unaffected, and warm, and...*gleeful*, that her enthusiasm was quite infectious. While she had no notion who these people were, and what 'this year's diamond' meant, still it seemed adventures lay ahead of them. So long as she had Anna and Izzy by her side, she would meet the challenges head-on. And surely she would have more opportunity to discover clues about Mama's identity if they were out in society. Bravely, Rose decided to speak up.

'It is so kind of you to welcome us, Lady Ashbourne. What your brother asks is no little request, and we appreciate it.'

Lady Ashbourne eyed her evenly. 'I am happy to admit that I experienced some qualms, after replying to say I would do it. But so far, I find you to be pretty-behaved and respectful, and I believe you may do well. However,' she raised a hand in warning, 'I shall expect obedience from all three of you. You have no notion of the ways of the *ton*, and you must respect my edicts, even if they make no sense to you at the time. Understood?'

They all agreed, Rose with some trepidation. Ahead lay unknown waters—a new world with its own rules and expectations. The thought of being out in public, in an unfamiliar place, and with unknown rules she must obey, was more than a little daunting.

What if I get it wrong?

'Naturally, we shall be guided by your greater experience, Lady Ashbourne,' Anna responded evenly, cool and practical as always.

Rose stole a glance at Izzy. Of all of them, she struggled most with rules and strictures, and had frequently come into conflict with some of the teachers at Belvedere. There was a hint of storminess in her expression, but wisely, she had nodded in agreement along with Rose and Anna.

One thing was bothering Rose though... Who was the gentleman she had encountered last night? And were they going to see him again? He had been occupying her thoughts almost constantly since the encounter on the landing, and each time she thought of him her body reacted in the same way as it had at the time.

It was a shock, she thought sagely. *And I am not yet recovered from it.*

Who was he? They would be living here with Lady Ashbourne for months, and yet they knew little about her, apart from the fact she was a widow. She was not old enough to be the man's mother, yet the age difference between them was such that he was unlikely to be her peer. A cousin, perhaps? On her husband's side?

Lady Ashbourne clapped a hand to her head. 'I have just had the most diverting notion!' She paused, frowning. 'Let me think it through...dancing lessons... music...presentation... Three of them...all at once... quite the stir.' Suddenly she grinned, and Rose held her breath.

'I have changed my mind, girls!' she announced, an air of excited triumph about her. 'Instead of going out about town we shall remain here in Ashbourne House, and I shall send for the dressmakers and milliners to come to *us*. I shall also arrange for a caper merchant and a music teacher, for I shall want to assure myself of your ability to dance, sing, and play. We have two weeks until your presentation at Court, and we must make the most of them.'

'So...' Anna's brow was furrowed. 'You mean for us to *not* meet anyone until Court?'

'Exactly! Clever girl!' She rubbed her hands together. 'I shall try to keep you unobserved and secret until your debut in a fortnight's time. That will give you all the chance to—to *settle* properly, focusing on your preparations. All of the other sponsors—all those aunts and mamas and grandmothers—have had months if not *years* to prepare their girls for their come-out. I have two weeks, and I intend to make the most of it—not waste my time in house calls and eating ices at Gunter's!'

'Ices? I should love to eat ices, my lady!' As ever, Izzy seemed unafraid to challenge an adult—although she was smiling.

Lady Ashbourne smiled back. 'A girl after my own heart! Never fear, you shall have your ices—just not yet.' She tapped the side of her head. 'I am not perhaps the *cleverest* woman in London, but I can just imagine the reaction to the three of you when you make your debut! It will be so much more entertaining if no one knows beforehand you are identical. I mean—identical triplets! Who would have thought such a thing was even possible?'

Their hostess's plan was beginning to sink in, and

Rose liked the sound of it. Two weeks of lessons… of solitude? Two weeks confined within this opulent mansion—which surely had a library? Two weeks of not having to engage with strangers? It sounded heavenly. Rose felt her shoulders relax. The anticipated ordeal was put off for two whole weeks! Dreamily, she imagined two blissful weeks of reading, and simply being with her sisters and the welcoming Lady Ashbourne.

Anna was nodding thoughtfully. 'Shall we be quite alone in the house, Lady Ashbourne?'

Abruptly, Rose focused again on the current conversation. Who was even now in the house with them? Who was the man she had seen?

Their hostess started, clapping a hand to her head. 'James! I must swear him to secrecy. My nephew, the current Viscount, lives here when he is in London. Well, naturally he does, for all of this belongs to him now. He is such a kind boy, for he would have been well within his rights to banish me. Instead I keep house for him, and he tells me I shall remain mistress of his establishments until he marries.' She nodded thoughtfully. 'I shall have to speak to the butler and housekeeper to ensure the servants do not tittle-tattle, for if word gets out my plan would be entirely spoiled.' She rose, a decided air of vigour about her. 'Now, if you have all completed your breakfast, let us retire to the drawing room to make plans!'

Dutifully they followed in her wake, Rose ruminating on Lady Ashbourne's statement. *Nephew. Unmar-*

ried. So he would be there, in this house, throughout their visit. Disquiet rumbled through her. Unused as she was to the company of gentlemen, she hoped they would not be too often in the Viscount's company—despite his looking like someone Michelangelo would wish to carve or paint.

Shrugging off the memory she trailed after her sisters, and moments later found herself upstairs in the same elegant drawing room where they had met their hostess the night before. In daylight it looked even more sumptuous, with twenty-foot-high ceilings etched in gilt, and silk-satin curtains billowing at the three long windows overlooking the street below. Seeing it boasted not one but *two* fireplaces, Rose reflected wisely that in winter the power of two fires would surely be needed to heat such a large expanse. The walls were adorned with various paintings framed by plaster cartouches, while the furniture was an elegant series of settees, chairs, and tables along with a cedar-wood desk. After lowering the writing flap, Lady Ashbourne passed them all paper, pens, and ink, directing them to seat themselves at a table and write to various dressmakers, shoemakers, and milliners for, as she declared with fire in her eye, the sooner the messages were sent, the sooner they could begin.

Having complimented the girls' penmanship she signed the messages, and footmen were then dispatched to deliver the notes to the various places of business. When that was done she bade a housemaid bring 'all the copies of *La Belle Assemblée* from my chamber', practically rubbing her hands together in enthusiasm as she contemplated the tasks ahead.

'Take one each, girls, and let us see if anything takes your fancy.'

Rising, Rose took a copy from the proffered pile, murmuring a word of thanks to the housemaid. Retaking her seat she began flicking through the pages, discovering as she did so that any maiden, it seemed, might have an interest in fashion—even her own bookish self. Along with her sisters she joined in the *oohs* and *aahs*, showing her favourites to Lady Ashbourne and learning as she did so that her taste was a little different to the others.

'Excellent!' Lady Ashbourne beamed in delight. 'I do declare this is such fun! It has been years since I experienced such amusement! Now, I—'

The door opened, and in walked the gentleman from last night. Instantly Rose's mouth went dry, her hands clammy.

He is even more handsome than I remembered.

Dark hair, dark eyes, and a fine figure...

Lord!

'Good day, Aunt,' he began. 'I hope I am not disturbing you, but I—'

He stopped, blinking and looking from one to the other as they rose for the formalities.

'Quite,' murmured his aunt. 'James, may I introduce my guests to you? These are my brother's wards. Miss Lennox, Miss Isobel Lennox, and Miss Rosabella Lennox.' He would not have noticed—although

Rose did—the way Lady Ashbourne's gaze flicked to the coloured trims of their dresses as she was introducing them. 'Girls, this is my nephew, the Viscount Ashbourne.'

They curtseyed in unison and he blinked again, while Lady Ashbourne clapped her hands in delight. 'Such perfect harmony, girls—a pretty trick, and one which I hope you will use again!'

Trick?

'It is no trick, ma'am,' offered Izzy. 'But we are always together, and so we often—'

'Do things together,' Anna completed the thought.

'We are very close, you see,' Rose explained.

'And you are lucky to have each other,' Lady Ashbourne declared firmly. 'Please sit, James, and tell me, how was your evening?'

He shrugged. 'The usual. People are beginning to arrive in Town now, so the club was fairly busy last night.'

His voice was deep, and was sending mysterious shivers through Rose.

What on earth—?

As she clasped her hands firmly together in her lap, she noticed that they trembled a little. Thankful to be one of three, she knew he could have no idea which of the sisters he had encountered last night. And a good thing too, for otherwise her mortification would know no bounds.

'Shall you dine there again this evening, James?'

A slight frown marred his forehead. 'No,' he replied slowly, 'I believe I shall dine here, if it does not inconvenience you, Aunt.'

'Not at all, my love! You know you are always welcome to dine here. It is your home now, after all.'

His gaze softened. 'I thank you.' His gaze drifted to the triplets. 'So you are the sisters my aunt's brother has sent to her for the season.'

Was it Rose's imagination, or was there now a little hardness in his expression? Perhaps not. Perhaps it was only the contrast with how he had looked at his aunt, whom he clearly held in high regard.

Buoyed by relief in not being identified, she replied boldly, 'Yes, and we are eternally grateful to them both. Mr Marnoch is the best of men, and Lady Ashbourne has welcomed us so warmly. It is so much more than we deserve.'

'As to what you *deserve*, I can say nothing. Yet,' he murmured, and Rose's eyes widened. One could read his statement any number of ways, but she was suddenly convinced he meant to criticise. Shock made her blink, and sudden anger flared through her.

'Do let us know,' she offered sweetly, without pausing for consideration, 'when you have come to a conclusion. I am sure we shall all be fascinated to hear your verdict.'

Lord, what am I doing?

Normally, she did not speak to strangers at all, unless absolutely necessary. Her pounding heart and racing pulse must be affecting her usual demeanour.

I am suffering from some sort of temporary madness I think.

Her sisters' expressions indicated surprise, and a hint of warning for her unusual boldness, while the Viscount gave a wry smile. '*Reserve thy judgement*, eh?'

Recognising the quote, she gave him another from the same play. 'Aye, and *give thy thoughts no tongue.*' Her tone was saucy, almost snappish, and entirely out of character.

Lord, stop! she told herself. *Just stop!*

Lady Ashbourne tutted. 'Now then, let us have no more literariness, for it quite wears me out, as you well know, James. Yes?'

The footman had returned, with news that not one but two tradespeople had arrived in response to her messages.

'Well show them in, then!' Turning to her nephew, she added, 'You may wish to make yourself scarce, James, for we mean to begin ordering the girls' new wardrobe.'

Grimacing, he rose hastily. 'I shall retire to my club for a few hours, then. I shall see you at dinner.' As he bowed, Rose threw Lady Ashbourne a meaningful look. Thankfully she understood it.

'Oh, James—say nothing of the Belles.'

'The Belles?' His voice rose questioningly, even as he glanced their way.

'Yes. No one is to know of them until they make their debut. At least—I have mentioned their arrival to some of my friends, so people already know of their *existence*. But I did not know myself they are identical until they arrived. No one in society has yet *seen* them, and I mean to keep them from view for the present.'

After a fleeting frown of puzzlement his face cleared. 'Ah, I see your game, Aunt.' A dimple danced in his cheek and Rose, fascinated, watched it, 'And I wholeheartedly approve!' he continued.

Bowing again, he saw himself out, leaving Rose decidedly torn. Who was he, this handsome man? Someone who judged, and would find them wanting? Or someone with humour, and character? And why did it matter so?

Chapter Four

Rose stood with her sisters in the antechamber, awaiting their turn to be presented. Her heart was pounding, hands clammy, and mouth dry. On the other side of the enormous double doors was the Queen, as well as the entire court. In Rose's mind the Queen—like all of the royals—had always been more of an *idea* than an actual person. Today would change all of that, for she was about to come face to face with her. Queen Charlotte herself.

Lord Ashbourne and his aunt had accompanied them in the carriage, and when they had finally reached the top of the long queue of carriages outside St James's Palace, it had been something of a relief.

The sooner this is over, the sooner I can be calm again.

The Viscount had just left them, going ahead into the council chamber—the long chamber in use today as the Queen's drawing room for the presentation of debutantes. Bowing, he had wished them luck and told them in an offhand tone that they all looked beautiful.

His gaze had roved over all three of them equally, and he would have no way of knowing who was who today.

This guaranteed anonymity was something of a relief, for naturally Lady Ashbourne had informed him of their preferred colours, and so for most of the past two weeks he had known which sister was her. Strangely, his impartial gaze today seemed to her to lack something. Normally, she realised, she saw a slightly different look in his eye when he addressed her. It was…humour, and something else. Something like interest. Or warmth, maybe. *Strange.*

Having been much more restrained since her waspish responses to him that first morning, Rose felt she had been succeeding fairly well at treating him as just a…a person, of no greater or less significance than anyone else.

He himself, Rose had had to acknowledge, was looking particularly handsome today in the formal clothing required for court.

Or perhaps all young gentlemen look handsome in this garb.

The tight breeches and well-fitting jackets that were so fashionable at present certainly showed off the male figure to advantage, Rose reflected. Of course, the only gentlemen she had ever seen formally dressed before today were the Viscount and Mr Marnoch— and their figures were entirely different.

On the way here it had been a tight squeeze even for Lord Ashbourne's generously proportioned carriage, what with five people, including three dressed in elaborate gowns with hoops and trains and with tall feathers on their heads.

We must look ridiculous! she thought now, and yet... the Viscount had said they were beautiful. *Beautiful.* She had never been beautiful before.

As their sponsor, Lady Ashbourne was required to accompany them as they approached the Queen. She had gone over the details with them a hundred times, until Rose's nerves were a mangled mess.

Still, she thought dreamily, *all will be well.*

'Girls! Girls!' Lady Ashbourne called now in a low voice, and Rose abruptly focused again on the here and now. Turning, she leaned in to hear what their sponsor had to say. The antechamber was almost empty, as most of the other girls had already gone inside.

'Well!' declared Lady Ashbourne, 'I must say I have outdone myself! By dint of a recent fortuitous conversation with the major-domo, I have managed to ensure you will be the very last to be announced. Indeed it was in the end a fairly easy task,' she assured them, 'for normally no one wishes to be last, when the crowd may be restless, the Queen bored, and the debutantes miserable with anxiety.'

'But—you prefer for us to be announced last?' Anna's puzzlement came across clearly in her tone.

'Indeed I do. You will make an impact, girls, I know it. First or last—never the anonymous middle!' She eyed them all. 'Miserable with anxiety? Ha! Not my girls!' she declared, clear pride in her voice. 'Why, you are as serene as a bevy of swans!'

Only because you cannot see my knees quaking!

Still, Rose had to acknowledge that some of the other young ladies had looked much more anxious than she. Perhaps there was some advantage in knowing so little of London customs, and having avoided spending years dreading this presentation. In addition, the girls' deportment lessons in Belvedere had included guidance on appearing calm even when one was agitated inside.

And of course being always one of three helps.

It would be so much harder for all the other girls, entering the Queen's drawing room as the only debutante from their family.

Waiting until the doors closed behind the last girl apart from them—Miss Chorley, accompanied by her mother—Lady Ashbourne turned to them, the air of excitement about her even more pronounced.

'Veils off, girls!' The heavy face veils had been a clever notion from the mantua-maker who had created their elaborate court dresses. The face veils had been donned just before leaving the carriage. The fabric masks were fine enough not to cause discomfort, yet gauzy enough to prevent people from realising they were identical. While the other girls and their mamas had glanced curiously in their direction, their disguise had not been penetrated. With the assistance of the four palace maids, Lady Ashbourne now ensured that the girls' veils were removed, their dresses and lappets were straight, their four-foot-long trains extended, and that they were arrayed as agreed.

'Is that you, Anna?' she asked, and Anna nodded. As the eldest she was in the centre, with Izzy a step behind and to her left, and Rose another step behind and to Anna's right. 'Now remember, walk slowly,' she added—unnecessarily, as the girls had been rehearsing this walk for the past three days in the Ashbourne ballroom, long curtains tied to their waists and nodding feathers behind their tiaras, just like today's elaborate headdresses.

The court gowns, each containing yards and yards of pure white satin, were almost identical, at Lady Ashbourne's decree. The trimmings were of delicate silver thread with myriad glass beads which, when they caught the light, made it seem as though the dresses were sewn with diamonds. The diamonds set within the tiaras loaned to them by their hostess were, however, all too real. The effect was spectacular, and Rose could not have imagined ever wearing anything so beautiful. And while the dresses were almost identical, each tiara was unique—the only noticeable difference between them as they stood quietly facing the double doors that led to their future.

'Tiaras are normally for brides, you know,' Lady Ashbourne stated conversationally as they waited for the footmen to open the doors. 'However, they are perfect with the dresses and feathers. You look beautiful, my dears.'

'Thank you,' they all murmured.

Glancing down, Rose noted the sparkles on her bodice, the unnaturally wide skirt below, the details on the back of her sisters' gowns.

I know not if we are actually beautiful, but today I feel beautiful.

An increase in the crowd noise from the presentation chamber drew her attention and she lifted her head. She caught her breath. Ahead, the doors were slowly being opened. *It is time!*

James stood among the restless crowd of courtiers, suppressing a grin as he anticipated his aunt's revelation. This year's presentation had gone on for nigh on two hours, and the crowd standing about in the Great Hall had clearly had enough. He glanced to the Queen, who was currently engaged in a side conversation with her ladies, even as Miss Chorley made her way towards the dais at the far end of the room from the doors.

In the antechamber just now he had witnessed a near-altercation between the Chorleys and the impassive major-domo, who had simply kept repeating that the young lady could not be presented earlier in the sequence, as she was last to arrive. In vain had Mrs Chorley spoken of the carriage accident that had caused them such inconvenience as they had travelled from their townhouse in Soho. His aunt, an expression of kind concern on her face, had offered to let Miss Chorley enter before her own girls, and the Chorleys had accepted with churlish gratitude.

Oh, Aunt, you are a wonder! was his thought now,

anticipating the Chorley chagrin when his aunt finally unleashed the Belles on an unsuspecting court.

The past two weeks had been fascinating to say the least. Despite his intention to dine at home only once in order to assess the young ladies and their impact on his well-meaning aunt, he had found himself dining every night with the ladies. Well, it stood to reason that he would need more time than he had anticipated, given how utterly identical they looked.

The colours helped distinguish them, and he was beginning to form an impression of the Belles. Anna was sober and sensible, and often managed the other two with an even look or a frown. Isobel, the middle one, was irrepressible and on occasion headstrong. Once they were out in society she was the one he thought most likely to behave rebelliously. Yes, he would need to keep an eye on that one.

And as for Rose…he pictured her in his mind's eye. She unsettled him greatly, and he was unsure why. Each time he saw the sisters he instinctively sought her out, and it was to her that he addressed many of his comments—although he was careful not to make it obvious. He frowned briefly. At least, he hoped so.

They all, herself included, described her as 'the quiet one', and yet that was not his impression at all. Yes, she seemed to disappear in a daze of thought at times, but it had been she who had challenged him on being too quick to judge, that first day. And time and again, in the relaxed setting of his aunt's dining room, she had shown herself to be entirely capable of holding her own in the discussions at table. Of the three she was the most bookish and, although it was unfashionable for ladies to be thought of as bluestockings, it certainly made for more interesting conversation than he was used to in the company of ladies.

Naturally, there was also much talk of fashions, frills, and furbelows, for Ashbourne House had it seemed been invaded by an army of dressmakers, milliners, and cobblers—all sworn to secrecy by his enterprising aunt. He also understood that the Belles had had singing and dancing lessons, and hoped they had learned enough to be deemed passable at the interminable balls and musicales he would no doubt be forced to attend these coming weeks.

A creature of habit, he tended to breakfast alone in his chamber, disliking too much cheerfulness early in the day. He usually called briefly in the drawing room on his way out, then spent the day at his own pursuits—meeting friends, attending the boxing saloon or the fencing studio, completing social calls— before returning each evening for dinner. As he took his Parliamentary duties with the utmost seriousness he would also continue to spend a significant amount of time in Westminster. The bill to invoke the Regency had been debated long and hard a year ago in the House, but in the end, the sad decline of the King had left the lords with little choice.

Sighing, he recognised that his aunt's responsibilities would likely limit his own freedom somewhat this season. Still, she had need of him, whether she realised it or not. It was only two years since she, too, had lost the people in the world most precious to her—her beloved husband, and her brother- and sister-in-law. James nodded. His aunt was dear to him—indeed she was the only family he had now—and he would not see her put upon. Somehow, he would manage all of it.

Miss Chorley and her mother had reached the Queen. They curtseyed, exchanged a few words with Her Majesty, then moved backwards to stand to the side. Instantly, his gaze swivelled to the double doors at the back of the hall. Despite himself, he discovered he was a little nervous, hoping the girls would not trip or faint, or disgrace themselves in any way. For his aunt's sake, naturally. The doors opened and he held his breath.

Chapter Five

The major-domo's voice rang out. 'Your Majesty, Your Highness, my lords, ladies, and gentlemen. The final debutantes of the day. Lady Ashbourne presents the wards of her brother, Mr Marnoch. Miss Lennox, Miss Isobel Lennox, Miss Rosabella Lennox!'

Rose moved forward in step with her sisters, the perfect distance behind and enough to the side that she did not risk standing on Anna's train. To her left and right she sensed hundreds of people watching—courtiers, other debutantes, and their families. Keeping her eyes fixed ahead she concentrated only on walking in perfect time with her sisters, following Anna's lead. The sensation of nodding feathers on her head, along with the tiara heavy with actual diamonds, was novel, as was the hoop under her full skirt and the weight of the long train dragging behind her.

Elegant. Calm. Unhurried.

These were the words the girls had intoned in unison as they had practised in Lady Ashbourne's ballroom, and they now served to keep Rose from thinking about who might be watching.

The room was high-ceilinged, ornate, and very long. To Rose's left, bright sunshine bathed them all in warm light through three long windows hung with curtains in a gorgeous shade of rose-pink. Taking it as a reassuring sign, Rose stepped on, noting that the throne ahead was set beneath a canopy and backdrop of luxurious draped fabric—again in rose-pink, this time trimmed with gold braid. On either side of the Queen sat her ladies, but Rose kept her eyes steadfastly on the Queen herself.

Vaguely, Rose noticed that the sounds around her were slowly changing. First a hubbub, then—now—slowly decreasing. There had been quite a level of noise when they had been announced, but by the time they were halfway up the long aisle, a strange hush seemed to have fallen on the assembly.

Yes, we are identical, she thought tiredly, used to shocked responses from strangers.

The familiar response ironically gave her comfort, and what seemed an instant later they had reached the dais.

Taking one final step forward to stand to Anna's right and exactly in line, Rose knew Izzy would be doing the same on the other side. A moment later, Anna began the curtsey. Rose dipped in exact time with her, and to the exact same depth, all the while keeping her eyes fixed on the Queen.

'Well,' said Her Majesty. 'Well!' She was gowned

à la française in a heavy open robe of brocade satin, with lace-trimmed elbow sleeves and a fortune in emeralds about her neck. While the Queen's appearance was not in keeping with current fashions, it occurred to Rose that such fashions had predominated when her own mother had been young.

Did Mama first meet my father wearing just such a gown?

Perhaps Mama's hair had been powdered, like the Queen's, or might Mama have been among the new wave of ladies to insist on wearing their natural hair?

Attention! She must not allow her mind to drift.

Lady Ashbourne, who had made her own procession up the aisle behind the girls, had also now curtseyed, for Rose could plainly hear the rustle of her hostess's satin gown.

'Lady Ashbourne!'

'Yes, Your Majesty?'

'Where have you been hiding these delectable creatures? I declare I have never seen anything so pretty! Sisters? Yet they are so alike!'

'Triplets!' declared Lady Ashbourne, and a murmur of surprise rippled through the crowd.

'Triplets, I declare!' The Queen fluttered an elegant hand. 'La, and I thought only puppies were born in threes!'

This earned a titter from those within earshot—apart from a blond gentleman standing to the Queen's right who was decked out in regalia denoting royalty.

Why does he look so cross? Rose wondered briefly,

but her attention was abruptly drawn back to the Queen, who was rising to address the assembly.

We need to move aside, and swiftly!

Pushing her train out of the way, Rose took two careful steps backwards, half-turning. Anna came to the right with her, while Izzy and Lady Ashbourne gave way to the left. Thankfully no one got caught up in their own train.

The Queen smoothed her gown, then raised her voice. 'My friends, I declare we have found our diamond of the season. And not just one—but three of them!' With a gesture, she indicated the Belles should face the crowd. 'Take your bow, my dears, and then come and sit by me!'

Bewildered, Rose curtseyed to the crowd—again in time with her sisters—and tried not to show on her face her shock at the applause and cries from the crowd. 'Delightful!' declared one elderly gentleman, while most of those without debutantes of their own seemed to agree.

Afterwards, and feeling a little as though she and her sisters had just become an act in Cooke's Marvellous Circus, Rose sat on the dais in one of the chairs hastily vacated by Her Majesty's ladies, making polite conversation with the Queen—although, to be fair, Lady Ashbourne carried most of their side of it. Yes, they were orphans. No, her brother had no information on their mother's or father's family, save that the mother was a lady—this said with a meaningful nod.

Their dowries were…respectable. Yes, they had been gently educated, and were the *sweetest* girls.

Hearing the sincerity in Lady Ashbourne's voice, Rose felt a wave of warmth towards her. It was clear that their hostess had taken a risk by presenting them at Court, for their success or failure would undoubtedly reflect upon her. She had staked her own reputation based on her brother's recommendation and a brief acquaintance with them.

I shall not disappoint her! Rose thought fiercely.

'Tell me your names again! And which of you was born first?' the Queen ordered, and they did so.

'I am Annabelle, the eldest.'

'By twenty minutes!' Isobel clarified, a hint of humour in her voice. 'I am Isobel.'

'And I am Rosabella. I was born a half hour after Isobel.'

'Three babies in one confinement! Your poor, poor mother!' She turned to Lady Ashbourne. 'Tell me more, my friend.'

'Well, they were each apparently known as "Bella" or collectively "the Belles" in school,' offered Lady Ashbourne. 'Until I learn which is which, it is how I refer to them.'

'Belle, Bel, and Bella,' repeated the Queen. 'Yes, I see. Entirely apt.' Turning slightly, she raised an eyebrow at the royal gentleman Rose had noticed earlier, and he stepped forward.

'Claudio, may I introduce Lady Ashbourne, Miss

Lennox, Miss Isobel Lennox, and Miss Rosabella Lennox.' Rising, they curtseyed to his bow.

He is very handsome!

Vaguely, she was aware that, while she saw and acknowledged his good looks, he did not leave her heart pounding as it did when she reflected on the handsomeness of the Viscount.

How odd!

'It is an honour to meet you,' he murmured, yet something in his tone was not quite right. Something more than his accent.

What on earth?

'Lady Ashbourne, Belles,' the Queen continued, 'this is Prince Claudio Friedrich Ferdinand of Andernach, a distant cousin of mine. He is considering making his home in England. Is that not so, my dear?'

'Nothing is as yet decided,' he replied non-committally, and the Queen laughed. 'Ah, but I always have my way in the end, Claudio. You know it!' Turning back to Lady Ashbourne and the Belles, she declared, 'Now, you diamonds must all go and mix with the assembly, for how are you to get husbands sitting here with two old ladies?'

'Not *old*, Your Majesty, surely?' returned Lady Ashbourne, a decided twinkle in her eye.

This earned a short laugh. 'Yet not young either, my friend!' The Queen patted Lady Ashbourne's hand briefly. 'We bear our trials well, you and I.'

'We do.' A moment of shared understanding passed between them. Rose now knew that Lady Ashbourne had lost her husband just two years earlier, and of course the King was known to be unwell. He had reportedly gone into a decline on the death of Princess Amelia, their youngest child, some months before, and the Prince of Wales had been confirmed as Regent last year.

The Queen certainly has trials to bear.

Not even royal status could prevent the pain of illness and of loss. Rose felt a wave of sympathy for the two women, followed swiftly by gratitude at having her sisters by her side.

If Mama could only have been here!

Then they were rising, and curtseying, and stepping off the dais. Instantly, or so it seemed, they were surrounded. Lady Ashbourne, besieged on all sides, accepted the compliments of the ladies and gentlemen on the girls' behalf, providing introductions and explanations at a rattling pace, so much so that Rose's head was practically spinning. Never would she be able to remember half the names.

A few stood out though. Lady Mary Renton, a darkhaired debutante with a shy smile, stood silently as her mother conversed with Lady Ashbourne, then told Rose in a quiet tone that she thought Rose and her sisters were beautiful.

'I am glad you think so,' Rose replied helplessly.

Beautiful? Us?

'It must be these wonderful gowns and headdresses.' Eyeing Lady Mary's pretty face and delightful satin gown, she added, 'I think *you* are beautiful! And I am Rose by the way!'

They both laughed then, and Rose felt as though she could be friends with this girl. A moment later, Lord Ashbourne joined them. Rose introduced Lady Mary, her pulse suddenly skipping.

'And you are Rose, are you not?' His dark eyes pinned hers, making her mouth go dry.

Determined not to allow him to see the effect he was having on her, she eyed him quizzically. 'I am, but how—?' Her face cleared. 'Were you listening just now? I have just told Lady Mary my name.'

'Nope!' He grinned, and her eye was drawn once again to that elusive dimple, high up in his left cheek. 'Truth is, I tried to memorise the tiaras when you were approaching the dais. The one you are wearing was a gift to my aunt from her husband, on the twenty-fourth anniversary of her wedding day. I wonder if he suspected that he would not live to see their twenty-fifth?' His gaze drifted to the front of the tiara. 'Rose-cut diamonds in a gold and silver setting of myrtle.' His eyes met hers again. 'Myrtle symbolises love.'

Rose lifted a gloved hand to touch the tiara, ruthlessly ignoring the fact her heart was suddenly pounding even more loudly than before. Not even meeting the Queen had affected her as much as hearing him talk of love and seeing him look at her with those eyes.

'How tragic! And yet, how moving!' Thankfully her voice sounded reassuringly steady. They were speaking of Lady Ashbourne and her husband. No one else.

A thought struck her. 'How did he die, the former Lord Ashbourne?'

'Carriage accident.' His tone was clipped, his expression closed.

Oh, dear! I have upset him.

Before she could apologise—indeed, before she could even think of what to say, to their right, the musicians struck up the introductory bars to a quadrille. 'Might I have this dance?' he asked formally, bowing.

'I—yes, yes, of course.' She eyed him dubiously.

But what of Lady Mary?

It did not seem right to simply walk away from her.

Glancing about, she saw that both her sisters' hands had also been claimed by gentlemen, but to her great relief another approached their group just now, Lady Mary agreeing graciously to dance with him. Exhaling, she took the Viscount's hand and walked to the space that had been cleared for dancing during their conversation with the Queen. With some difficulty she hooked her train twice around her left arm as the other young ladies were doing, then lifted her eyes to his to indicate she was ready.

He bent his head to speak in her ear. 'I almost thought you were going to refuse me just now!'

'Refuse you? No! The dancing master was most clear with us.' Her tone was prim as she repeated M. Dupont's words. 'A lady must not refuse an invitation to dance unless she is genuinely indisposed, for gentlemen expose themselves to rejection each time they ask.'

He laughed, to her great relief—for she did not like to think her enquiry before had caused him hurt.

'I am glad to hear it!' he declared. 'Imagine the shame of being rejected by one of this season's diamonds!'

Diamond?

Yes, the Queen had used that word. 'So why did it occur to you to wonder if I might say no?'

'Well,' he offered, as they took their places for the first figure. 'I thought you might insist I dance with Lady Mary at the same time!'

Her jaw dropped. 'I did not think my thoughts were so transparent.'

This seemed to strike him, for he looked rather startled for a moment, but said only, 'Perhaps I am getting to know the Belles a little.'

'As we are getting to know you!' she retorted, part of her noting the fact that she would not speak so freely with anyone else. But then, he was part of her household now, which made everything feel different. That was the reason why she could be less guarded with him. There was something about him—something that intrigued her, and made her bolder with him than she had ever been with anyone.

As they moved through the figures they continued to converse. 'What does it mean, to be a diamond?'

'Not just "a" diamond,' he replied. '*The* diamond. Or diamonds, in your case.'

She sent him a puzzled look.

'Each season, the ladies of the Court make judgements on the debutantes.'

'They do?'

He nodded, a glimmer of amusement in his eyes at her shocked expression. 'They judge young ladies on their looks, behaviour, connections, and of course, on the size of their dowry!' His mouth twisted cynically. 'The larger the dowry, the more beautiful the damsel!'

This made no sense. 'And the diamond?' she prompted.

'Normally,' he emphasised, 'that accolade is saved for a young lady who has universal favour. The Queen has rather pre-empted matters this season. But do not concern yourself, for no one will dare contradict her!'

The dance took them apart again, giving her a moment to think. Out of the corner of her eye she spotted one of her sisters in the next set, dancing with Prince Claudio. An actual prince!

Is this truly happening?

When the figure brought her together with the Viscount once more, she was ready with her next assertion. 'What you have said defies logic.'

'In what sense?' His eyes were alight, and she had the sense he was enjoying their raillery.

Good, for I am too.

A sort of heady giddiness was pervading her, and she had to force herself to behave with composure. She must not let dear Lady Ashbourne down by being loud, improper, or in any way vulgar.

'What you have said is nonsensical, for my sisters and I are unknown in London. Also, we are not well-dowered, and have never before been described as beautiful.'

He looked thunderstruck. 'Never?' He shook his head. 'You are bamming me, Miss Rosabella!'

'Indeed, I would not do such a thing!' She reflected on this. 'Actually, that is not quite true, for I might, in some circumstances. Regardless, I assure you I am not—er—*bamming* you at this moment.'

His eyes danced at her admission—or perhaps it was her use of his cant word that had amused him. Either way, he seemed determined to stay on point. 'Your statement is flawed in three ways.' Taking her free hand, he lifted their joint hands as they stepped towards one another—so close his warm breath briefly fanned her face.

She blinked, her heart skipping, but a moment later they both took the required step back, then moved on to the next partner in their set. Her pulse was still racing, and it occurred to her that she had not had this reaction to little M. Dupont during their dance lessons.

'Firstly,' he declared when they met again—just as though they had not been interrupted, 'being unknown is a good thing. The impact of novelty is well-known—and today, my aunt has certainly made the most of it. Secondly—'

They parted again.

He is doing this deliberately!

A gurgle of laughter bubbled up inside her.

'The matter of small dowries is less of a problem, so long as it is known from the earliest opportunity. I have no doubt my aunt has ensured the Queen is fully informed. And thirdly—'

This time she knew what to expect and her expression remained serene as they made their way up the set.

'Thirdly, I do not believe you when you say you have never been described as beautiful.'

'You—excuse me?' Unaccustomed to being accused of telling falsehoods, she lit on this point first.

'How old are you?' he asked directly, and she pressed her lips together.

'Shocking! You must know it is impertinent to ask a lady her—oh, very well.' She grinned, unable to maintain the pretence. 'We are one-and-twenty!'

'One-and-twenty? Most debutantes are but seventeen.' This seemed to surprise him, but after a moment his expression grew thoughtful. 'Actually, that explains certain matters. Your poise. The lack of giggling.'

'You think we cannot giggle? Well, you are mistaken, I assure you. And I dearly hope to still be able to giggle in my dotage!' Not giving him a chance to reply, she ploughed on, returning to his earlier assertion. 'And how can it be a good thing to be unknown? I understood the *ton* valued connections above all else.'

Losing the teasing look, he appeared to give this some thought. 'Not solely connections, no. They value *breeding*. New wealth is to be abhorred, unless accompanied by centuries of old poverty. The mother's line, and the father's, plus an ability to behave without vulgarity.'

'So they hate misbehaviour and ordinary people then?'

'Not *hate*, no. They value good behaviour. Is that so bad?'

She sniffed. 'I suppose.' It all sounded rather arbitrary.

Abruptly his look was serious, his tone dark. 'Miss Lennox, let me advise you. Do not criticise the *ton*, or you will find their approval vanishes in an instant.'

Recoiling from what felt like a clear attack—and an unwarranted one at that—she lifted her chin. 'I have no need for your advice, sir.'

They glared at one another, the amity of just a moment ago vanishing like mist in the morning. Rose was conscious of a sense of hurt beneath the anger. Almost, she had dared to like this man. To trust him a little. Had she been mistaken to do so? Was it in his nature to be judgemental, and even prejudiced?

The comment about giggling which she had taken to be light-hearted just moments ago now took on a darker meaning. Did he think young ladies were fit only to giggle? Had he no appreciation of the depth of character and *differences* of character even among young ladies raised together? And who had given him the right to *advise* her about anything?

Finishing the dance in stony silence, Rose left him with a shallow curtsey and a frozen expression. His was unreadable, his demeanour stiff. Where had it gone, that feeling in her chest from a few minutes ago? In its place was a profound disappointment. She had, she realised, been perfectly ready to anoint the Viscount with all good qualities, based on what? His handsome face and figure? The fact that she had spent time with him at his aunt's house? In an instant, he had turned from possible friend to—to *judge*, and she did not like it. Not at all.

Seeking the comfort of her sisters, Rose spotted Izzy leaving the dance floor and made directly for her.

Oh, dear!

Izzy's expression was turbulent, her face flushed with anger.

'What happened?'

'Insufferable man!'

'Who? Who is insufferable?' Rose glanced about, but it was unclear to her whom Izzy was speaking of.

'That prince person! He thinks a great deal of himself, that one.'

'As does the Viscount Ashbourne!' Rose retorted. 'He dared to try and *advise* me, as though I were a junior girl at Belvedere!'

Anna had now joined them, and immediately wished to know what had got them in such high dudgeon. As always, she responded calmly, pointing out to Izzy that the Prince was literally a prince, and could think as highly of himself as he wished, while the Viscount was no doubt trying to be genuinely helpful. As she spoke, the anger left Rose like an over-mixed cake deflating when taken out of the oven.

'How do you do that?' Rose asked her.

'Do what?'

'You make things feel instantly better, just by talking to us.' While she was still convinced the Viscount was wrong, it was possible he had acted out of a mistaken sense of helpfulness.

Perhaps, after all, my reaction was a little strong.

Yet the feelings of hurt, and wariness, and—almost *betrayal*—remained.

I am being ridiculous.

To have feelings this strong was neither reasonable, nor proportionate, nor in any way logical.

Anna shrugged. 'I just try to take the sensibility out of it, and look for the good sense beneath.'

'We can always rely on you, Anna.' Glancing at Izzy, who looked no less stormy following Anna's intervention, Rose added brightly, 'Still, we are here at the palace, and dancing in court dresses. Who would have thought it possible just two months ago?'

'Well, I should much rather be back at school, sewing, than suffering such arrogance!' Izzy was unrepentant. 'And, Anna, you are wrong. Just because he happens to be a prince does not mean he can treat others with disdain!'

'Izzy!' Anna breathed in warning, even as the Prince reached them.

Bowing, he smiled politely, showing no sign that he had heard Izzy's outburst, even though he could hardly have failed to do so. 'Having already danced with Miss Isobel,' he declared urbanely, tilting his head unerringly towards Izzy, 'I should now like to dance with each of her sisters.' He looked from Rose to Anna and back again. 'Which of you is Miss Lennox, the eldest?'

Anna identified herself and walked away in step with him, her hand on his arm, while an instant later two other gentlemen came to claim Rose and Izzy for the boulanger. As Rose danced she reflected that Prince Claudio had clearly known which of them was Izzy—probably by the expression on her face. Or, more likely, that he had heard Izzy's angry words. *Oh, dear!*

And Rose herself was little better. Anger still burned within her, fierce and bright. It seemed that gentlemen of the *ton* might have a predilection for arrogance which, when she thought about it, was hardly surprising. They had clearly been reared to consider their own opinion to be always correct—particularly when debating with ladies. The anger burning in her chest, and which she had seen reflected on Izzy's face, was an unexpected challenge though. They had rarely had occasion for anger in the sheltered world of Belvedere. Occasional bickering between the sisters when one of them was feeling low, or cross, was about the height of it.

Yes, navigating the world of the *ton* was likely to be thornier than Rose had anticipated. Not only was it going to be exhausting, but it was also likely to be maddening.

I shall have to learn how to bite my tongue.

Having been genuinely cross with the Viscount, she

had behaved entirely out of character in arguing with him, and in public too.

Glancing at Izzy, Rose felt a sudden sympathy for her sister. Izzy was quick-tempered and felt things deeply. It was no wonder she spoke out of turn at times. Rose and Anna had at least learned to hide anger in public. She grimaced.

Apart from today.

Unable to prevent herself from doing so, she scanned the room for the Viscount. There he was, dancing with Lady Mary. While she could only be glad that Lady Mary was not short of dance partners, she was astonished to find a streak of what felt like angry possessiveness within.

Yes, the Viscount lived in Ashbourne House, where the Belles currently resided. Yes, they had spent some pleasant evenings at dinner. But that did not mean anything. Logic told her he was free to dance with whomever he wished. But as the day turned to evening and he danced with multiple young ladies, logic had no explanation for the vexation within her.

I dislike him! I argued with him. He is rude, and judgemental, and he spoke to me as though I were a child!

Yet her eyes followed him wherever he went.

It simply made no sense.

James went through the steps of the dance unthinkingly, his mind elsewhere.

Lord, Miss Rose is the most frustrating, the most...

He had only been trying to help, to advise her. She had never been among the *ton* before, and clearly had no idea just how vicious its members could be.

And while she and her sisters had all the advantages he had mentioned—the impact of their dramatic unveiling, accurate information in circulation about their no-more-than-respectable dowries, their beauty—here he paused, allowing himself to recollect Rose's perfect visage—deep blue eyes fringed with dark lashes and dancing with humour and intelligence, flawless complexion, rose-pink lips that curved delightfully...

He shook himself out of it, bestowing a kind smile on Lady Mary, and complimenting her dancing. She replied shyly, and he stifled a flash of boredom. This was his typical experience while dancing with debutantes—they had little to say, and had been made so terrified of making a *faux pas* that it often seemed they had no character, no individuality.

Not like Miss Rose Lennox.

And what he had not yet told her—for he had not had the chance—was that, for all their advantages, still the *ton* would be waiting and ready to judge the triplets harshly if they did anything to incite comment—much more harshly than most of the other debutantes. The stain of illegitimacy could be borne by a child of a king—indeed, dukedoms had been offered to many a Fitzroy in the past. But a trio of debutantes from rural Scotland, with neither a father nor a mother to their name...that was *quite* a different matter.

Chapter Six

'Yes, put them over here please, Burton.' Lady Ashbourne directed her butler to place the latest vase of flowers on one of the few remaining empty side tables. It was barely an hour since breakfast, yet the gentlemen of the *ton* had already arranged for multiple bouquets to be delivered to the Belles.

'More flowers?' Anna looked as bewildered as Rose felt. 'Who are these from?'

Burton, with a bow, handed his mistress a small card, before departing.

'Mr Kirby.' She pursed her lips. 'Five thousand a year and a pretty property in Kent, but frightfully dull, my dears!' She glanced at them in bewilderment. 'Now what have I said?'

Anna was first to recover. 'It was the *way* you said it. So seriously, and yet it ended so…so…'

'So badly!' declared Izzy, sending them all into paroxysms of laughter again. Lady Ashbourne helplessly joined in, and they all had a good laugh together.

'Well!' she said, a little later, drawing a delicate

handkerchief from her reticule. 'I cannot remember when I last laughed like that.' She dabbed at her eyes. 'Thank you, my dears.'

The door opened, admitting her nephew. 'Good morning, James! I trust you are well.'

'Never better,' he declared, in a clipped tone. 'Good morning, ladies.' His eyes narrowed, focusing on the handkerchief clutched in his aunt's hand. 'Have you been—are you upset, Aunt?' Swiftly, he took a seat beside her.

She patted his knee. 'Not at all, my dear. The Belles and I have just been indulging in a bout of laughter. I have not felt so contented in a very long time.'

His brow cleared. 'Then you must share the joke!'

By this stage Rose was feeling decidedly uncomfortable. Once he heard what they had been laughing about they would no doubt come in for more criticism—or *advice*, as he would have it. Only this time, Lady Ashbourne might also be on the receiving end of his fault-finding. That she could not allow.

'Ah, but to do so might earn your disapproval,' she declared tartly. 'We are not to criticise the *ton* in any way, manner, or shape. Is that not correct, my lord?'

'Naturally.' He raised an eyebrow. 'I do hope you have not been leading my aunt into committing an indiscretion.'

'Oh, no!'

'Never!'

Anna and Izzy spoke in unison, while Rose sat impassively. Naturally, she did not think their innocent humour to be anything like an indiscretion, but he, being Lord *Judginess* Ashbourne, would surely not agree. And she would not have their kind hostess upset for the world.

Lady Ashbourne was frowning slightly. Anxious to divert the conversation away from the comment about Mr Kirby, Rose indicated the multiple flower bouquets adorning the room. 'Are these blooms not beautiful, my lord?'

He looked about, his expression neutral. 'I believe self-consequence is unbecoming.' He snorted. 'Looks like the west side of Covent Garden around four in the morning,' he declared dismissively.

Her jaw dropped.

Self-consequence? Really?

As she had that first day, she found words pouring from her tongue without any restraint.

'You think it self-consequence for me to draw your attention to the flowers, my lord? That I drew your attention to them because of pride or conceit, and not simply because they are genuinely beautiful?'

He shook his head sadly. 'They have clearly been sent by your admirers, poor souls.'

His aunt slapped his arm playfully. 'Oh, James, do stop teasing us! I for one am delighted that the Belles were such a success at their presentation.' She glanced about. 'To be fair, we do have enough for a market stall, if one were so inclined!'

Rose was still not ready to let his barbs pass without further comment. 'And are you familiar with Covent

Garden at that time of day, my lord?' she enquired in a deceptively sweet tone.

No doubt he is the sort of man who regularly stays out half the night carousing or tomcatting!

'Miss Rose.' A hint of hardness in his tone set Rose's teeth on edge. 'I can tell you that I am familiar with many different parts of London, and many different times of the day or night. Is there a particular reason for your curiosity?'

'Oh, no,' she declared innocently. 'None at all. You may do as you wish.'

'Oh, but I do.' Now there was a definite edge in his voice.

'I do not doubt it.' She matched it, and their eyes met, she refusing to look away. The moment stretched, and suddenly aware that her sisters and Lady Ashbourne were eyeing their exchange with surprise and a hint of concern, Rose added brightly, 'I declare the pink tulips are my favourites!'

'Oh, no! The *roses*, my dear!' Lady Ashbourne contested. 'Roses have always been my favourite flower!'

As her sisters joined in the conversation, Rose stole a look at the Viscount. He sat there, self-satisfied and oh-so-sure of himself. What she would not give to see him at a disadvantage! Her nails dug into her palms.

Yes, his advice *may* have been kindly meant last night—although she had her doubts. But his way of delivering it had been offensive, with implied criticism of her for daring to suggest his beloved *ton* was not perfect in every sense!

And it was not—no, not by a long way. She was not blind. As well as the delightful pageantry of the court, she had been alive to the subtle and not so subtle slights and put-downs. The people whispering behind fans, tittering about others in the room. The married ladies flirting outrageously with game young bucks above their innocent daughters' heads. Yes, being one-and-twenty rather than seventeen at one's come-out certainly had its advantages.

And to think she had been on her way to quite liking him! What madness had briefly overtaken her, she did not know. But the scales had now fallen away from her eyes and she had seen him for his true self— someone smug, and knowing, and—and cocksure! His demeanour today was a clear continuation of the arrogance he had shown last evening. Her refusal to simper at him, thanking him for his advice and submitting to the notion that he was fit to advise her, was no doubt surprising to him.

Well, she had been raised by the most excellent teachers at Belvedere to think for herself. Deportment and good parlour manners notwithstanding, she had a quick mind and would not surrender it. As the others continued to converse, she reflected on this. As a young lady used to the self-deprecating humour and openness of the enlightened Scots, her first encounters with the *ton* had left her less than impressed. The sooner they could all return to Scotland, the better.

But first, she had work to do. Work that was much more important than prancing around on dance floors, or giving any weight to the opinions of handsome men. Now that they had been successfully launched, the Belles needed to try and find out more about their beloved mother.

Putting the vexing Viscount from her mind, she considered the matter. Who had she been, Mrs Lennox? Had Mama made her debut before the Queen, as her daughters had yesterday? Surely a lady giving birth to triplets would be extraordinary enough to be remembered, even more than twenty years later? Or had she left town before her condition was known? With little to go on, Rose and her sisters would have to use every ounce of wit they had to uncover the story of their own origins.

The door opened, jolting Rose from her reverie. The footman was announcing some callers—two gentlemen who had conversed with the sisters the night before. As they rose, preparing to greet the visitors, the Viscount bowed generally at his aunt and the Belles.

'I must take my leave of you,' he declared curtly, disappearing through the door with a muttered word and a swift bow to the gentlemen as they entered.

Lady Ashbourne sent the triplets a wry glance. 'Suitors, early in the morning—it is too much for James,' she mouthed, before turning to greet the visitors. 'What a delightful surprise! Welcome!'

That was just the beginning. The day passed in an abundance of visitors, and flowers, and even poetry. As gentleman after gentleman arrived to converse, and discuss, and compliment, Rose gradually found herself wilting, like the tulips in the vase in her eyeline. The heavy scent from so many flowers was overwhelming, and if she heard one more reference to the three Graces, she was sure she would be forced to run from the room, screaming like a Fury.

Instead she sat, and smiled, and pleased, allowing her sisters to carry most of the conversation—of which they were well capable. Oft-times she took refuge in reverie, smiling absent-mindedly while allowing her thoughts to drift away. Anna and Izzy were well capable of maintaining the social niceties, and Rose simply could not keep up with all of this chatter as they seemed to.

Some ladies visited them too—the mothers or sisters of the gentlemen—but some also came in their own right, Lady Mary being one of them. She and her mother arrived in the late afternoon, by which time Rose felt as though her smiling muscles would shortly begin to ache. Despite this, her smile was real as she walked across to greet Lady Mary, whose mama was already busily engaged in conversation with Lady Ashbourne.

'Lady Mary, it is a delight to see you again!' She held out both hands to the young lady, noting again as she did so how pretty Lady Mary was, with her dark hair and flashing dark eyes. 'I enjoyed our conversation last night, and wished we could have more time to talk.'

Lady Mary's face lit up. 'It was you! I confess I worried how I was to know which of you was the Miss Rose Lennox I had talked with.'

'I shall give you a clue,' Rose said in a confiding tone, leading them both to a satin-covered settee near the piano. 'My favourite colour is rose-pink.' She indicated her gown—a sprig muslin morning dress with clusters of pink flowers printed throughout.

Lady Mary's eyes widened. 'That is helpful indeed!'

A gentleman was now hovering near the settee. Ruthlessly, Rose ignored him, having had quite enough of conversation with gentlemen to last her a lifetime.

He can go and speak with Lady Ashbourne, or one of my sisters.

By this stage the long room had multiple different clusters, including one for their hostess and one for each of the Belles. There were also small groups of gentlemen conversing by the fireplaces and by the window.

Why, it is like a party—and this is just a series of afternoon callers in a drawing room!

An enormous drawing room, to be fair.

'Miss Lennox—' Lady Mary began, the hint of a warm smile in her eyes.

'Oh, do call me Rose! There are too many of us to all be Miss Lennox.' Abruptly, the Viscount's image was in her mind, and he was frowning. 'That is, if such a thing is permitted? I should not wish to appear *forward*, or to do anything I ought not!'

'It is perfectly acceptable between friends,' declared

Lady Mary with a smile, 'and I do hope we shall become friends.'

They chatted for a while, about everything and nothing, Rose feeling decidedly relieved to be once again in the easy, uncomplicated company of a lady. She talked freely of their childhood in Elgin and their time at Belvedere, while Lady Mary told her of her very different upbringing in London and in the family home in Sussex.

'My childhood was all very different from—' Rose waved a hand at the drawing room generally '—*this*, I assure you!'

'Your looks reminded my mama of someone,' offered Lady Mary casually, and Rose's heart skipped a beat. 'Do you have family in London?' she continued. 'Who are your parents?'

'As to that, we know very little,' Rose replied. 'Our guardian assures us our mama was a lady of the *ton*, but unfortunately he knows only her married name, Mrs Lennox. Might you have heard of the family?'

Lady Mary frowned. 'Lennox…the name is not familiar.' She shrugged. 'Were you born in London?'

'Honestly, I do not know.' She frowned. 'I do not think so. We lived somewhere else until we were five and I think we were born there…but I do not know where *there* is!' Her shoulders slumped. 'We lost our mama when we were ten, you see, and so we could not question her about such matters.'

'How sad!' Lady Mary looked genuinely sympathetic. 'Well, if your mother left London before you were born then *if* my mama met her it would have been when she was a debutante herself.' She grimaced. 'That would have been a very long time ago.'

'I understand.' Rose, with some effort, clamped down on her feelings—hope and excitement vying with the expectation of disappointment. Hopefully none of it was showing in her voice. 'I should dearly love to know something about her. Even her own true name—before she married Mr Lennox, that is.'

Lady Mary's brow was furrowed. 'Let us ask my mother.'

Rising, they waited until her mother had completed her current conversation and was ready to speak to them. Mary then introduced her to her mama again and as Rose curtseyed she thought she saw something hard or calculating flashing fleetingly in Lady Renton's eyes. It was only brief, and perhaps Rose had imagined it. After a moment Mary explained they knew little of their own family background, reminding her mama that she had said she thought the Belles looked familiar.

'Well, I did say so,' Lady Renton replied, 'but it has not yet come to me why. In the *ton*, Lennox is an earldom, not a family name. The earldom sits with the Stuarts, I believe. So Debrett's will be of no help, I think.' Her eyes narrowed. 'It would be *such* a shame if the diamonds turned out to be little Fitzstuarts!'

Not certain what she meant by this, Rose concentrated only on the possibility that here, finally, was a hint about Mama's identity.

'We should be for ever grateful if you could help us discover our mother's identity, Lady Renton,' she declared eagerly. 'Any hint, no matter how obscure, will help.'

'Well,' her ladyship sniffed, 'I am sure it is in everyone's interests for the truth to come out—no matter how unpalatable a truth it may be.'

Unpalatable? What can she mean?

Lady Renton had turned to her daughter. 'Mary,' she hissed, 'I have told you before, stand up straight! And—oh, for goodness' sake! One of your hairpins has come loose. Fix it, please!'

Mary, blushing, fumbled to find the offending pin.

'Here, let me help you… There!' Rose smiled reassuringly at her. 'Hairpins are the most irritating things, are they not? I declare my sisters and I are for ever fixing one another's hairpins.'

'Thank you.' Mary's voice was quiet, all animation gone from her pretty face.

'Now then, enough of this—young ladies conversing together!' Lady Renton's smile did not quite reach her eyes. 'There are numerous gentlemen here today—just as I predicted, Mary! I declare I see the Earl of Garvald by the piano. Have you made your curtsey to him yet today?'

'No, Mama.'

'Then let us approach him.' She sent Rose a half smile. 'It has been delightful to meet you again, Miss Lennox.'

Clearly dismissed, Rose turned away—only to have

her attention instantly claimed by Mr Kirby and his companion the Honourable Geoffrey Barnstable. The first was—as Lady Ashbourne had so naughtily described him—utterly dull, while the other made her shudder as he blatantly ogled her form, lifting his quizzing glass to focus it on her bosom, all the while muttering words like 'delightful!' in the most odious manner.

This ordeal lasted for quite twenty minutes until Izzy rescued her, calling her away to settle something with her new acquaintance Mr Gavigan—a gentleman on the wrong side of forty with a merry demeanour. Afterwards Rose managed to perform a similar service for Lady Mary, noting that her mother was engaged in deep conversation with two ladies of a similar vintage and mien. Lady Mary, meantime, had been trapped in conversation with a young gentleman by the fireplace and was looking decidedly uncomfortable.

'Rose! Thank you for rescuing me, for I do not know how much longer I could cope with listening to Mr Fitch talk about his horse!'

Rose giggled. 'So that was Mr Fitch? I declare there are too many names, and I am already all muddled in my head!'

'I know exactly what you mean. Still, Mama has told me the only people I need to focus on are the most eligible bachelors. Only certain gentlemen will do.'

'Your mama is doubtless thinking of your best interests.'

'I know.' Lady Mary's shoulders slumped. 'And it

is not unreasonable of her to hope I will make a brilliant marriage, being the daughter of an earl and all.'

'Indeed.'

There was a pause. 'Was it hard for you, growing up without a mother?' Lady Mary's eyes were sad.

Accepting her clear wish to change the topic of their conversation, Rose shook her head. 'You need not pity us, for as I mentioned we had our mama until we were ten years old. I can remember her clearly—her smile, her eyes...they were a hazel colour, with flecks of green as I recall. Her hair was fair, like ours.' Shaking away the memories, she gave Lady Mary a smile. 'It was only much later that we realised we knew nothing of her own home and family, or my papa. We have no memories of him, and we cannot recall her speaking much of him, save to say he was a good man who loved her. If we can find out more about either of them during our time in London I shall be content.'

'Then—you do not intend to stay?'

'Stay? Here?' Rose looked at her blankly. 'Well, no. At least—I had not thought about staying.'

Lady Mary looked puzzled. 'But—are you not here to find a husband?'

Unbidden, the image of a certain dark-haired gentleman filled Rose's inner vision. 'A husband? No. At least,' she frowned doubtfully, 'I do not believe so.'

Hearing her own uncertain words, her confusion increased. Finding the truth about herself—that was why she was here, was it not? Husbands were for other ladies—not for girls like her, freshly out of the school-room, even if she was one-and-twenty.

And yet, something within her had responded to the notion. Responded with a force that was shocking in its intensity, and which was now sending her mind reeling in hitherto unknown directions. She gripped the arm of the settee, as if to guard against a sudden spiralling dizziness. There was a roaring in her ears and her heart felt as though it had jumped into her throat, so strong was the pulse beating there.

No! she declared inwardly.

She would not allow her own imagination to run away with foolish notions, to distract her from her aims of discovering who Mama was and then return-ing to Belvedere to become a teacher.

Why, I do not even like the man!

Chapter Seven

'A hit!'

James grinned as Angelo the Younger, the fencing master, acknowledged his jab. Finally he was beginning to master the new technique the man was teaching him.

'Enough for today, I think. Thank you.' Picking up a damp towel from the table at the side of the room, he cleaned his face and neck, then retied his cravat in front of the mirror before donning his waistcoat and jacket. Having been reunited with his cape, boots, hat, and cane, he left the premises in as light a mood as he had experienced in a long time. Whistling softly, he made his way through Angelo's and out onto Bond Street, where he spent the next ten minutes moving slowly through the throng, lifting his hat to acquaintances and being generally affable.

'Ashbourne!' Instinctively, James turned to discover who was calling his uncle, then remembered with a cold sinking feeling that it was *he* who now bore the title. The title, and all of the responsibilities that came with it.

'Robert! Well met, my friend.' Clasping his friend's hand warmly, they exchanged pleasantries, and before long Robert suggested they take their conversation to their club, or alternatively to the nearest tavern.

Momentarily tempted, James shook his head. 'I cannot, I am afraid. There is a damned mountain of work on my desk—I am under the orders of my steward these days, sadly.' He chuckled. 'Not like when we were at Oxford, that is certain!'

'Indeed, no.' They grinned at one another as memories of various foolish antics flashed through James's mind.

Robert indicated to his left. 'I shall walk with you a little way, if you permit.'

James was delighted with this arrangement, and so they walked together as far as Grafton Street, talking of everything and nothing.

'We arrived in town just last night, and I have seen almost no one yet. What of the Queen's presentations? Were you there?'

James, trying not to recall the beautiful, infuriating Miss Rose Lennox, confirmed it in the briefest of responses. His friend, though, seemed determined to pursue the topic.

'Well? Who is to be the diamond of the first water this season?'

James could feel himself tense up, but managed a nonchalant tone. 'My aunt is sponsoring her brother's wards—identical triplets, if you please. Apart from them, the talk is all about Lady Mary Renton, Miss Chorley, and Miss Anderton.'

'My sister is to make her own debut this year, and is quaking in her boots about it. She is to be presented at next week's session.' He frowned. 'She is no diamond, but is pretty in her own way, and good-hearted. I pray she manages to navigate the season safely.'

James grimaced. 'It seems we will both see the season from a different perspective this year. I do not want my aunt to be vexed by her new duties. Not after the challenges of the past two years.'

'No indeed! Let us, then, approach the balls and soirées with fortitude, and with an eye to our womenfolk. At least we are both in the same situation, my friend.'

They had reached James's home. Politely, he invited his friend inside for tea, but Robert declined with a smile and a wave of his hand. 'I shall take no responsibility for distracting you from your viscountly duties, James! Besides, we have all of the season to see one another—as we chaperone young ladies about! Lord, who'd have thought it!'

James's smile faded as he climbed the steps and entered Ashbourne House. Crossing the threshold, he felt once again the burden of history settle upon his shoulders. For the sake of his parents, his uncle, and all of their ancestors, this duty was his now. And for the sake of his aunt, who had lost the man she loved...

I shall do this.

Two years was the blink of an eye, and still he ached

to see his mother smile once more, or to seek counsel from his wise uncle. And as for Papa…his throat tightened. No. It was time to work, not to wallow in sadness. Squaring his shoulders, he made for his library.

'You are not seeking to marry this season?' Lady Mary's astonishment was evident. 'But that is the whole purpose of making one's debut before the Queen!'

'It is?' This was surprising news, although Rose was now recalling the Queen's comment about getting husbands.

Lady Mary leaned closer. 'It means you are now part of the marriage mart.'

'The *what*?' Rose had heard of a cattle mart, a fish mart, even a flower mart. But a *marriage* mart? 'Do you mean mart as in market?'

'That is what they call it.' She raised an eyebrow. 'It is a little vulgar, to be sure. People simply mean to refer to the fact that unmarried debutantes come to London at this time of year—the season—and any bachelors or widowers considering marriage may attend the same balls, routs, and soirées, in order to select a bride.' Lady Mary grinned. 'Is it not the strangest thing?'

'They call it a mart?' Rose reflected briefly on this. 'And we are the cattle, I must suppose.'

Lady Mary looked a little uncomfortable. 'Has no one explained any of this to you before?'

'Our guardian had said he would like us to enjoy

a season in London, and that he believed our mother had had a season. I simply took it to mean spending a season here, enjoying social events. I had no idea… *Must* we choose a husband?'

'Well, no.'

'I am glad to hear it!'

'But—' Lady Mary looked confused. 'Do you not *wish* for marriage? A household of your own, and children?'

'I have not given the matter much thought,' said Rose, surprised by the questions. Not only did she consider herself too young, but as far as she knew there were no eligible gentlemen in Elgin, and so on the rare occasions when the matter might have occurred to her, she would have assumed she would probably never marry. The very idea was theoretical to her—not in any sense real.

At least, not until a moment ago, when a very specific gentleman had popped into her mind, unbidden. *Strange.*

Lady Mary's eyes widened. 'But you have been educated in household management?'

'Oh, yes.' Rose nodded. 'Our school was most thorough. But you understand if I do not marry, I must still manage my *own* household. I had thought to become a teacher.' At this, Lady Mary was eyeing her as though she had two heads. 'What? It is no more outlandish, I assure you, than a marriage mart!'

Lady Mary laughed at this, shaking her head. 'Very true. I had not thought about it in such a way before.'

Her gaze sharpened. 'If a gentleman was to catch your eye, though…'

Rose considered this, frowning.

'…or your heart!' Lady Mary's eyes were shining. 'You would be open to the possibility, yes?'

'I suppose so. But from what I have seen so far, that is an unlikely prospect.'

'So you do not oppose the notion of matrimony? Your own mama was married, of course, to Mr Lennox.'

Rose made an unladylike sound. 'Much good it did her, for he very inconveniently died at the worst possible time, leaving her with not one but *three* daughters!'

Lady Mary's eyes were dancing. 'Ah, yes, gentlemen can be most inconsiderate!'

Feeling slightly guilty, Rose added, 'I am sure he did not *wish* to die!'

'No, of course not.'

Feeling she had redeemed herself a little, Rose proceeded to quiz Lady Mary on all the details of the marriage mart, which she was more than delighted to provide. And by the time the guests departed, she felt well on the way to having cemented her new friendship.

'And so, we are to hope for vouchers to an assembly room called Almack's, which is the height of this *marriage mart*.' Rose's tone was scathing as she uttered the last two words.

She and her sisters were in Izzy's room—the central

of the three bedchambers. It had become their habit every night to meet there to talk after Lady Ashbourne and her nephew had retired. When Rose had suggested it on their second night there, she had carefully omitted the tale of her encounter with Lord Ashbourne in her night-rail, and she had made certain to don a peignoir over her nightgown before venturing out of her chamber each night.

It was the first time she had held such a secret from her sisters, but in truth she was unsure what to make of her response to the Viscount, and worried that if she spoke of her shocking encounter, it would both earn censure from her sisters and potentially expose the fact that she... What? Was drawn to him? That she was unsure what she thought of him? That he made her heart flutter in ways that no other man did? Reluctantly, she was beginning to admit that her body's response to him could not still be due to their unexpected first encounter, but was as yet unable to name or define what was occurring. She was still cross with him, that much was clear, and disappointment was uppermost when she thought of him now.

Tonight, unusually, the Viscount had not dined at home—a fact which Rose *knew* had to do with their falling out last night, a falling out that had been reinforced by their conversational fencing in the drawing room this morning. Well, naturally she could not *know* it, not for certain, but she was convinced of it.

'Well!' Anna's and Izzy's faces bore identical scandalised expressions. 'So the whole thing is one enormous social whirl, designed to fire off their daughters?' Anna sounded incredulous.

Rose nodded. 'And as for the gentlemen... I suppose they circle about, making judgements on the *worthiness* of the young ladies?' Izzy's expression was fierce. 'I can just imagine... Ugh! How appalling!'

'The thing is...' Anna's brow was creased, 'from a purely *practical* point of view—'

'Uh-oh.' Izzy sent a look of glee towards Rose.

'Here we go. *Practical*,' Rose added, then grinned at the daggerish look coming at her from Anna's direction. 'Do continue, dear Anna.'

Anna rolled her eyes, but clearly her need to complete her point was greater than the irritation she was feeling at her sisters' raillery. 'As I was saying, from a purely practical point of view it would make sense for us to marry.'

About to ask why, Rose refrained, since they all knew very well that wives and even widows had much more freedom and financial security than spinsters. 'It is just... I had not really considered the possibility before.'

'Well, why should we have done so,' Anna persisted, 'when the only men we encountered at home were either too old, too young...or not gentlemen?'

It was true. There *had* been men of marriageable age at home, but they had all been farmers and innkeepers and the like.

I had not realised we had been raised with such strong notions of class.

And yet it was hardly surprising, for the differences between the classes were everywhere.

Izzy's thoughts had clearly gone in a similar direction. 'Our mama was from the *ton*. We know this already.' They eyed one another. They had always half-understood it, yet here in Mayfair at the start of the social season, they were understanding the significance for the first time. It was no little thing, to be a member of what was known as 'the upper ten thousand'—people with wealth, and influence, and standing.

'We really need to find out who she was,' declared Izzy. 'Rose, that is your quest. Have you discovered anything so far?'

Rose grimaced. 'Not much. Lady Mary's mother, Lady Renton, thinks we look familiar, and wondered if she had made her debut during the same season as Mama. She has gone away to think about it.'

'Good, for we do not accidentally wish to marry Mama's younger brother or some such nightmare!' Anna's eyes were dancing at the very idea.

'So let us only flirt with gentlemen who cannot possibly be closely related to Mama or our unknown papa,' asserted Izzy. They all laughed at the notion of flirting—something that would have been unthinkable just days ago. London was very different to Elgin.

'But seriously, how are we to do so, when we have no idea of Mama's maiden name?' Anna frowned, then an idea seemed to come to her for she added, a hint of slyness in her tone, 'I suppose foreign princes must be a safe option, eh, Izzy?'

Izzy glared at her. 'Not at all, for the prince in question let slip that his own father lived here for a few years, more than twenty years ago. Besides—' she tossed her head '—I could never consider aligning myself with anyone so arrogant.'

While wholeheartedly agreeing with the sentiment, Rose's attention went to the lack of logic in Izzy's assertion. 'But the Prince's name is not Lennox!' How could someone whose name was Friedrich of Wherever marry a lady who was then known as Mrs Lennox? And besides, the man had clearly already been married, for Prince Claudio looked to be about their own age.

Izzy opened her mouth, then shut it again. Turning to Anna she said in a flat tone, 'Are you going to tell her, or shall I?'

Rose looked from one to the other. 'Tell me what?'

'Lord, Rose, you are such an innocent!' Izzy sounded frustrated.

'What she means to say, Rose...' Anna seemed to be choosing her words carefully, 'is that the reason Mama might have ended up in Scotland, with no husband, is because she never had one.'

'Never had one?' Rose eyed her blankly. 'But—but I do not—oh!' Abruptly, Anna's meaning sank in. 'Lady Renton said that Lennox is a Stuart earldom in the *ton*, not a surname, and speculated we might be Fitzstuarts! At the time I did not understand her meaning, but... I do now.' It had never occurred to

Rose that Mama might not have been married—even though she knew such things occurred.

'Quite. To be with child is ruinous for an unmarried lady of the *ton*. Perhaps Mama ran away—'

'Or was rejected by her family—'

'Because she was with child.'

'With child…*us*?' Rose's hand went to her mouth. 'Oh, poor, poor Mama!'

'That may not be what happened,' cautioned Anna. 'We simply do not know. Our first step must be to discreetly discover who she was.'

'That will then lead us to him—our father, I mean. If any of his family are here, we should confront them!' added Izzy, her eyes blazing with passion. 'I would know the truth, and soon! Why was she abandoned so? Was it her family's fault? Or does the responsibility lie at our father's door? Perhaps these Stuarts—'

Anna's tone was scolding. 'Lord, Izzy, quit being so devilish, and take your head out of those gothic novels. This is not a story in a book. This is *real*. And real life is always more…'

'Practical?' offered Rose.

'Yes, more *practical* than a storybook. Our papa died, remember? And Mama always described him as a good man. The truth may be entirely prosaic—she may have simply married someone her family disapproved of. But speculation is useless, so I suggest we quit guessing and instead focus on finding out if anyone in the *ton* remembers Mama.'

They said goodnight soon afterwards, and as she

padded barefoot back to her chamber Rose's head was reeling. First, the marriage mart, and now this.

There may be no Mr Lennox.

Had Mama been seduced by some vile adventurer, and been rejected once it became obvious she was with child? Oh, Rose could well believe it. Not that she could make any judgements about her poor mama. But had she not seen for herself the arrogance of certain gentlemen? And the antics of some of the people in the Great Hall yesterday?

She was no moralist, and had known of cases even in Elgin—the kitchen maid who had been sent away amid rumours she had been 'involved' with the butcher's assistant, such involvement resulting in her being in an *interesting* condition. The two girls ahead of Rose at school who had spoken openly of their status as the illegitimate daughters of gentlemen. They had seemed content with their lot, she recalled, and grateful that their natural fathers had paid for them to be educated. They had also, Rose recalled, had no expectation of being acknowledged by their fathers, nor marrying well.

No such intelligence had ever been presented to Rose about her own situation, and yet she knew that such a possibility must now be considered. Well, that would certainly put paid to any notions of success in the marriage mart! From what little she knew so far of London society, they would not for an instant countenance an alliance with a lady born on the wrong side of the blanket. The notion was both lowering and strangely freeing all at once.

I do not need to play their games.

Climbing into bed, she tried to imagine the Viscount's response if it were confirmed that the Belles were illegitimate. He seemed very proper. Might he tell his aunt to send them away? Perhaps their determination to uncover the truth about their origins might lead to unexpected news.

She caught her breath. Had Lady Ashbourne even considered the possibility? Their kind-hearted hostess had done nothing but good for them. Rose would hate to think she could be hurt if it were discovered she had been harbouring cuckoos in her nest—girls who should be nowhere near polite society. On that troubling thought, she blew out the candle.

Chapter Eight

With some trepidation, Rose raised the matter at breakfast the next day. Waiting until the footmen had departed after serving the food, she began by telling their hostess about Lady Renton's comment.

'Indeed?' Lady Ashbourne raised an eyebrow. 'Well, that does sound encouraging. My brother told me he knew little of Mrs Lennox's background. Her given name was Maria, I believe.'

'It was?' Rose was astonished. 'I never knew that.'

'It sounds familiar to me,' Izzy offered thoughtfully, 'although I cannot say how. Perhaps she mentioned it sometime.'

'We called her "Mama" of course,' said Anna. 'And everyone else called her "Mrs Lennox".'

'Our father, had he been alive, would have called her Maria,' Izzy offered. 'As would her own family.'

'But she was alone.' Rose's voice faltered. Alone, and never to be called by her own name again. A lump of hard, cold sadness pierced Rose's chest.

I am sorry, Mama.

'I am almost certain it was Maria. I shall check my brother's letter to me later, to be certain.'

'Then—you do not mind us trying to find out about her? Or about our father?'

'Not at all!'

'Even if—' She faltered.

'Even if it turns out she was unmarried?' Izzy, naturally, finished the sentence when Rose found she could not.

Lady Ashbourne raised an eyebrow. 'Then you have thought to consider the possibility?'

'We have.' Anna's tone was sober. 'But what would it mean, Lady Ashbourne? For us, I mean?'

'And for you?' Rose added quietly.

'That rather depends…' Lady Ashbourne paused, as the first footman had returned with freshly boiled eggs. Gradually, the kitchen staff were adapting to the different tastes of their guests. More porridge, rolls, and eggs at breakfast. Less meat and smoked fish. 'Today,' she declared, changing the subject entirely, and without even a hint she was doing so, 'I mean to take you on some house calls with me. We were at home yesterday. Today we shall call on others.'

Taking her cue, the girls steered away from all controversial topics while the servants were present. Afterwards, safely ensconced in the drawing room, Lady Ashbourne picked up the thread of the conversation.

'You asked me earlier what it would mean if you were discovered to be—that is, if Mrs Lennox was not, in fact, *Mrs* Lennox. As I was saying, it would rather depend. What the *ton* detests above all is three-fold: deceit, vulgarity, and a lack of breeding, you see.' Before she could expand the door opened, admitting her nephew. 'Ah, good morning, James. I trust you are well.'

After the formal greetings—Rose ensuring as much as she could that her facial expression remained impassive—Lady Ashbourne took up her explanation yet again.

'I was just explaining to the Belles some of the rules of the *ton*. The *unwritten* rules,' she added wryly.

'Fascinating! Do continue.'

Seating himself on a gilded chair near his aunt, he was directly in Rose's line of vision.

Why should he be so handsome? she thought crossly, even as her eyes roved hungrily over his dark hair, the strong line of his jaw.

As ever in his company, her heart had begun racing in a most inconvenient manner, and a now-familiar breathlessness beset her. And this despite the fact she remained out of charity with him.

His face should instead match his personality— dour and judgemental.

And how strange it was to think it was he who had come to mind when Lady Mary had mentioned marriage.

It must simply be due to his being the gentleman I see most frequently in London.

Yes, that was undoubtedly the reason.

'Well, my dears,' Lady Ashbourne continued, bringing Rose's attention back to the present, 'the *ton* detests deceit. Someone who pretends to be something they are not. An assumed heiress who turns out to have a small dowry, perhaps, or a person who tells falsehoods about their own accomplishments. Even someone who is puffed-up may invoke censure.'

'Puffed-up?' Strangely, the image in Rose's head at the words was that of a society gentleman in the guise of a ram that had escaped shearing for two summers in a row. Puffed-up and ridiculous.

'It means they exaggerate their own virtues or achievements. They boast and bluster, skirting always on the edge of honesty while not *actually* saying something truly dishonest.' She sent them a reassuring smile. 'Not that you Belles have any need to worry about such things. No, your company manners are impeccable, and you are refreshingly straightforward, I think. No simpering or enacting tragedies with you three! However—' Her smile died. 'My brother tells me your dowries are no more than respectable, which is hardly to be wondered at since there are three of you. Still, I ensured the Queen knew it from the first. The correct information will therefore circulate about you, and the fortune hunters will look elsewhere.'

Rose shuddered. 'Fortune hunters? Then it truly is a cattle mart—in more ways than one.'

The Viscount sent her a piercing glance. '*Reserve thy judgement*, Miss Lennox,' he advised, alluding to their previous conversation. 'There are men encumbered with titles or estates or both, but with a sorry lack of funds. For such men it is sensible to consider the matter of the dowry in their selection of a bride. Madness not to do so, in fact.'

Her eyes met his, and there it was. The same strange broiling turbulence within her. It was both physical—affecting her innards from chest to nether regions—and pertaining to the emotions. She was feeling *something* very powerfully, but could not really just tell what the emotion was. Anger? Anxiety? Warmth? Strangely, those all seemed to be part of it. In the end, the overriding emotion became clear: *vexation*.

'Their *selection*?' she asked, tossing her head and feeling as though she had accidentally stepped into Izzy's slippers. 'And might the young lady have any say in the matter?'

'Well, of course she does. He may ask, and she may refuse.' He shrugged. 'It should not be a matter for great sensibility.'

His coolness inflamed her further. It was as though he was presenting himself as a bastion of sense against her railing illogicality. 'For a gentleman it may not be. But for the heifer—that is to say, the *lady*—it may matter a great deal!'

'And no one is suggesting a lady should be forced into an alliance she does not like.'

'Then you are saying that the young matrons we met who were married to men twenty and thirty years older were happy to be in such alliances?'

Lady Ashbourne spoke quietly. 'My husband was

twenty-two years older than me, yet I loved him dearly.'

'Oh, dear!' Rose swung around to eye her hostess, putting a hand to her mouth. In truth, she had almost forgotten the presence of the other ladies. 'I did not mean to suggest—that is, I—I apologise if my words caused you any distress.'

Lady Ashbourne patted her arm briefly. 'Not in the least! I am simply grateful to have the opportunity to inform you young ladies.' She fanned herself, eyes twinkling. 'I do declare I am feeling quite motherly, and I must say I like it very much!'

'But you cannot be old enough to be our mother, my lady!'

Lady Ashbourne chuckled. 'It is kind of you to say so, but I made my debut at seventeen and was married at eighteen. Had I been blessed with children they would now be your age or even older.'

I am wrong again.

Every time she spoke she seemed to err. Rose, mortified, could not help but glance in the Viscount's direction. The quizzical raised eyebrow was all it needed.

Gritting her teeth together, she vowed never again to speak if he was so much as in the same room as her, never mind within earshot. Such a vow should not be too difficult to maintain, given that it was her usual behaviour when in company. The vexing Viscount had won this particular battle, and she had been silenced. She would just have to remember to treat him as *company*, and nothing more, even though they happened to be staying in the same house. That way she could avoid repeating such humiliation in future.

Her sisters had no such anxieties to address. Instead, they smiled at Lady Ashbourne for her 'motherly' comment, then carried on with the conversation just as though the barbed exchange between Rose and the Viscount had never occurred.

'So that is the deceit aspect,' mused Izzy. 'What of vulgarity?'

Lady Ashbourne sighed. 'Some of those who have gained access to society due to a combination of wealth and an advantageous marriage do not behave...that is to say, it is possible to discern... I mean—' Her voice tailed off as she sought the right words.

'What I think you mean to say, Aunt, is that people of the *ton* can detect vulgarity from fifty feet away. And here amid the *ton*, reputation is everything. No one in their right mind could ever be careless of their reputation.'

Can he even hear how arrogant he sounds?

Her mind drifted to their housemaid in Belvedere. A plain-speaking woman from a farming family, Agnes would likely be judged to be vulgar by the likes of the pompous Viscount. To be fair, Agnes's way of speaking was blunt, to the point, and occasionally peppered with the language of the farmyard. Did that make her vulgar? Perhaps it did, here in London. But Agnes's heart was warm, and good, and she was kind and generous. Did the *ton* value these things?

'Indeed, James.' Lady Ashbourne thought for a

moment. 'Too much jewellery is often a sign. Or the wrong jewellery for the time of day. But sometimes it is in the manner of speech, or the gait and posture, or even in the air with which they present themselves.' She looked at each of the Belles, who were wearing similarly confused expressions. 'Oh, dear, this is more difficult than I thought it would be.'

'Actually, I think you have explained it rather well,' her nephew declared.

'And I must add,' Lady Ashbourne declared firmly, 'that there is no sign of any vulgarity in any of you Belles!'

'I am relieved to hear it! But—how is it so?' Anna looked confused. 'Is it to do with our education? With the teachers at Belvedere and their classes on deportment and the like?'

'I should imagine so.' Lady Ashbourne nodded vigorously. 'And if they themselves are gentlewomen, then they perhaps acted as pattern cards for appropriate behaviour.'

The girls glanced at one another, nodding thoughtfully. Rose knew they, like her, would be reflecting on the less obvious lessons they had received at Belvedere.

'But it was not just school,' said Izzy. 'I remember how gentle Mama was, how polite, how…'

'Ladylike!' Anna declared.

'Well, we know she was a lady, the daughter of a gentleman, and well-educated, as my brother reported. We just do not actually know who her family were.'

'Mr Marnoch told us she had a season.'

The Viscount was frowning again. 'Wait—I know that information about the Lennox family history was meagre. Do you mean to say you do not know *anything* of the young ladies' background, Aunt?'

'Not a bit of it!' she declared cheerfully. 'Now, do not look at me like that, James! I know you like to be cautious in all things, but you can see for yourself the Belles have the sweetest manners, and behave just as they ought! Besides, you have just heard that their mother had a season, so it is clear she was a lady.'

They behave just as they ought...

For some reason, the look the Viscount flicked in Rose's direction made her think of the first time she had ever seen him, when she had been walking about the house wearing nothing but her nightgown. Her flush began in the pit of her stomach, radiating out until every part of her was consumed with mortification, and discomfort, and a strange pulsing sensation in her nether regions that was entirely new to her. How he had looked at her!

No, on that occasion she had most certainly *not* been behaving as she ought! And even now, both she and Anna continued to leave their chambers to visit Izzy's on a nightly basis after the household had retired.

And if the Viscount is out, we know he does not come home until much later, and so it is safe to do so!

Reminding herself he could not possibly know which sister he had seen that night, she turned her eyes away from him with determination.

This time it was Anna who prompted the conversation.

'It is all very well knowing our mama was a lady, but it is true we know nothing of her family—*our* family. The third item on your list, Lady Ashbourne, related to *breeding*. Am I to assume this refers to one's parentage and ancestry?'

'Indeed. And that is where you may run into some trouble. You see, I have been checking in Mr Debrett's book which lists every member of the *ton*, and there is, I am afraid, no Mr Lennox who married a lady called Maria around twenty or twenty-five years ago. Which means...'

Her voice tailed away. Her nephew, undeterred, completed the thought. 'It means that either your mother married someone not of the *ton*, or she did not marry anyone.' His tone was flat, but Rose thought she saw disapproval lurking in his expressive dark eyes.

'I see.' This was confirmation of their own speculation. 'And so...ought we not to have been presented to the Queen?' Anna sounded uncharacteristically uncertain.

'As to that—' Lady Ashbourne now sounded more confident again '—I refer you to my previous comments regarding deceit. When Her Majesty asked me again about your parentage that day, I was brutally honest with her. "Unknown," I said. "My brother believed the girls' mother to be a lady, but nothing is known of her family—or indeed the girls' father." So you see, she knows. And her ladies will ensure that, by the end of the week, everyone will know.'

'I see.' Izzy's lips were pressed tightly together. 'Everyone. I see.'

'So what does it all mean for us? For you?' As ever, clear-sighted Anna cut to the heart of things.

Lady Ashbourne grimaced, pausing to gather her thoughts.

'It means,' declared the Viscount in a harsh tone, 'that with small dowries and the possibility of illegitimacy, you are unlikely to receive stellar offers. Realistically you should look for husbands among the older gentlemen, or those at the fringes of society desirous of a marriage to someone who will appear ladylike.' There were gasps from all four ladies at this. 'It also means that my aunt has staked her own reputation on you. If any of you do anything which may lead to gossip, anything which can be portrayed as vulgar, then not only will you be ostracised from the *ton*, my aunt may be cut along with you!'

Chapter Nine

The carriage had turned out of the main thorough-fare and into a quiet avenue. Normally, Rose would have been taking in every detail—mansions and town-houses, messenger boys and jarveys. Yet she could not, for her mind remained full of the conversation earlier about her parentage.

Who am I?

She was… Miss Lennox. But was that her true name? Did she even *have* a name—a father's surname, gained honestly and legally as the result of her parents' marriage? She had her sisters, and she was lucky to have Mr Marnoch for a guardian and his sister for a hostess. But she and Izzy and Anna had no one else. No grandparents, uncles, aunts, or cousins. No history.

Where are my people from?

She loved Scotland and still thought of herself as Scottish even though both parents, she now realised, were likely to have been English. There was no sense of *place* inside her, beyond Belvedere and the town of Elgin.

Who am I? she thought again.

Really, she had no idea.

The carriage pulled up outside yet another elegant townhouse, and Rose mentally braced herself once again to be in society with others. Unlike Izzy, who seemed to thrive on company, Rose found that being in social situations for any length of time usually tired her out—and since this would be their fourth—no, *fifth* visit of the afternoon, she was rapidly reaching her limit. There was only so much tea Rose could take.

Lady Ashbourne seemed not to notice her weariness, which encouraged Rose into thinking she was managing to hide her feelings well. *Good.* Life in London, it seemed, involved the frequent need to hide away one's true feelings.

Once the coachman had opened the door and let down the step, Rose followed Lady Ashbourne and Izzy out of the carriage, hearing Anna descend behind her. They were wearing day gowns trimmed with their preferred hues, Rose's cream muslin gown finished with cream lace and with tiny pink rosebuds along the hem, bodice, and sleeves. Mr Marnoch had been generous indeed, for the girls had been provided with an entire wardrobe of new clothes—everything from gowns, spencers, and pelisses to half boots, slippers, bonnets, shawls, gloves, and even parasols. They also had new nightgowns, corsets, stockings, and handkerchiefs, despite arguing to Lady Ashbourne that no one would know if they used their old ones.

'You are mistaken!' she had replied firmly. 'For *I* should know!'

And so they had acquiesced, and Rose was secretly thrilled at her delightful new wardrobe. However, the thriftiness in her continued to be troubled by what surely must have been a significant expense.

Unbeknown to Lady Ashbourne, the girls had begun to unpick their enormous court dresses, adorned with expensive silver thread and precious glass beads, and were cutting the yards of silk-satin fabric with the intention of remaking them into new gowns. Rose estimated she would easily get two overdresses out of her presentation gown—a gown she would never wear again. *Not* to remake them would be shocking, in her view.

Why, the four-foot train alone would easily form a short-sleeved bodice and overdress. She just needed some pretty fabric in a contrasting shade for the slip...

Perhaps I could use my old pink Sunday gown...

The front door was already open, the butler himself coming to show them to the drawing room. Already, Rose knew this was a singular honour, as most guests were escorted by footmen. Lady Ashbourne was well-respected in this household, it seemed.

Who are we visiting now?

Lady Kelgrove, Rose recalled. An elderly widow, Lady Ashbourne had reported, and one who exerted considerable influence within the *ton*.

Very well.

Squaring her shoulders, Rose prepared to please.

Half listening as the butler asked Lady Ashbourne for their names, Rose looked about her. The first thing she noticed was, as ever, the impressive proportions of the rooms. High ceilings, gilded plasterwork, large Adams fireplace, elegant furniture—all present and correct. Having lived in Ashbourne House for nigh on three weeks now, and having seen the inside of four other townhouses today, Rose could see that the *ton* had a preferred style when it came to furnishings. It was all very different to the elegant simplicity of the Belvedere parlour—the grandest room she had known for most of her life.

The butler—an elderly gentleman with a stiff demeanour but kindness in his eyes—led them up the wide staircase and along the sumptuous landing, and Rose braced herself to smile and once again play the part of the demure debutante.

The second thing to come to her attention was that there were *three* people in the drawing room, not one. Lady Kelgrove had other visitors it seemed, or perhaps these were family members. All three people—two ladies and a gentleman—were rising to greet them, and Rose formed a quick impression of them.

First, the elderly lady. Lined face, piercing black eyes, grey hair peeping out from beneath a lace-trimmed cap. She had been slightly hunched while seated, and yet now pushed herself upright with the aid of a stick, standing ramrod straight with shoulders back and chin raised. She clearly had had some stringent deportment lessons in her youth. Her silk gown had a fuller skirt and a lower waist than was currently fashionable, yet it suited her.

'Thank you, Brooks,' she murmured to her butler, easing Rose's apprehension a little. Lady Kelgrove might look terrifying, but she was respectful to her servants. That was something.

Turning her attention to the couple, Rose subtly assessed them as she made her curtsey. They were older than Lady Ashbourne—on the wrong side of fifty, certainly. Both were dressed in the expected costumes for the time of day—jacket, waistcoat, cravat, and breeches for him, his boots polished to a high gloss and his hair carefully dishevelled over his brow. His lady was wearing a round gown in a deep orange shade, with three rows of lace at the hem, long sleeves, and a neck ruff. Her cap was in the same fabric, and trimmed with the same expensive lace. Yes, more fashionable people—and quite how Rose was expected to recall all the names and relationships, she did not have any notion!

The formalities completed, they took their seats and Lady Kelgrove ordered tea. Under her breath Rose was repeating her list of people from earlier today, for fear she would forget them.

Lord and Lady Wright, who had had little to say beyond banalities. Mrs Anderton, who had had much to say, also banalities, and her daughter Miss Anderton—haughty, with red hair. And Lady Jersey, who was something to do with Almack's, the place where the marriage mart reached its apogee.

Well, she had, at the end of their visit, promised to send vouchers to Lady Ashbourne, which apparently was a good thing. Rose shrugged inwardly.

Who else?

Mrs Phillips, her son Mr Phillips—nice smile—and her daughter Miss Phillips—quiet.

And now these three. Mr and Mrs Thaxby, and Lady Kelgrove. The elderly lady was, in Rose's view, an Original. No sooner had the tea been served than she began questioning Lady Ashbourne at length about where the Belles were from and what *exactly* the Queen had said to them during their presentation.

Mr and Mrs Thaxby, having attempted a few conversational sallies—consisting mainly of gossip and put-downs—eventually conceded the floor to their hostess, seemingly accepting that she was determined to focus on Lady Ashbourne and her protégées rather than themselves. Looking decidedly put out at no longer being the focus of Lady Kelgrove's attention they recalled another engagement and departed, and Lady Kelgrove gave a wicked cackle once they were gone.

'Ha!' she said, thumping her stick off the wooden floor. 'They can take a hint, it seems! Good, for if I was forced to bear their company much longer I might have had a sudden fainting fit or bad turn. Nothing, I assure you, can clear a room more quickly than illness!'

Lady Ashbourne chuckled. 'You are a wicked, wicked woman, Lady Kelgrove.'

'Ah, but you know me well, Sarah,' she replied,

leaning across to tap Lady Ashbourne's hand with clear affection. 'I am eighty-four,' she added, directing this to the Belles. 'And when one is eighty-four one can say and do almost *anything*.'

Izzy's eyes were dancing. 'Then I can barely wait to reach eighty-four, for at twenty-one one can say and do almost nothing at all!'

'Is that so?' Lady Kelgrove's tone was sharp, and Rose caught her breath in fear.

Really, Izzy ought not—

'I see you have some opinions, Miss Lennox. Which one are you again?'

'I am Isobel,' Izzy replied, undaunted. After a moment during which they held each other's gaze, Lady Kelgrove gave that cackle again. 'Ha! I predict you will do well, Miss Isobel.'

Swinging her gaze back to Lady Ashbourne, she resumed her questioning, asking first about their dowry, then their parentage. Clearly Lady Ashbourne and her nephew had not exaggerated when they had spoken of the importance of these matters.

So why am I so cross with him?

The answer came immediately.

Because he is right, and I am wrong, and I do not like to feel so exposed.

Rose—the quiet one, the considered one, was used to feeling calm, knowledgeable, in control, only speaking when she was sure of herself.

Helping the Belvedere teachers with the younger girls had been a delight—not just because she genu-

inely liked to teach, but because she liked the feeling
it gave her.

I know things, and I teach others.

Being the learner again, adrift on a sea of uncertainty, had severely unsettled her. And besides, his
manner was deliberately vexatious. She was certain
of it.

'Are there any clues as to their parentage?'

Turning her attention back to the conversation at
hand, Rose forced herself to pay attention. At eighty-
four, Lady Kelgrove had been around the *ton* for a very
long time. Perhaps she might know something helpful.

'None. There is no Lennox listed in Debrett's.'

'Hrmmph. Not good. A tradesman or servant perhaps?'

'Perhaps.'

'It would not be the first time. Nor will it be the last.
Still, they are pretty as well as being pretty-behaved.
They should attract some offers at least.'

Rose blinked. Lady Kelgrove was speaking as
though they were not even present!

'Who knows, Sarah?' she continued. 'They might
even outgun the Gunnings!'

Rose and her sisters exchanged blank looks at this,
Anna shrugging subtly to indicate she had no notion
what or whom Lady Kelgrove was referencing.

Seeing their confusion, Lady Ashbourne explained.
'The Gunning sisters took the *ton* by storm when they
made their debuts in—Lord, I heard of it but cannot
remember exactly...'

'It was 1750,' Lady Kelgrove declared. 'Luckily, I and my Baron were already wed by then. I was two-and-twenty and already a mother too, for my daughter, Judith, was born earlier that year,' she mused. She sent them a quick glance. 'Yet here you are at twenty-one years of age with not so much as a single husband between the three of you! You are leaving it late, girls!' Her gaze became distant. 'These two sisters, Elizabeth and Maria Gunning, arrived from Ireland to be feted as great beauties and great wits. By 1752 Elizabeth had married the Duke of Hamilton, and after he died she married again. Her second husband also eventually inherited a dukedom. Not many women can be said to have been married to two dukes!'

Izzy looked fascinated. 'And what of her sister, Maria?'

'Ah, Maria…' Sadness flickered briefly across Lady Kelgrove's face. Recovering herself, she continued. 'She married Coventry, but died a few years later. Too young. Much too young. They say ten thousand people came to view her coffin.'

Maria…

Rose briefly considered the possibility, but the timing was wrong. Mama would likely have been born sometime around 1770, much later than the Gunning sisters. And besides, Maria was a common name.

'Maria Gunning had a tremendous rivalry with Kitty Fisher, as I recall,' Lady Kelgrove continued, 'once Kitty became involved with Coventry. They even argued in the park one day. How I should have loved to witness it!'

Rose's eyes widened. *Involved?* Did that mean—? Exchanging glances with her sisters, she saw that Izzy's shock was mixed with fascination.

'Yes, well, perhaps we should not speak of such matters,' said Lady Ashbourne primly, with a nod to the Belles. 'At least, not in present company.'

'Stuff!' declared Lady Kelgrove inelegantly. 'I firmly believe that girls should know of the real world once they make their debuts. I wish I had known more than I did. And I wish I had been more open with my own daughter and granddaughter.' She shrugged. 'But I can do nothing now about might-have-beens.' She focused her piercing gaze on Lady Ashbourne once more. 'Let me advise you, Sarah. Ensure these girls are well-informed and well-prepared. They have good faces and fine figures, their manners are good, and they have you as sponsor. The Gunnings had no dowries to speak of and had even performed on the stage before their debuts. If anyone asks me, I shall say that your protégées may look as high as they wish for a husband!'

Lady Ashbourne thanked her, and soon afterwards they took their leave. In the carriage, however, she took the opportunity to counsel them against putting too much faith in Lady Kelgrove's final pronouncement.

'The Gunning sisters had their season sixty years ago. What happened then was highly unusual and has never been repeated. I fear my nephew has the right of it when it comes to London society today.'

The Viscount was right. I was wrong.

Not that Rose cared about their marriage prospects. No, she had a perfectly reasonable plan for her life. Return to Elgin, live out her days in Belvedere, relish the joy that would come from teaching. It was just his infuriating *rightness*.

'So we should not expect offers of marriage from anyone of note?' Anna's voice was low.

Lady Ashbourne grimaced. 'I cannot lie. It will be highly unlikely with the possibility of illegitimacy hanging over you. You may look perhaps among the professional classes, but not the *ton*. Or at least, none of the titled gentlemen.'

'Well, that is a good thing,' declared Izzy brightly, 'since we have not come here to search for husbands, but to search for information about our parents.'

It was more than that.

We have come here to find out who we are, thought Rose, and a wave of sadness suddenly washed over her.

All of the people they had met today would doubtless be able to recite their own family history and connections back for generations.

Mrs Thaxby, in the brief time they had spent with her, had managed to mention that her maiden name had been Fletcher, and on hearing they had grown up in Scotland had stated that she and her husband owned Glenmore House in Edinburgh, which had been in the

Fletcher family for generations. No, despite growing up in Scotland the Belles had not heard of it, which had seemed to disappoint her greatly.

Everything is about pride, and wealth, and family history, Rose thought now, recalling the displeased look on Mrs Thaxby's visage.

'Should we have asked Lady Kelgrove if she recalled anyone who might be our mama?' Anna asked.

And we are no different—at least with regard to the history part.

'I did think of it,' said Lady Ashbourne, 'but we need to be careful. We first need society's leaders— the likes of Lady Jersey and Lady Kelgrove—to accept you for who you are now. And by that I mean you are beautiful, quick-witted, and well-brought-up young ladies. The Queen's approval is already given, and will be of significant assistance, but I must ask you to be patient in your search for information. We do not wish for the *ton* to think "possibly illegitimate" every time they see you.' She grimaced. 'I apologise for speaking so plainly, Belles, but it had to be said.'

Feeling a little guilty, Rose repeated her conversation with Lady Renton about Mama, and Lady Ashbourne frowned. 'Hmmm. Do not vex yourself, child. If Lady Renton remembers something useful, I am sure we should all be glad to know it.' She thought for a moment. 'The daughter is a sweet child, but Lady Renton is one of the most ambitious mamas of the season. She is determined to achieve a stellar match for her daughter…and she may well achieve it.' She marked each advantage off on her fingers. 'Title, wealth, family history, a good-looking and pretty-behaved girl...indeed the only barrier as I see it is Lady Renton herself. If there are gentlemen who can stomach having her for a mother-in-law then Lady Mary may do very well indeed.'

As they made their way to their final house call Rose felt more than ever that they did not belong in this place, with these people. Oh, Lady Ashbourne was a darling, and Lady Kelgrove an interesting old harridan whom she would like to know better. Lady Mary, too, was a sweetheart, though as Lady Ashbourne had highlighted, her mother was clearly ambitious—too ambitious on behalf of her quiet daughter? But people like the Thaxbys seemed also typical of the *ton*. In the brief time Rose had spent with them, she had formed the impression they were self-focused, small-minded, and judgemental.

And the Viscount? Honestly, Rose could not be sure which category he belonged to. He was an enigma. At first she had liked him. Liked him too well, probably. And then he had shown his prejudice and quickness to judge, and she had come to heartily *dislike* him. Yet throughout, she could not deny she was drawn to him in some unique way. Even thinking of him was making her heart skip in a most confusing manner.

It is simply because I have never been intimate with a handsome young gentleman before.

It was true. While she had, naturally, *seen* handsome men on occasion—like the man who ran one of the inns in Elgin, who was renowned for his good looks—never before had Rose lived in the same household as someone like the Viscount.

My sisters probably have the same reaction to him. The notion was lowering. Well, why would they not? They had eyes in their heads, did they not?

He is not the only attractive man among the ton *though.*

The Prince was good-looking, as was the Earl of Garvald, and even Mr Phillips, whom they had met earlier today, was attractive in a non-handsome way. He had a warm, winning smile, and seemed less conceited than some of his more handsome fellow gentlemen.

Pleasing manners are, if anything, more attractive than pleasing looks, Rose mused.

There were a few others too, and Lady Ashbourne had remarked on what a good year it was for bachelors.

'Some years, girls,' she had commented, 'the pickings are rather meagre, as the matchmaking mamas would confirm.'

This had made them laugh a little, but on more sober reflection now Rose knew it was a good thing that, unlike many of the other debutantes, the Lennox sisters were not desperate for a match.

And a good thing too, since we may well be b— illegitimate.

Even in her head, Rose could not bear to utter the word *bastard*. Still it lurked there, regardless.

* * *

London was in darkness when James quietly entered Ashbourne House, the hall clock gently chiming three. Arriving home before a hint of dawn was in the sky always seemed to him a sort of achievement, somehow. Absent-mindedly thanking the footman who had waited up to let him in, James made his way up the carpeted silence of the main staircase, candle in hand. His focus was elsewhere, on the conversations at his club tonight. His aunt's protégées were the talk of the gentlemen's clubs and, being unaccustomed to feeling any sort of connection or indeed *responsibility* for young ladies, he had been made to feel decidedly uncomfortable.

More than once tonight conversations had ceased abruptly when he joined a group, but he had gleaned enough information via careful eavesdropping to understand the threads of interest. Firstly, there was widespread agreement that they were beautiful. *Well yes.* Any man with a vestige of virility within him would say so. But secondly, the *ton* gentlemen had noted that their *manners* were pleasing, and they were willing to say so. It seemed the gentlemen were mightily impressed by the Belles' faces, forms, and friendliness. When it came to *finances* however, the matter was altogether different.

'A pity,' he had heard more than one half-inebriated gentleman mutter tonight, 'that the dowries are so limited. And of course, the *parentage*...' The tone in which this last word had been uttered had engendered within James an entirely irrational desire to plant the blackguard a facer.

How dare they speculate in such an odious way?

Yet he was forced to admit had he not had a personal interest in the Misses Lennox, he too might have joined in such idle chat. As he himself was not on the hunt for a wife—there were quite a few years ahead for him to consider such matters, he reminded himself—he did not normally engage in such conversations from the perspective of suitor. Instead he would normally play the role of disengaged observer, passing judgement on each year's debutantes with casual disregard for any sensibilities on the subject.

Regarding the matter of his own future marriage, he reflected again that he had been right when he had decided to wait. At just seven-and-twenty, there was plenty of time for him to address the issue—particularly as he was still coming to terms with his duties and responsibilities as Viscount. Knowing himself to be constitutionally cautious—despite a welcome wildness during his university years—he acknowledged ruefully that he could not imagine how he would manage to make such an important choice when the time came.

Briefly, his mind ran through some of the factors he must consider. Breeding, poise, good sense—and yes, beauty too, if he could find a lady who combined all of the Graces. No man could wish for ugly offspring. Sighing, he shook his head.

Impossible!

How on earth he would manage to select an appropriate bride when the time came, he did not know.

He paused, frowning. Having reached the first floor, he saw a chink of light ahead, coming from one of the rooms. Had the servants failed to douse a candle somewhere? He tutted. Such an error—both wasteful and dangerous! Instead of continuing up the next flight of stairs to the bedchambers on the second floor, he made his way down the dim hallway, his eyes focused on that thin line of light. The door to the library was ajar, but it made no sound as he pushed it open.

At least that.

The servants may have omitted to check the candles, but at least the hinges were all well-oiled. While he gave little thought to the running of the household, leaving such matters in his aunt's capable hands, he nevertheless expected a certain standard to be upheld.

His gaze swept towards the light.

There!

A single glowing candle in a branch of three, set on an oak side table. With a disapproving headshake he moved towards it, and as he did so his attention was caught by a slight figure curled up in a comfortable armchair. His gaze roved over her form, noting the letter *R* embroidered amid the pink flowers and pale green curls and tendrils on the thin muslin.

Miss Rose! I might have known.

Abruptly his heart was thumping in his chest—not simply at the sight of a beautiful woman, but because it was the one woman who was rarely far from his mind. Her face was relaxed in sleep, her beauty breathtaking. Helplessly, his gaze took in the gentle curves and planes of her countenance, noting in an instant the sweet bow of her lips, her finely arched brows and long lashes—darker in shade than her golden tresses, which were unpinned and fanning out beneath her.

As if sensing his presence she shifted slightly, and he caught his breath, his eye drawn inexorably to the movement of soft curves beneath the thin fabric.

Should I wake her, or simply leave?

She did not look uncomfortable, it had to be said, and the night was warm… Perhaps he should just tiptoe out.

Too late. The book open on her lap, disturbed by her movement, slid to the floor with a thump that sounded like thunder in the stillness of the night. Startled, she awoke, her eyes wide with confusion as she pushed herself upright.

Lord, I should not be here, watching her like this!

Feeling strangely like a schoolboy caught at mischief, James pushed against such a lowering notion. Seeking refuge in censure, he squared his shoulders. 'You really ought not to be falling asleep with a candle alight, Miss Lennox. Particularly—' he gestured at the floor-to-ceiling bookshelves '—in a library.'

Rubbing a hand over her face, she shook her head. There was a silence, as James found himself rooted to the spot. She, adorably bemused. He, hoping his own bewilderment was not evident in his expression.

Lord, she is like a goddess!

Their eyes met, and instantly the atmosphere was charged with possibility—as tense as the air before a thunderstorm. The urge to kiss her was almost overwhelming... There was puzzlement in her gaze, as well as—Lord save him—desire. She desired him!

But no. She had likely never even been kissed, and might have no notion what she was feeling. Focusing on her clear confusion, he reminded himself sternly that she was his aunt's guest, and he the master of the house.

I am a viscount, not some green boy free to dally with a chambermaid.

And she was no courtesan or merry widow, but a young lady of quality.

Breaking her gaze, he brushed an imaginary speck from his right sleeve, then pretended to stifle a yawn.

'It is late. I was surprised to see a light in here.'

Hearing her exhale in something like relief, he was conscious of a strong feeling of disappointment.

'Yes, of course. I apologise, my lord.'

He nodded, then briefly, daringly, he allowed his gaze to sweep once more over her form, delightfully hinted at through the thin fabric. As he watched, transfixed, she tied the belt on her sheer peignoir—a garment trimmed, he noted, in rosebud pink.

'I could not sleep, you see,' she continued, 'and so I came downstairs to choose a book...' Confusion briefly flashed across her face and she looked about, bending to pick the book up from the floor.

'Oh, dear! I do hope I have not damaged it!'

Rising, she inspected the small tome, turning towards the candle on the table to see better. Unfortunately, this gave him an unhindered view of her delectable rear, glorious golden curls cascading down her back, her shapely legs outlined through two layers of thin, candlelit fabric. Stifling a groan, he turned away. 'I shall bid you goodnight, Miss Lennox.' He threw the comment over his shoulder as he made for the door. 'Do try not to burn my house down, I beseech you.'

On that note he left the room, marching briskly to the staircase that would take him to the sanctuary of his own chamber. Lord, he had expected his quiet life to be disturbed by his aunt's debutantes. Just—never had he expected the disturbance to be quite so...personal.

Chapter Ten

'Welcome, Lord Ashbourne, Lady Viscount Ashbourne! And all the Misses Lennox! How delightful to see you all!'

Lady Renton, splendidly dressed in a sumptuous evening gown of jonquil silk, offered a gracious hand. She and her husband were tonight hosting a musicale, and the Viscount had chosen to accompany his aunt and her protégées.

'I need to ensure you will not disgrace us!' he had declared in an attempt at humour as they had left Ashbourne House. Anna and Izzy had laughed easily, which Rose found astounding. Did he genuinely not vex them as he did her? Could they not see that his so-called humour contained barbs of criticism?

Since their encounter in the library two weeks ago, Rose had been avoiding the Viscount as much as she could. Twice now, she had been indiscreet, and had been *seen* by a gentleman while in a state of undress. She shuddered at the very thought of what Miss Logie, the Belvedere headmistress, might say about such behaviour. And it had not been just any gentleman, but the *same* gentleman, on both occasions.

She eyed him balefully. Between his relentless teasing, the unwished-for reaction of her body to his presence, and the lowering feeling that she had not behaved as she ought, the Viscount Ashbourne irked her at every turn.

Naturally, he had noticed her stony lack of response, and as Anna and Izzy followed Lady Ashbourne out to the carriage he had leaned down to add in Rose's ear, 'Especially you, Miss Rosabella.'

Unable to prevent herself, and refusing to notice that his deep tones had sent a curious shiver through her, she had fallen for his bait. 'And why especially me, my lord?'

'Because,' he had returned smoothly, 'you are so easy to tease!'

He had turned away then to murmur a thank-you to the footman, not allowing her the opportunity to answer. Not that she could have answered anyway. He seemed to have a talent for taking away her powers of thought, never mind speech.

Irritation rose again within her now as she made all of the expected noises towards Lord and Lady Renton, then made her way up to their drawing room. In the weeks since their presentation, the Belles had barely paused for breath, or so it seemed to Rose. Every day they were either at home, calling on others, or out and about in London's fashionable places.

The ices in Gunter's, to be fair, had been delightful, and shopping for ribbons and stockings in the impressive bazaars an interesting experience, yet Rose's favourite moments had been spent in the parks. Hyde Park, the Green Park, St James's Park…each one more beautiful than the last, and each one giving Rose the chance to *breathe*, to inhale air unblemished by smoke or noxious odours. If she closed her eyes now she might almost imagine herself in that meadow with the milch herd, or wandering by the Serpentine, or ambling along the King's Road—but no, for she was in the *other* London, the London of the polite smile and the curtsey, and she needed to have her wits about her.

They had not yet attended a ball, but they had been to two 'small soirées' as their hostesses had inaccurately described them.

Small?

With forty people or more milling about the public rooms—most of them the same forty or fifty people who called upon them, and whom they visited in turn. There were many others, too—people Rose had met only once and would be hard-pressed to recall when she met them again.

It was clear though that some among the *ton* were determined to attend *every* event, visit *every* day. Rose listed some of them in her head. The Rentons. Mrs Chorley and her daughter. The Thaxbys. The Prince and his friends. Lady Kelgrove—who, despite her advanced years, was often to be seen in the drawing rooms of Mayfair and St James's. The horrid Honourable Geoffrey Barnstable. The taciturn Earl of Garvald.

I am quite the debutante, getting to know so many tonish people! she thought now, accepting a glass of— something—from a footman. *Strange to think we were in Belvedere less than two months ago.*

A pang went through her as she recalled her bedroom at school, the classrooms, the Belvedere parlour…yet surprisingly she could not truly say she was pining for home. Allowing her sisters to carry the conversation for now, she reflected on this. Of the three, she had been the most reluctant to leave Elgin, the one for whom this had been the biggest wrench. Anna took everything in her stride, while Izzy had been positively eager to leave home and go somewhere different.

I came for Mama, and to discover who I am, she reminded herself.

And yet she was finding something more in this busy place, full of activity and intrigue, fashion and false smiles. The *ton* was beginning to fascinate her. As the most bookish of the Belles her sisters had often accused her of having her head in the clouds, but Rose *noticed* things, and thought deeply about them. Yes, she sometimes failed to be as commonsensical as the others—well, how was she supposed to think that Mama may not have been married?—but when she noticed something or someone she tended to *really* notice them.

Glancing around the room at the throng, her eye immediately picked out the people she was drawn to, intrigued by. Lady Mary, speaking to a servant about some aspect of the evening's entertainment. Lady Kelgrove—currently pronouncing from a winged armchair by the ornate fireplace. And the Viscount.

She sighed. Yes, he intrigued her. Why, she could not say. Unlike some of the others he did not always attend *ton* events, but when he was present Rose had to fight to keep her eyes away from him, and when he was not her eyes were constantly on the door, filled with anticipation… Strangely, events where he was not in attendance always seemed to her to be dull, or flat.

Perhaps I secretly enjoy his baiting!

Yes, that must be the explanation, strange as it seemed. And yet, it did not feel enjoyable in the moment when it was occurring. No, it felt frustrating and strange and yet, she had to concede, curiously invigorating.

Her fixation with him was entirely unwelcome, and also it differed from her interest in the two ladies—one young, one old. Lady Mary was now a friend. Even at school when they had always had each other, the Belles had also developed friendships among the other girls, each to their taste. Rose had always been drawn to shyness, to bookishness, to people who understood the beauty of silence. Lady Mary had a quiet stillness about her that Rose instinctively liked.

Yes, I enjoy the company of Lady Mary.

Lady Kelgrove was fascinating for other reasons. Having lived through the key historical events of the last eight decades, she had plenty to say about them—

and had found in Rose an avid listener. What had begun with the story of the Gunning sisters had now developed into a habit where Rose would seek out the old lady at every event, gently encouraging her to speak of her youth, her life, and the events that had shaped London and the world. Lady Kelgrove seemed delighted to find such a fascinated listener, and Rose was learning about everything from the Great Terror to the challenges of walking elegantly through a crowded room wearing enormous panniers and a tall, powdered coiffure. Lady Kelgrove was also blunt and open about matters about which the Belvedere teachers had been decidedly coy, like childbirth. Yes, Rose would surely find the opportunity to sit with the old lady again tonight.

Who knows what I shall learn?

While she was developing a decided affection for the two ladies—and, naturally, for Lady Ashbourne, who was just as kind-hearted as Rose had initially surmised—her feeling of being drawn to the Viscount was more complicated. He vexed her, he teased her, he irritated her intensely at times, yet sometimes when he looked at her *just so*, her breath would catch in her throat and her heart would pound in a most curious manner. Deep down, she was vaguely aware she wanted him to like her—sometimes believing he did. Yet other times when he was critical or standoffish or vexing…

She sighed, bringing her attention back to Lady Renton's drawing room. Once again her mind had drifted back to the Viscount Ashbourne—as, unfortunately, had her eyes. Dragging her gaze away from where he was chuckling handsomely with Mr Phillips, she focused instead on Izzy, who was muttering about someone being arrogant. The Prince, Rose surmised, listening to confirm her assumption. It was always the Prince. While Anna replied in a calming manner, Rose excused herself, for Lady Mary was now free.

They shared a friendly embrace and complimented one another's gowns, then made their way to a quieter corner where they found a recently vacated settee. 'The music performances are to be after supper,' Lady Mary offered, in a confiding tone, 'and I am already all a-quiver at the notion, for Mama means for me to perform first!'

Rose patted her hand. 'I am certain all will be well, Lady Mary. What will you perform?'

They exchanged plans—both intending to play the piano, although Rose planned to sing while accompanying herself. 'I am not nearly as talented on the piano as Anna, and would not dare to play anything so complicated as her Beethoven piece. No, a simple song will do me very well.'

Lady Mary seemed genuinely anxious, and so Rose set out to soothe her nerves. Soon afterwards the unwelcome presence of the Honourable Geoffrey made itself known, and the girls endured quite ten minutes of his leering above them—quizzing glass deployed to uncomfortable effect—before Lady Ashbourne rescued them, claiming she needed Miss Lennox to settle an argument instantly, and that Lady Mary's opinion was also required.

'So here we are, girls,' she declared, bringing them to where the Viscount was still chatting to Mr Phillips. 'Now then, James, I have brought Rose—er—' she quickly glanced at Rose's pink-trimmed gown as if to make certain '—yes, Miss Rosabella and Lady Mary to be entertained by you. They say supper will be called soon. Now, do not let me down!' With this obscure pronouncement she swept away in a flurry of feathered headdress and rustling silk.

There was a brief silence, during which Rose noticed two things. First, that both Mr Phillips and Lady Mary were each looking a little flustered as they saluted one another, and second, that the Viscount was giving her *that look* again. Performing her own curtsey—aimed more at Mr Phillips, as naturally she did not need to formally greet the Viscount—she sensed a thunder in her ears and a tightness in her throat. It was uncanny, really, the effect he had on her. Every time.

'Lady Mary!' Mr Phillips was giving her friend his best smile. 'You look delightful!' Turning to Rose, he added in a more measured tone, 'As do you, Miss Lennox!'

'Thank you,' Rose responded, carefully keeping her voice free of any dryness. Despite herself she could not resist catching the Viscount's eye, and his dark gaze was brimful of humour. Allowing him to briefly see she shared his understanding, she looked away before her mouth was tempted to quirk up at the corners, focusing instead on the ongoing, fairly stilted conversation between Lady Mary and her admirer.

'Oh, yes,' Lady Mary was saying, 'Mama has ordered all sorts of delicacies for supper!'

'Might I—?' he swallowed. 'Might I have the honour of accompanying you to supper, Lady Mary?'

'I should be delighted.'

His timing was perfect, for at that moment the gong sounded, and people began drifting out towards the staircase. Supper was to be served downstairs it seemed. Wordlessly, the Viscount offered his arm and Rose inclined her head, tucking her hand into the crook of his arm. His arm was warm, and *oh!* she had to walk close to him—so close she could even feel the movement of his chest against her arm as he breathed. While part of her brain was doing all the usual things—walking, nodding occasionally to acquaintances, being careful not to trip on her gown as they descended the staircase—her real self was entirely focused on the sensation of his breathing, his warmth, his size—tall and strong beside her. On him.

It took almost ten minutes for them to reach the front of the supper line, and she was conscious of a feeling of loss as she slipped her hand away from him. Their eyes met briefly, and once again his expression—unfathomable, dark, intent—made her insides curl with breathlessness. Shaking his head briefly, he made some remark about the food, helping her fill her plate with her favourite delicacies.

'Now, let me see…you would dislike the eels, I

think,' he murmured, pointing instead to a dish at the back of the long sideboard. 'This lobster would be more to your taste. Am I right?'

'You are,' she said, with some surprise. 'Clearly you have been observant at dinner these past weeks.'

He grinned. 'Anna enjoys pastries, Izzy has a weakness for rich sauces with poultry, while you have a decided preference for shellfish.' He added lobster to her plate. 'And these!' At her nod, he added a selection of French beans, asparagus, and peas.

'I must admit I am impressed.' The words were forced from Rose, for—despite breathless looks and strange flutterings—their usual interactions were based almost entirely on raillery and barbed jesting. 'I cannot reciprocate, I am sad to say, for it seems to me you like all of it!' She indicated his plate, which was filled with a much wider range of dishes than her own.

He laughed at this, looking around for a place to sit, for they had reached the end of the food line. 'Follow me!' he declared, waving away the footman offering to find them a place and she did so, knowing his height gave him some advantage in the crowded interconnecting rooms. A moment later, he drew out a chair at a table already occupied by Mr and Mrs Thaxby, and Rose suppressed a sigh.

After seating her he joined them, making light conversation with the Thaxbys while Rose picked at her food, suddenly feeling not so hungry. Something about the Thaxbys bothered her. Mr Thaxby, though not overtly dissipated as was the Honourable Geoffrey Barnstable, nevertheless made her skin itch in an unpleasant way, while his wife was everything vain, shallow, and selfish.

'Just look!' she was saying, seemingly oblivious to Rose's antipathy. 'The Prince is talking to Miss Chorley! As if someone like *her* could marry a prince!'

'So who,' asked the Viscount casually, 'in your estimation, should marry the Prince?'

She sniffed. 'Someone with class, and breeding, and a strong family line. No one with the smell of the shop or the hint of—' her eyes flicked towards Rose '—questionable parentage, that is for certain! A prince could never consort with anyone *vulgar.*'

Vulgar! Rose gripped her cutlery tightly, clamping her jaws shut in case she was tempted to speak. *Thank goodness it is me at her table, and not Izzy.*

Given this provocation Izzy would have struggled to hold her tongue.

'Vulgarity,' murmured the Viscount in a mild tone, 'is in the eye of the beholder, do you not think?'

Ouch! Rose sent him a searing glance. *Be careful!*

'And what do you mean by that?' Mrs Thaxby's tone matched her sharp glare.

He shrugged. 'Simply that there are some who may find Miss Chorley perfectly amiable.'

Rose was conscious of a tightness in her shoulders. She had always found conflict difficult, and the air around their table just now was tight with tension. Conscious of Mr Thaxby's scrutiny, she forced herself to eat another forkful of French beans.

'And the mother? Surely *her* vulgarity is undeniable?' It was clear Mrs Thaxby was not ready to let the matter go. 'The father exists, I am told, but is not fit for our drawing rooms!'

He paused, seemingly busy chewing a morsel of fine beef. 'We cannot choose our relations, it is true. But we can choose our companions. Thankfully I am blessed to be surrounded by those who are both kind and sensible.'

Does he mean us? Me?

She held her breath, for it seemed he had more to say.

'What of your own relations, Mrs Thaxby? Perhaps there is some trouble somewhere in your family tree? I know I was the despair of my father in my youth.'

Interesting.

Since he was fairly young now—Rose estimated he was in his late twenties—by his 'youth' he must have meant when he was her own age, just a few years ago. Had he been wild while at Oxford? Perhaps he had not always been so stuffy and judgemental as he sometimes seemed. She frowned. His challenge to Mrs Thaxby was perfectly reasonable, sound, and just, and his defence against the implied criticism of her and her sisters forced her to evaluate again her impression of him.

Something flashed briefly in Mrs Thaxby's eyes then, looking exceedingly uncomfortable, she gave a tight smile. 'My family has never—*never*—been accused of vulgarity, I assure you, my lord!' She dropped her gaze, adding, 'Although we have had our fair share of unhappiness. We lost my dear brother many years ago, and of course Mr Thaxby and I were never blessed with children.'

Mr Thaxby patted his wife's hand ostentatiously, yet Rose felt a pang of sympathy. There was a clear lesson for her here, and one that she should have recalled. Even the most unattractive of people—the coldest, the most unappealing—had their own troubles to bear.

'So, Miss Lennox—' Mrs Thaxby turned to her, eyes glittering with arrogance bordering on contempt. 'I believe you and your sisters are trying to discover who your parents may be. Have you had any success?' Her tone was scathing, making it clear what she thought of such a scheme. Before Rose could answer, she continued. 'I declare I would not have had the audacity to foist myself on society if there was any doubt about my parentage. Thankfully I can trace my own family heritage back for generations. Why, the Fletchers likely go back to the Conqueror. Sadly the name died with my brother, and the bloodline will die with me.'

Faced with such an overt attack, Rose was at a loss. *What should I say to this?*

Thinking quickly, and trying to imagine what Anna might do, she limited her reply to a simple statement. 'We have had no success thus far in finding information about our mother's family.'

'Humph.' Clearly losing interest—perhaps because

Rose had managed to sound unperturbed—Mrs Thaxby turned to her husband. 'Have you finished, my dear?'

Mr Thaxby set down his fork, which had been half-way to his mouth. 'Yes, my love. Shall we return to the drawing room?'

They made their farewells and left, Rose exhaling in relief and allowing her shoulders to relax as she watched them walk towards the door.

'How do you, Miss Lennox?' The Viscount was eyeing her keenly. He had clearly not been fooled by her even tone and bland response just now.

'Better now,' she declared wryly. 'Mrs Thaxby really is an unhappy person, is she not?'

He nodded, his expression serious. 'I must apologise to you, Miss Rose.'

Her brow creased. 'For what?'

'For exposing you to that woman's ire.'

'But you are not responsible for her actions.'

'Oh, but I believe I am—in this instance at least. If I had not angered her with my comments on vulgarity she would not have turned her venom on you.' He grimaced. 'She is not well-liked, but in one thing she is correct. Behaviour that would be judged as vulgar or unseemly in anyone else is excused for Mrs Thaxby, simply because she is a Fletcher by blood, and the *ton* values bloodlines.'

'Then—' Rose frowned, seeing the inference. 'My sisters and I must behave perfectly, lest our lack of bloodline expose us to accusations of vulgarity?'

'Exactly.' His eyes held a hint of sadness. 'I do not

say it is right—indeed, I wholeheartedly reject such notions—but I know the *ton*. What may be excused in a Fletcher or a Renton would be condemned in a Miss Lennox or, indeed, a Miss Chorley.'

'I see,' Rose replied thoughtfully. 'So when you constantly warn us against unbecoming behaviour...'

Reaching out, he touched her arm lightly. 'I mean only to be helpful—and as I told you earlier—' he grinned '—you are altogether too easy to tease!' His smile faded. 'I have not always explained such things in an articulate way.' He ran a hand through his thick, dark hair, and helplessly, her gaze followed it. 'Lord, this is difficult! I am unused to having to think of such matters, not having ever been responsible for the conduct of a debutante before—never mind three of you!'

'But Lady Ashbourne...'

'My aunt is all that is good, but I do not wish for her to carry this burden alone.'

Rose's hand flew to her mouth. 'We are a burden to her?'

He shook his head. 'Much less so than I had anticipated, I admit. Yes, she has staked her reputation on you, and she is busy from early morning till late into the night being determined to see to your interests, but so far she seems to be thriving on it all. Truthfully, I feared she would exhaust herself. Since my uncle died she has lived fairly quietly.' He grinned. 'I have not seen her so happy since we lost him, to be perfectly honest.'

'It relieves me to hear you say so.'

There was a companionable silence as they each enjoyed the food before them. Inwardly, Rose was considering his words—particularly the part about Lady Ashbourne.

'You said your aunt is busy "from early morning". Does she not then sleep late, as we do?' She flushed a little. 'It still seems shocking to me that we are out almost every night until three or four, then lie abed until after midday. Our teachers would be horrified if they saw us now!'

He chuckled at this, but explained. 'I exaggerated when I referred to *early* morning, but it is true that my aunt is about much earlier than you. I believe she has chocolate in her room then rises to meet with the servants. By the time formal breakfast is served, she has already spent two or three hours on household matters—meeting with the servants, dealing with correspondence and the like.'

'I see!' Rose declared, much struck. 'Poor Lady Ashbourne!'

'Poor nothing!'

His eyes held hers, and her heart stood still. Being in charity with him again was surely the most wonderful of feelings!

'She is in her element, I assure you!' Around them, most people were now rising to return upstairs. He stood, holding out a hand. 'Shall we?'

Placing her hand lightly in his, she allowed him to keep it while she rose.

I have much to think about.

Chapter Eleven

James made his way upstairs, Rose's little hand tucked once again into the crook of his arm. His mind was awhirl, and he was unsure why. The incident with Mrs Thaxby just now was not unusual. Such people—unhappy, bitter, and self-important—were common in the *ton*, yet never before had he experienced such visceral anger at comments about supposed 'vulgarity'. Oh, such talk was commonplace, with self-appointed arbiters judging everyone who came across their path while oblivious to their own shamelessness.

Recalling the conversations that night in his club just after the Belles had been presented at Court, it occurred to James to wonder about the more ribald comments that had no doubt inspired the dirty laughter emanating from a couple of the conversations at White's. For the first time it occurred to him that the Belles might be in danger of insult from one or more of the more licentious members of the *ton*—those who might believe the lack of information about the Belles' background made them fair game. Ladies like Mrs

Thaxby would show their disdain with barbed words and contemptuous looks. Gentlemen might show it in…other ways. He had heard of a number of unsavoury incidents over the years…

But no. He tried to reassure himself. The girls were under the protection of Lady Ashbourne, and, by extension, himself.

Yet, he mused, *it may do no harm to let certain people know I am no* laissez-faire *observer, and that I will not hesitate to take a hand in my aunt's scheme if needed.*

His mind briefly flashed him an image of Rose at the mercy of some upstart who believed that the Belles' unclear ancestry meant he could take liberties. Instantly his gut clenched in fear. Fear for Rose—for all of them—and a deep burning anger. No, he could not stomach such a possibility.

Giving Mrs Thaxby a subtle set-down just now should have posed no difficulty—something he would not even think about a moment later. Yet when he recalled the stricken expression that had briefly flickered across Rose's face—despite her even tone—rage against Mrs Thaxby's casual cruelty blazed within him. Yes, the Belles were unsure who their parents had been, but that did not mean for certain that they had been born out of wedlock. It certainly should not make them subject to rumour, gossip, and conjecture.

Quite when he had moved from worrying about his aunt to focusing on the Belles themselves, he could not say. To be fair, following her initial doubts his aunt had approached the entire undertaking with enthusiasm, and was clearly taking it all in her stride, and—as he had told Rose just now—she was positively enjoying having three debutantes to launch. His own doubts had persisted much longer than his aunt's and yet, as he had become accustomed to the Belles' presence in the house, he found that his views had slowly changed. It struck him now that he was quite enjoying being in the company of young ladies who neither simpered nor flirted. They enacted no dramas either, and he could not recall so much as a single female headache in the month and more since they had come into his life— never mind a faint or fit of the vapours.

Do they even wish to find husbands?

The thought was a novel one, yet everything he knew of the Belles suggested they were more inter- ested in the experience of London, and being part of the *ton*, rather than actually being on the hunt for a husband.

Perhaps that is why they are all three so popular.

For popular they were, with both gentlemen and ladies—apart from those high sticklers who seemed determined to keep them at a distance pending news of their parentage. The reason, as far as he could un- derstand it, was straightforward: they were *likeable*, with no pretensions, airs, or graces. Of course, most of the *ton* could not tell them apart, and so judged them in the collective rather than as individuals. He, though, knew better. Although he mixed up Anna and Izzy at times, he was by now skilled in identifying Rose's face when all three were together. He was also gaining a deeper understanding of their character, knowing that Izzy—Miss Isobel—was filled with pent-up energy, and that Anna was self-contained to the point of being rather inscrutable.

As for Rose—his pulse skipped as he allowed his thoughts to dwell on her. *Something*—something nameless, and profound—was happening between them. He could not ever recall experiencing anything like it before. It was unlike the *tendres* he had experienced in his youth—brief infatuations with flirtatious, beautiful, unattainable ladies. No, this was altogether different, for Rose had no arts to attract, and his notion of her was founded in the *reality* of her, rather than some romanticised view. She was temptingly easy to tease, and yet at times they enjoyed stimulating raillery where she gave back as much as he doled out. Had she been a gentleman, he would have called her friend, yet because she was a lady—and a beautiful one at that—his amity with her was coloured by decidedly carnal complications.

Even now, mounting the stairs with her hand in his arm, he was surprised by the strength of his body's reaction to her. Feeling rather guilty—for he really should not be indulging such earthy thoughts in a public place—he diverted himself by asking if she and her sisters intended to perform.

'Oh, yes,' she responded calmly. 'I do love music—although I am not particularly talented. I know Lady

Mary is feeling quite anxious about her performance, so I hope it goes well for her.'

Kind, he thought, adding it to the reasons why the Belles were well-liked. The Belles rarely criticised others, and were often to be seen carrying out small acts of kindness.

'You can be sure Lady Mary has some musical talent, for Lady Renton would not have hosted a musicale otherwise.'

She glanced at him, nodding. 'That makes sense, and is reassuring. Thank you.'

'Come now,' he chided her. 'Must we be in tedious harmony all the time? Is it not more entertaining when we are fencing with words, trying to best each other?'

This earned him a side glance. 'I am sure I do not know what you mean,' she declared primly, making him chuckle.

'Very well, Miss Lennox,' he said, deliberately leaning his mouth towards her ear. 'But I do hope that our normal verbal pugilism will soon return, for without it my days will be sadly dull!'

There!

Had she shivered as his lips had almost caressed her delicate ear? But with what? Desire? Or disgust that he was being over-familiar? No, he could not believe so. He hoped—had reason to believe—that perhaps she felt the same frisson that was currently pounding through him.

Lord, I must stop this!

Thankfully they had reached the drawing room,

and he managed to find her a seat near the fireplace, standing alongside her chair as if he belonged there.

Belonged?

These notions were becoming quite absurd. 'Would you like a drink?' he asked, conscious that his tone sounded rather brusque.

A frown appeared briefly as she declined, her tone clipped.

She is matching my coolness.

It pierced him—the loss of intimacy occurring in just a few seconds. Lord, this thing—whatever it was—was turning him soft! Never before had he been so sensible to the least nuance of another person's response to him. Suddenly he felt raw, exposed. The feeling was unwelcome, and so he pushed it away.

Lady Renton introduced her daughter to the gathered throng, and he sensed Rose's anxiety as Lady Mary began to play. While he cared not whether Lady Mary was a success or no, it occurred to him that he did not like to see Rose distressed or vexed—apart, of course, from the moments when he himself was the source of her vexation—and that of course was only in jest. Most of the time, anyway.

Thankfully Lady Mary's execution was competent, and his gaze met Rose's as they applauded at the end.

I knew it! he signified with a raised eyebrow, and she acknowledged it, nodding in some relief.

As the musicale continued, with both ladies and gentlemen singing and playing, he realised he was listening much more intently than usual, and with a different perspective. Tonight, as well as all the usual nameless, indistinguishable debutantes, three were under the aegis of House Ashbourne. That was clearly why he was so intent on judging the standard set by the others, so he might know how well or poorly his aunt's protégées performed.

Miss Isobel was the first of the Belles to take the stage, and thankfully she gave an accomplished performance, earning polite applause and a few wry acknowledgements from those who may have assumed that a limited dowry and unknown parentage necessarily meant a poor education—or vulgarity. No, Izzy had challenged the views of the more small-minded among the *ton* with her skilful playing.

Miss Phillips was next, and James instinctively looked to her brother—to see exactly the same hint of tension on his friend's face as he imagined must be on his own. Robert was a good friend, and he was still desperately hoping his sister would *take* on her debut. 'I do not need for Charlotte to be a diamond,' he had confessed to James earlier, 'I just wish for her not to be an antidote.'

Thinking of this now as he watched Miss Phillips give a creditable performance on the harp, it occurred to James to wonder if Rose might be able to assist Miss Phillips. Like Lady Mary, Miss Charlotte Phillips tended to be quiet and rather shy...his thoughts wandered in this direction until, abruptly, he realised Miss Phillips had finished her piece. Applauding with everyone else, he saw Lady Renton nod towards Rose to indicate she would be next to entertain the gathering, and instantly his gut twisted with anxiety on her behalf.

'And now we shall have another of the Lennox sisters,' Lady Renton announced, and her tone had a patronising edge to it. 'Which one are you, my dear?' she asked condescendingly as Rose made her way to the piano.

'I am Rosabella,' Rose replied calmly, and James felt a strange swelling sensation in his chest.

I believe I am proud of her!

To maintain such composure in the face of Lady Renton's disdain—particularly given the incident in which Mrs Thaxby had showed her viciousness earlier—showed a quality that many here present could learn from.

Rose cannot be having a good evening, was the next thought and he squirmed slightly.

As someone who had all his life been part of the *ton*, it occurred to him that tonight he was seeing society with fresh eyes. The eyes of Rose and her sisters.

The nerves in his gut remained as Rose settled herself at the piano, a look of concentration settling across her beautiful face.

But she is adorable!

And that was even before he heard her sing.

Her voice, pure and clear, called beautifully throughout the room, and her fingers moved dexterously across the piano keys in accompaniment. While she would never match the professional singers who graced the stage at the opera, for a drawing room her performance was proficient. Polished, even. As she finished her song and stood to respectable applause, he realised he had been half holding his breath. Exhaling in relief, he had managed to compose himself reasonably well by the time she had retaken her seat.

'Well done. Your performance was excellent.' Leaning down to murmur the words close to her ear, he saw that she was charmingly flushed. The room was, to be fair, becoming uncomfortably warm, as the performances had attracted guests from the card rooms and the terrace below. They were all held a little more closely together by the press of the crowd, and many of the ladies were deploying their painted fans.

'Thank you.' She smiled mischievously. 'I must admit I am glad my piece is done.' She glanced about the room. 'Ah, Miss Anderton is next.' A frown creased her brow. 'I wonder when it will be Anna's turn?'

'So you cannot be easy until your other sister performs?'

She shook her head. 'Not at all. Anna will be fine. Now hush, for Miss Anderton is about to begin!'

About to remonstrate with her, he closed his mouth as the opening bars of Miss Anderton's piano piece rang out. The girl clearly considered herself something of a virtuosa, swaying spectacularly at times and banging on the keys for dramatic effect during fortissimo sections. She was, he had to admit, fairly accomplished, with only a handful of wrong notes and mistiming during the demanding piece.

Flushed with success, she took a curtsey as enthusiastic applause rang out, meeting her mama's eye with a look of wild delight.

Yes, James noted sagely, *it will likely be Miss Anderton they will speak of in the drawing rooms tomorrow.*

With tonight's performance, she had increased her social prominence in an effective way. Glancing briefly towards Miss Anderton's mother, he noted the triumph in her expression and realised his own loyalty to the Belles was leading him to a rather partisan wish that they, and not Miss Anderton, might have triumphed at the musicale. Pathetic of him, no doubt, and yet it had made a fairly tedious evening pass in a rather more interesting fashion than usual.

And of course the Queen has declared them to be diamonds—no little accolade.

With this comforting thought he brought his attention back to Anna, who had seated herself at the piano and was currently arranging her sheet music on the stand. Given Rose's confidence that Anna would be fine, and the fact that both Rose and Isobel had clearly had some good teaching and applied themselves well, it was likely that Anna would be equally accomplished.

The first notes rang out and he raised an eyebrow, recognising the piece—a piano sonata by Beethoven, and one renowned for being extremely difficult to play. The movement was lively and intricate, but Anna's playing was astonishing. The hush among those present was absolute, and James—with some effort—made himself glance around the room. Everyone seemed entranced—even the Earl of Garvald, who was a noted connoisseur of music, and whose sensibilities were often offended by some of the performances wrought by ladies and gentlemen of the *ton*. As Anna segued smoothly into the melancholic second movement, there was absolute silence among the guests. Even the footmen, obeying the butler's frowning command, had ceased circulating with trays of drinks.

A few moments later Anna finished, the piece dying away gently with repeated triads softening to silence. There was a moment's pause, and then wild applause broke out all around the enormous drawing room.

'Brava, Miss Lennox!'

'*Bravissima*, Bella!'

Catching Rose's eye, he allowed her to see his astonishment. 'Your sister is very talented,' he declared, bending towards her to ensure she would hear him amid the jubilation.

Her flush deepened. 'I thank you. Yes, Anna is the musical one, and Izzy excels at art.'

'And you?'

She grimaced. 'I excel at nothing, I am afraid. When the good fairies blessed Mama's birth, they must not have expected a third baby to endow with gifts and talents.' Her tone was matter-of-fact, but he wondered if there was pain beneath it.

'Come now! There are more talents than those of

the arts!' He held her gaze, trying to show her how extraordinary she was to him. 'Did you not tell me before that you have a knack for teaching? That is just as much a gift as musical or artistic talent.'

'I suppose.' There was a slight crease between her brows. 'It is just that it is less *visible*, somehow.'

'Well, it will not earn applause such as this, that is for certain.' The noise was beginning to die down now, as the crowd abandoned their applause in favour of excited babble. Still he kept his head lowered to hers. It was better that way. 'But it will have a significant impact on those you teach.' He paused. 'Your own children someday perhaps?'

She shook her head. 'I wish to be an actual teacher. In a school.'

His jaw dropped, and he was conscious of a feeling of severe disappointment, quite disproportionate in its intensity. 'Then, you do not intend to marry?'

'I think the possibility of my marrying is low.' She shrugged. 'My sisters and I are not wealthy, and so we must make our own way in the world.'

'But if you marry well, you need not consider such things!'

'Ah, but we cannot marry well,' she reminded him with a twinkle. 'You and Lady Ashbourne were most clear about that, and Mrs Thaxby would no doubt agree! With dubious parentage and small dowries, it matters little how talented we may be, for we are destined to be banished to the fringes of the marriage mart, I fear!' She shook her head, clearly amused at the notion such matters might be considered important. 'Still, we must endure this sad state of affairs with fortitude!' Her eyes were dancing. 'And so, I may be forced into a life as a teacher, rather than as a wife. Such hardship!'

Her expression indicated she thought it not a hardship at all, which was unfathomable. 'So—' He struggled to put his thoughts into words. 'You would be perfectly content to *not* marry? To never have a home and children of your own?' As he spoke his mind unhelpfully supplied him with an image of a small child—a child with her blue eyes and his own dark hair.

'I—well, naturally, I—' Her voice faltered, and their gazes held.

Abruptly, there was a rushing in his ears, as though the mighty tides had decided to sweep through a London drawing room and take his legs out from under him. Everything he thought he knew was changing. Now. In this instant.

She swallowed, and her flush deepened. 'I—I apologise, my lord. The heat in the room...' She pressed her hands to her flushed face.

Instantly a lifetime of good manners compelled him to action. 'You are unwell, Miss Lennox! Can I procure you some lemonade, perhaps? Or perhaps you might like to go to the terrace?' He flushed slightly, in case she should assume he had ill intentions. 'I mean—er—it would be cooler. And it is well-lit, and there are usually many people on the terrace.'

His discomfiture may have eased any concerns she might have had, for she nodded, saying, 'I think I should. Besides, both my sisters have performed now, as has my friend, and so I believe I can safely take a few moments outside.'

She led the way and as he followed her through the oblivious throng, he was conscious that he was in a high state of agitation. The reasons for it were myriad, and currently they were tumbling through his mind and heart like a troupe of chaotic acrobats. Chief among them was confusion, as he tried to make sense of it all.

In the past couple of hours he had felt pride, and shame, desire, and affection, and…something more. Something deeper, and terrifyingly potent. It was as like to those boyish infatuations as a candle to the sun. He only knew that Rose… *Rosabella, beautiful Rosa*…was precious to him, and that he must do everything and anything to ensure her happiness and comfort. And, naturally, he would continue to tease her, for their raillery was currently one of the most stimulating parts of his life.

Her hand was resting in the crook of his arm as they descended the staircase—just as it had been an hour ago. And yet, in the time between, something had changed.

When had it begun, this fixation with Rose? It had its origins in their earliest encounter on the landing over a month ago, he knew. That night when he had first seen her in her night-rail. Oh, he had known all along it had been Rose, for earlier that day he had heard his aunt direct the housekeeper to allocate the bedrooms in birth order, giving the eldest the largest room. Which meant that when he had disturbed her listening at the middle chamber door and she had bolted, she would have made for her own room—which in turn meant she must be the youngest sister. The next morning when the formal introductions had been made, it was the youngest Belle, the one in the rose-trimmed gown, to whom he had paid most attention, for she was the maiden who had disturbed his dreams.

Then there had been that encounter in the library, which had haunted him since. In his imagination he had replayed it a thousand times, and it had always ended in a kiss.

Every time.

As he followed her now along the hallway and through the supper room to the terrace beyond, it occurred to him that his life, and his aunt's, had indeed been turned on its head—as he had feared it might. Not however, through strife and friction and drama. His prediction had been correct, yet incorrect, for the changes the Belles had brought were good ones.

Tonight he was not missing his club, nor the company of his old friends—the friends he had happily drunk and gamed with until two years ago. No, not in the slightest, for here, in his own world, was a new friend. Rose. A friend with whom he enjoyed weighty conversations as much as light-hearted ones. A friend who was dazzlingly female, and who was causing him disturbed nights and lustful days.

She is a true lady.

A lady who was kind, and quick-witted, and refreshingly humble. A lady who was fond of serving him a fine trimming each time he irked her! A smile flashed briefly across his face… Perfection, really.

And yet…she had no notion of marriage. Or so she claimed. Yes, he could understand her desire to teach, particularly as she had identified it as her own personal talent. But surely, the stricken look he had seen flash briefly in her eyes had been telling? Marriage, a home, children…

She had her sisters, but since losing her mother at a heartbreakingly young age, she had lived in a school.

A school!

No matter how caring the teachers had been, it could not possibly be anything like his own childhood, in a loving family. He himself had been sent to school from the age of fourteen, but had always been able to rely upon the home that was waiting for him at the end of each half term. A school could never be a home.

As to the rest, the notion that she must not look too high for an offer of marriage…

Until he had met Rose and her sisters, he would have agreed. Had indeed spoken it aloud. Ladies whose parentage was unknown might turn out to be entirely unsuitable to be married to a member of the *ton*— and the Belles did not even have the inducement of being well-dowered! And yet…at this moment all he could do was wish that matters were otherwise. As she walked, he studied her as would an artist. Her golden hair, swept up and held with pins. Her graceful neck and a hint of smooth shoulders, revealed by her lace-trimmed gown. Her gait. The poise of her.

Shaken, he pulled his gaze away, to nod and smile to those passing. This *tendre* would surely pass, as had the infatuations of youth.

Caution. Prudence.

He must certainly not make rash decisions while experiencing what seemed a bout of madness. Delicious madness, yet madness it was.

Chapter Twelve

Rose could not account for the feelings rushing through her. She felt flushed, feverish, yet she was not ill. Her pulse refused to slow, and her thundering heart to settle. It was to do with *him*, she knew, but how? Why? Why should this one person cause her to feel so uncertain, so in alt, so...*frightened*?

Oh, she was not frightened *of* him. He was, she was now certain, one of the best, most upright persons of her acquaintance—even when he vexed her. Tonight had changed everything. Their conversation earlier had revealed he had truly had the best of intentions when attempting to counsel Rose and her sisters. But this...what she was feeling in this moment was the most intense, the most striking, the most disturbing, *beautiful* thing she had ever felt.

I do hope it is cooler on the terrace.

Her flushed face must be a giveaway to the tumult racing within her.

Why is it fear that I sense?

Fear of what?

As she made her way through the crowds to the terrace, she sensed him by her side, sometimes a little behind as he gave way to others in the throng. Her awareness of him was like a…a *tingle* in his current direction. Her entire life, it seemed, was focused on when she might see him next. And when he was there, it was about how long he would stay near her. When they would speak. Whether he might give her *that* look… That, then, was the fear, perhaps. He had disrupted and disturbed twenty-one years of her existence with something so new, so all-consuming, and so enticing, that it was truly terrifying.

Her own sense of fairness gave her pause. All he had *actually* done was to simply be there, being his own handsome self. Never had he blatantly flirted with her, or been over-familiar or ungentlemanlike—at least, never overtly. She did not have to feel uncomfortable with him as she did with the gentlemen who ogled young ladies, or even with the adoring young men who sent the Belles poetry and flowers.

Perhaps it was simply that she had not met many men like him. Good-looking, good-hearted, quick-witted, and upright.

Good-hearted? Well, yes.

Even though his methods were sometimes clumsy, his intentions were good. Had always been good, she now knew.

In truth he was, to her current mind, an exemplar of what a gentleman should be. And yet she might use exactly those same epithets to describe dear Mr

Marnoch. Apart from the good-looking, perhaps. So what was the difference about her response to Lord Ashbourne? To…to *James*. Deliberately she used his given name in her mind, just for the thrill of it. With him, there was assuredly something more. Something that made her flustered, and confused, and *alive*.

Is this why the serving maid in Belvedere allowed herself to be seduced by the butcher's boy?

The mystery as to why any maiden would risk ruin in such a way was abruptly, terribly clear. Not that she would ever do such a thing. No, of course not. She just understood it a little better now.

They had reached the terrace. Still he was with her—as he had been all evening long.

As he should be.

Quite where the notion had come from, she did not know. She only knew there was a feeling of rightness when he was by her side.

But such an arrangement could not possibly last. He would leave, or she would. This friendship—or whatever it was—could not continue like this, leaving her longing for more from him. They both knew the impossibility of it all. The Belles were not marriageable—at least, not to someone like Lord Ashbourne. Society would not approve, and Rose would do nothing to lessen his stature among the *ton*.

'There is something I wish to ask you,' he said, indicating they should move to the left side of the terrace, away from the gaggle of matrons and the solitary gentleman puffing meditatively on their meerschaum pipes—none of whom even glanced in their direction. Besides, it was perfectly acceptable for them to stand on the terrace together, in the company of other guests.

She glanced at him. 'Ask away.'

Lord, how handsome he is!

Starlight suited him. Starlight, enhanced by the warm glow of the flambeaux on the edge of the terrace. It was cosily dark, and Rose was grateful there were witnesses present, for otherwise her head would surely be going to places it should not.

'My friend Robert—Mr Phillips—has a younger sister. She is also a debutante this season. Are you acquainted with her?'

Rose's heart sank.

Does he like Miss Phillips?

And why should it matter to her if he did? 'Yes,' she managed with a casual air, 'I know them both—it was Mr Phillips who accompanied Lady Mary to supper, was it not?'

'It was.' He grinned, and her smile answered his, as they recalled together the sweet awkwardness between her friend and Mr Phillips. Rose had not known there might be something between them—nor indeed between Mr Phillips's sister and Lord Ashbourne.

But perhaps I am assuming too much.

She swallowed, but honesty forced her to continue. 'I find them both pleasant and likeable.'

'Miss Phillips is rather shy, and is, I understand, feeling a little overwhelmed by the expectations of the *ton*, and by the need to perform as she ought during her season.'

Instantly, all concerns about the Viscount and Miss Phillips left her mind, washed away by sympathy for the young lady.

'Oh, the poor girl!' Rose pictured the girl, her shy smile so like her brother's, and her heart went out to her. 'I knew she was quiet, but I did not know it affected her so. I shall make a point of inviting her to walk out with me. Has she no friend among the young ladies?'

'I fear not.' He took a breath. 'I must say... I knew this would be your response.' He made a formal bow, honouring her. 'I thank you, Miss Lennox. You are all kindness.'

She waved this away. 'Think nothing of it! If I knew more of the *ton* I might have noticed her isolation already. My sisters and I always looked after the younger girls in Belvedere in such a way. Oh!' This last was uttered in a tone of surprise, for some small creature had just brushed against Rose's legs. 'A cat! Hello, Puss.' She bent to stroke the animal who proved to be very friendly, purring and arching its back to enjoy Rose's attentions. Its markings were striking, being a mix of black and white with patches of striped tabby—a classic tortoiseshell pattern. 'Oh, you are pretty!' Picking it up, she held it close, enjoying the sensation of it rubbing its little head against her face.

'Careful!' the Viscount warned. 'It probably has fleas!'

'Ugh!' Bending, she set the animal down, making an interesting discovery as she did so. 'You are a mama, little one! Where are your babies, hmm?' The kittens could not be far away. Taking a single step into the darkness of the garden to test matters, Rose was glad to see the cat came too, mewing as if speaking to her and skipping ahead a few steps. She paused then, looking towards Rose as if checking she was following.

'I am here, little one.'

Turning, the cat stepped to the left, along the wall of the house and, curious, Rose followed.

'Miss Lennox!' Lord Ashbourne sounded perturbed. 'Rose! Come back! You should not—'

But Rose had had quite enough of music and smiling and doing as she ought for one night. Enough of having her heart race because he was there. Enough of lowering worries that he liked another lady. Enough. Just…*enough*.

Ignoring him, and the stern voice in her head that warned against entering the darkened garden, she walked on following the dim shape of the cat.

James stood immobile for a moment, shocked by Miss Lennox's disregard for his warning. One did not simply wander around *ton* gardens in darkness— particularly if one was a debutante protective of her reputation. One false step, a chance encounter with the wrong sort of man, and more than her reputation could be in tatters. What Miss Lennox probably did not know was that some of the more unsavoury gentlemen—those who were hangers-on at the fringes of events such as these—would think nothing of going to the garden to relieve themselves, should the withdrawing room be busy. And once there, if they came upon a pretty maid in the darkness, they might well assume she was seeking some sort of sordid adventure.

What to do? His innate sense of caution bade him hold back in the hope she might return immediately, for if he followed and they were discovered together, then her reputation—and that of her sisters—would be surely ruined. Yet if he did *not* follow, and some harm befell her, he would never forgive himself.

Gritting his teeth and choosing his moment when the others on the terrace seemed particularly distracted, he stepped off the terrace and into the darkness.

Rose hurried on, following the silently padding cat through the dimly lit garden. She loved animals and had always made a pet out of the Belvedere cats—much to the frustration of Agnes, who had declared the creatures would be useless as mousers if Miss Rose insisted on feeding them all the while. But Rose knew cats, and this mama cat was definitely intending that she should go with her. And so Rose would go, and enjoy the momentary freedom.

'So, Mama Puss, where are we going, eh?' She spoke softly. 'Do you want to show me your babies?'

This proved to be correct, for the cat disappeared

into a niche in the wall, her eyes gleaming briefly in the starlight as she turned back towards Rose. The high-pitched mews of kittens came faintly to Rose's ears, and she tentatively reached in, feeling soft furry bodies snuggling into their mother, who was currently nosing them in turn. Inexplicably though, the mother cat then moved again, emerging from her makeshift nest to walk a little further along, returning to wrap herself around Rose's legs and mew piteously.

'Are you hungry, little one? It must be hard work, feeding all those babies.' But the cat moved on, crossing to disappear under some undergrowth, crying all the while.

Bending, Rose tried her best in the darkness to see why the cat had left her babies to come here. A tiny, pathetic mew emanating from the undergrowth caught her attention. 'Another kitten!' Carefully, she reached her hand in, feeling around as best she could. The mother cat was there, tail twitching in agitation. 'Never fear, Mama, I mean your little one no harm.' Her fingers closed on something soft and, thankfully, warm. The kitten mewed again, and Rose felt the mother cat try to pick it up to carry it. There was some barrier there... The kitten had managed to wedge itself under a lattice of woody twigs, making it impossible for the mother cat to reach it.

'Miss Lennox! What on earth are you doing!'

Oh, dear!

Lord Ashbourne had followed her, and he sounded decidedly cross.

Deciding to meet fire with fire, Rose retorted, without turning around, 'I am *trying* to rescue a kitten, which you might have deduced had you applied your powers of reasoning to the situation!'

'But you are in a garden! After midnight! At a musicale!' Lord Ashbourne sounded astounded.

'And?' Making a frustrated sound, Rose withdrew her hand. 'I cannot loosen it. You will have to help.'

'To *help*? In knee breeches and dancing slippers? Are you quite *well*, Miss Lennox?'

She could not help it. A small giggle escaped. 'I suppose it is rather absurd, when you put it like that. Lord knows what I have done to my gown! Now, do you mean to assist or not?'

A sound of exasperation emanated from him, and Rose grinned in the darkness, knowing he would not be able to read her expression. 'Well?'

'I can *hear* your amusement, you know,' he muttered. 'You should not even be here. A young lady alone with a gentleman in a darkened garden…your reputation might be undone by such an event.'

'Then you should not have followed me, my lord, for if you had not, would there even *be* such a risk?' Brushing her skirts as best she could, she added, 'Really, you must admit you have caused this potential calamity yourself.' He made no answer to this, but she could sense the anger and frustration in him. 'I know you mean well, my lord, but the best option would be for you to assist the kitten, and then we could both return to the terrace immediately.'

With a muttered utterance that sounded suspiciously like an expletive, he crouched down. 'Where is the damn—the dashed creature?'

'It is stuck under the branches and roots. The mama cat cannot release it.' There was a brief silence as he felt his way beneath the vegetation. 'I expect,' Rose mused, 'the kittens were probably born here, but the mama moved them to a safer spot afterwards. All except that one.'

With a satisfied grunt, he withdrew his hand. 'Got you, you little fiend!' His tone was fierce, but with a hint of softness which made Rose's heart melt a little. 'Now then, Mama, quit your crying. Here is your little one.'

He straightened but Rose kept her eyes on the cat, who made no delay in trotting off, her wayward offspring held firmly by the scruff of the neck.

'And not even a thank-you!' she declared, turning her attention back to the Viscount, gratitude flowing through her. He was cross and frustrated, yet still he had rescued the kitten, and had done so in such a gentle way that it told her something new about him.

'So,' she continued, 'I shall thank you on her behalf.' Impetuously, she kissed his cheek, then froze, transfixed by the enormity of her impulse.

There was a strained silence. 'It is not the custom…' he offered, his voice sounding strange, 'for young ladies to kiss bachelors in a darkened garden.'

'Lord! I am sorry! I ought not to have done it!'

'Do not—' he bit off. 'Do not apologise, Rose. Not for that. Never for that.'

His hand reached out, tracing her face as if learning it by touch, and she caught her breath. His hand was warm, and gentle, the fingers firm and smooth, and where they trailed they left a line of sensation—rather like pins and needles, only a thousand times stronger, a thousand times more pleasurable. Now his thumb was on her lower lip, gently sliding across from one side to the other, and causing some sort of havoc to unleash itself throughout Rose's body.

'Rose.' It was half speech, half groan, and it proved to be her undoing.

'Kiss me.' Rose's tone was low, but in that instant she knew she had never wanted anything more in her entire life than she wanted his kiss.

He needed no second invitation. His arms slid around her back leaving a trail of tingling fire in their wake, and he pulled her close.

Closer.

Closer yet.

So close their bodies were touching—pressing—from chest to thigh. The feel of him—warmth, strength, his heart thudding against her—set fiery desire scorching through her. At the same time his cheek brushed hers and he turned his head, trailing his warm lips over her face. Closer, ever closer to her lips.

Rose was in heaven. The sensations generated by his lips on her skin, by their bodies tightly bound together, by his strong hands on her back, seemed almost too much, so potent were they. And his lips had yet to join with hers!

She could bear it no longer. Turning her head, she claimed his lips with her own, enjoying the sensation of a lover's kiss for the first time in her life. Instantly her pulse picked up yet more speed, now at a full gallop. Not quite knowing what to do she followed her instincts, covering his lips with hers, tilting her head slightly to fit. He moved his mouth then, ever so slightly, from left to right in a repetitive motion, maintaining just enough contact with her lips to maximise the sensations he was causing.

'Mmmhh…' The groan was hers and it seemed to inflame him, for he pulled her even tighter, pressing his hips to hers and moving them in circular motions which made her knees suddenly weak. Desperately she clung to him, knowing she could not possibly stand upright without him.

Now he parted his lips a little, kissing first her lower lip, then her upper one. Now the corner of her mouth, now the middle. And now… *Lord!* Now his tongue was touching her lips—just a little, now and then, but where it touched, she burned.

She groaned again, and this time her own lips parted a little. As though he had been awaiting this very eventuality, his tongue dipped inside her mouth—just briefly, just for an instant, but that instant felt so right, so delicious, that Rose immediately wanted more. Tentatively she brought her own tongue forward to caress his lower lip as he had done hers. Emboldened by his sharp intake of breath she explored further, eventually bringing her tongue directly into his warm mouth. His own met her there, and as their tongues met and danced, Rose thought she might actually die from sheer joy. The sensations coursing through her body were like nothing she ever could have imagined.

Now he was kissing her lips again, slowing it down, allowing his hips to relax away from her. The kiss was ending. With one final, gentle resting of lips on lips, they sighed, then leaned back a little. His gaze was too much for her, even in starlight. His eyes glittered with…something dark, and intense. Lowering her chin, she tucked her head beneath his, resting it in the hollow of his shoulder, allowing her breathing to settle a little.

Closing her eyes she savoured the moment, vaguely knowing she would need to remember this for the rest of her days. The sensation of his arms about her and his warm strong chest pressed against her, his thudding heart and ragged breathing, gradually slowing.

Naturally, he was first to come to his senses. 'We should return, before we are missed.'

'Yes, of course.' Her voice shook a little. 'That was…' She struggled to articulate her feelings. 'That was astonishing!'

There was just enough light for her to know that he smiled briefly, before becoming solemn again. 'It was. Quite, quite astonishing.' His hands now slid down her arms and he took her gloved hands. 'Are you well?'

She nodded. 'I am quite well, I thank you. More

than well, in fact.' She grinned, recalling his asking her a similar question just a few moments ago, in bewilderment at her request he assist the kitten.

A few moments, or a hundred years ago.

His kisses had changed her; she would never be quite the same person ever again. 'To be quite honest,' she added, considering the matter, 'I am *perturbed*.'

He made no reply, and it struck her that he might misunderstand her meaning. 'But in a *good* way, you understand.'

He chuckled. 'I am glad to hear it.' Together they walked back nearer to the terrace, just out of sight of those now present. 'Now, go you when they are distracted,' he whispered in her ear, sending a delightful shiver down the entire length of her spine. 'I shall follow after a suitable delay.'

She nodded, and they waited until a particularly raucous exchange developed among the matrons on the far side of the terrace. He pressed her hand and she went, slipping silently towards the nearest set of doors and making her way up the hallway directly to the ladies' withdrawing room, where she spent the next ten minutes gathering herself. The housemaids were busy, stitching hems and mopping wine stains from no fewer than three ladies' gowns. Rose was able to check her own appearance, thankfully finding almost no trace of her recent adventures, save a small paw-mark on the bodice of her gown.

'Oh, dear, miss! What happened?' The housemaid's question was entirely free from suspicion.

'There was a pretty cat on the terrace, and I picked her up briefly.' Rose made a face. 'I did not realise her paws were muddy.'

'Not to worry, miss. I shall soon sponge it out.'

While the housemaid worked on the offending stain which to Rose's relief, did respond to her clever ministrations, Rose tried very hard *not* to think about him. Lord Ashbourne. The Viscount. *James.*

She tried not to think of him when Izzy came looking for her, declaring that Lady Ashbourne wished to go home now that the performances had ended. She tried not to think of him all the way home in the darkened carriage, claiming tiredness when her sisters quizzed her on her silence. And she tried very, very hard not to think of him all the way through the night, when her mind insisted on showing her every detail of their encounter, over and over again, like a ceaseless waterwheel.

'James...' She spoke his name in the darkness of her chamber, remembering once again his tongue, his lips, his arms, his hips...

It was going to be a very long night.

Chapter Thirteen

James awoke with a start, his mind and heart buzzing as though a hive of bees had taken up residence within him. Less than a second after opening his eyes, memories swarmed through him. Delicious kisses in the darkness. Her nonchalant defiance of his advice to stay on the terrace. His pride as she sang. Anger at the Thaxbys. Back to the kisses again. Groaning, he rubbed his face with both hands.

What have I done?

He was a fool. An impetuous, irresponsible fool. To dally with a gently-born maiden—a maiden under the care of his own aunt—was reprehensible. Had he heard of another gentleman doing such a thing he would have condemned the man without hesitation. With a determined attempt to be objective, he tried to imagine how his actions might be viewed by those who frequented the gentlemen's clubs of London.

If the young lady involved was well-dowered it would be seen as a crude attempt to seduce or compromise her into marriage. If, like Rose, she was not, then her seducer would be seen as the wickedest of men, for to compromise the reputation of an ineligible maiden, knowing full well that marriage to her was not a prospect, was iniquitous.

Rose.

Her name in his mind conjured up her image. Rose, as she had looked while performing, her nimble fingers moving swiftly over the keys and the slightest frown of concentration between her brows. Rose, sending him a humorous glance at some absurdity that she knew he would enjoy. Rose, listening thoughtfully as her sisters opined on some matter. He closed his eyes. Rose, her mouth on his, his hands on her, her passion asserting itself…

Stop!

This was madness. Where was his penchant for caution, for order, for taking no action on important matters until he had considered every angle? Since inheriting the title he had been a pillar of vigilance and prudence. Caution had briefly left him last night and while he could not truthfully say he regretted kissing Rose, he did regret that he had kissed her.

That makes no sense!

And yet, strangely, in the fog of his disordered mind this morning, it did.

Of one thing he was certain. There could be no repeat. Now that he knew of his weakness for her he could guard against it. Grimly he rose, pouring cold water from the jug on his table into the matching bowl, and splashing it around his face and neck. The shock was just what he needed. No more could he indulge in a particular friendship with Rose—with any of them. Their guardian, his aunt's brother, had entrusted the girls to the care of the Ashbournes, and by God he would not break that trust. Distance was required, and caution, and he was well-practised at caution.

'I have been thinking, girls.' Lady Ashbourne, currently enjoying a hearty breakfast, was showing no signs of tiredness from the late night at the musical soirée.

But then, Rose surmised, *my lady has probably been up and about for a couple of hours already, and is fully awake, whereas I—*

'With regard to the search for your mother, I have a suggestion.'

Now, this was one of the few topics of conversation capable of distracting Rose from her sweet, perturbing memories. 'Yes?'

'As you all know, Maria is a fairly common name among the *ton*. My suggestion is that we put together a list of all of the Marias who had a season around that time. What year were you born, Belles?'

'Er...1791.' Anna looked intrigued by Lady Ashbourne's proposal. 'And we believe Mama was around nineteen when we were born.'

Just nineteen, and giving birth to triplets.

At twenty-one, Rose could barely imagine how Mama must have felt. How on earth had she managed?

'So if your mama already had a season at that point,

it would likely be between 1788 and 1791. Would that be correct?'

'Yes…' Frowning in concentration, Rose calculated Mama's likely age. 'Might she have been out at sixteen?'

Lady Ashbourne shrugged. 'It is possible, so I suggest we include all four years as possibilities. My own season was in 1784, which means your Mama was just a few years younger than me. Such a pity, for I did not take much interest in the debutantes who followed in the years after my own marriage. My husband and I were that most unfashionable of unions—a love match!' She shook her head rapidly as if ridding herself of distracting memories. 'Now, we shall need to speak to the archivists at St James's Palace, for debutantes would all have been listed in the Court Circulars. Copies of *The Times* newspaper may also help, for they publish the names every year. We should also consult the ladies of your mama's era—like Lady Renton—for their memories may be of use. Since she has already indicated to Rose that she finds you familiar, she may well be able to assist.'

'An excellent plan!' Izzy's eyes were shining. Anna and Rose joined in the excited conversation, as they discussed how they might record the information, and how they could eliminate as many possibilities as they could manage.

Afterwards, Lady Ashbourne excused herself, declaring she needed to speak to the housekeeper and would be in her morning room if anyone needed her.

Ignoring the ongoing conversation between her sisters, Rose followed their hostess, catching up with her in the hallway.

'Lady Ashbourne!'

She turned, an expression of surprise on her kind face. 'Yes, my dear?'

'I—' Conscious of the footman standing rigidly at his post nearby, and of the housemaid currently polishing a delicate side table a little further down, Rose faltered. 'Might I speak with you?'

A frown fleetingly flitted across Lady Ashbourne's face—so brief Rose might have imagined it. 'Yes, of course, Rose. Come with me.' By this point Lady Ashbourne seemed well used to the Belles' clothing colours, and rarely mistook one for another. Following her hostess to the comfortable morning room that was her preferred location when dealing with matters of household management, Rose took a seat in an upright chair, while Lady Ashbourne seated herself at her rosewood desk.

'Now, Rose, what did you wish to speak to me about?'

There was still an air of tension about her. 'I do not wish to seem indelicate, my lady...' Rose began, 'That is, I should not mean to imply anything, or make *assumptions*, but... Oh, dear! This is proving to be more difficult than I anticipated.'

'Spit it out, my girl.' Lady Ashbourne's tone was uncharacteristically blunt, her forehead decidedly creased. 'Although I may already have an inkling...'

Rose blinked. 'You do? Has Lord Ashbourne said something?'

'He has not.' Her tone was clipped, her mouth a rigid line. 'But I am not without perception, my child.' Her gaze softened. 'Just tell me.'

'Very well.' Rose took a breath. 'Lord Ashbourne told me that you spend many hours each morning dealing with household matters while we are lying in our beds. I wish to offer my services in whatever way I may assist you.'

Lady Ashbourne laughed aloud, a hint of relief in her expression. 'Is that all? I had thought you meant to speak to me of *quite* another matter.' Tilting her head to one side, she considered Rose's offer. 'I should welcome your assistance, Rose, and I thank you for offering. But are you quite certain? It might mean rising a little earlier…?'

'Oh, yes! For I am often awake quite early anyway. I simply laze away the first couple of hours each day with reading and chocolate, so it will be no great loss to rise earlier.'

Lady Ashbourne patted her hand. 'You are kind, Rose. Thank you. I certainly have much to do, between the usual household matters and then all of the invitations that must be responded to. Indeed, I have already sorted my correspondence this morning, although I have not yet had the chance to send replies. Would you mind writing responses to these?' She indicated a small pile of letters on her desk. 'We can attend all of these, but cannot go to these others.' She pointed at a separate pile.

'Of course!' Rising, Rose took the invitations and thumbed through them.

Lady Ashbourne crossed to the bell. 'You use the desk while I meet with the housekeeper.'

The next hour passed in a flurry of concentration— a helpful distraction from the warm memories lurking at the edge of Rose's consciousness. She wrote polite acceptances and regrets to all of the invitations, half listening to Lady Ashbourne's conversations with Mrs Coleby, the housekeeper. There was certainly much to be done, it seemed. The conversation between them ranged from menus for the evening, the prices of various provisions, and whether there would be availability of good salmon for the morrow, to the conduct of the female staff, including a housemaid who was causing Mrs Coleby some concern.

'She does not seem able to concentrate on her tasks, and can be dreadfully clumsy!' Mrs Coleby declared.

'Oh, dear! Which one?' Lady Ashbourne asked, her brow furrowed once again.

'Sally,' the housekeeper replied grimly, and Rose started.

She is the maid who looks after me!

Lady Ashbourne had noticed Rose's reaction. 'You have something to say, Miss Rose?'

'I—' Rose bit her lip. The last thing she wished was to get on the wrong side of the dour housekeeper. Still, her sense of justice compelled her to continue. 'Sally has been acting as my personal maid, and I have no complaints. Indeed, I would say she does an excellent job in that aspect of her work.'

There was a brief silence, and Rose held her breath. How would the housekeeper respond?

Mrs Coleby sniffed. 'I am glad to hear it, for she appears to have no interest in her other duties!'

The conversation moved on then, but Rose remained uneasy.

I am a guest here. It is not my place to interfere in matters between the lady of the house and her house-keeper.

Biting her lip, she bent her head to her task. A little later, the housekeeper left, and Lady Ashbourne sent Rose a keen glance.

'Well, Rose? How do you?'

'Oh! I have done all of the replies, and also created a list of every invitation we have accepted, arranged in order by date. With so many engagements it would be easy to miss something!'

Is she displeased with me?

'Thank you. Er—a word of advice, Rose.' Lady Ashbourne's tone was neutral, and Rose quivered.

Here it is.

'Yes, my lady?'

'Never show your fear to the servants. You did nothing wrong, my dear, but you need the *appearance* of courage when you speak out. Do you understand me?'

Rose nodded. Izzy and Anna always seemed so much more capable in challenging situations. Even a hint of controversy sometimes made Rose feel like shrivelling inside.

Which of course made the madness of last night's kiss even more incomprehensible. At the brief hint of memory Rose's heart instantly began to race, and she sensed a slow flush spreading along her face and neck.

Lady Ashbourne's eyes narrowed. 'On another matter, I...' Her gaze flitted away, then lifting her chin, she turned her gaze back to Rose. 'Until we find out about your parentage, you and your sisters would do well not to develop *tendres* for any of the more eligible among the gentlemen.'

Rose's jaw dropped.

Does she know what happened last night?

'Honestly,' Lady Ashbourne continued, 'the *most* eligible gentlemen—anyone with a title, for example—would be advised not to consider you as potential brides. Not while there is the possibility of scandal once your parentage becomes known.' She shook her head. 'And while your origins are *unknown* there is always the potential for a disastrous outcome. No family will risk that.'

Anyone with a title.

Rose swallowed. 'Of course! You have made that clear already.' She gave a bright smile. 'I am certainly not on the hunt for a husband and while I cannot speak for my sisters, I do not believe they are considering marriage either. Our focus is to discover more about our mother and if possible to discover something of our father.' She grimaced. 'Even if we were born out of wedlock. At least we would know.'

Lady Ashbourne gave a sad smile. 'I am sorry, my dear. But it had to be said. I would hate for you—for any of you—to develop preferences that cannot possibly be indulged, and so I shall advise Anna and Isobel too. There is no sense in wishing for the impossible.'

'No. Of course not.' Rose dropped her gaze to her hands, uncomfortable with the sympathy she saw in Lady Ashbourne's gaze.

'So!' Lady Ashbourne's tone turned brisk. 'Show me this list of engagements. The coming weeks will be busy, I think!'

Lady Ashbourne proved to be correct, for the next month passed in a whirl of social engagements. The sisters attended soirées, routs, and even their first ball, along with a trip to the theatre and the first country excursion of the season to see the views at Greenwich.

Every night Rose fell into bed in an exhausted state, grateful that tiredness meant she did not have to think about anything. Or anyone. Lady Ashbourne's warning had been an instant cure for the girlish dreams that she might otherwise have been tempted to indulge. No, there was no point in wishing for the impossible.

Instead she surrounded herself with gaiety, with friends, with her sisters. She regularly met Lady Mary for ices at Gunter's, took the shy Miss Phillips shopping, and accompanied her sisters on visits to the Tower, and Astley's, led by enthusiastic young gentlemen. In the mornings she assisted Lady Ashbourne with correspondence, and listened in as she met daily with Mrs Coleby, and with Burton, the butler. She came to greatly admire Lady Ashbourne's knowledge and insight into household matters, and reflected that the senior staff must be grateful to have a mistress who showed such understanding of their daily trials.

When she said as much to Lady Ashbourne, her hostess smiled broadly. 'Why thank you, my dear! And I must say I am grateful for your small interventions. That was a most useful suggestion you made today when we were considering how to best organise the footmen now that young John has hurt his hand.'

Rose blushed a little. 'I admit I am becoming fascinated with everything that must be done to keep the household running smoothly. I recall Miss Morrison—one of my teachers—comparing such tasks to the movement of a swan. We see it gliding serenely across the water, but its little webbed feet are paddling furiously out of sight!'

Lady Ashbourne laughed. 'An apt comparison, Rose. Bless you, child! I am truly grateful for your assistance. Now, I see there is a new batch of invitations to be dealt with.'

They set to work, and a little later joined Izzy and Anna in the drawing room. They were to be at home today, which was something of a relief to Rose. Although it still involved smiling and pleasing it seemed a little easier than doing the same in an unfamiliar setting.

I suppose I just prefer home, she thought as she took her seat in the drawing room, realising with a start that Ashbourne House had indeed become home to her.

At this point she knew every one of the rooms well—apart from most of the other family bedchambers and the servants' quarters, naturally. She had, however, visited the housekeeper's comfortable room in the basement a couple of times. The room had the benefit of a high window and even a small fireplace, denoting Mrs Coleby's status.

Rose had been there to help the housekeeper plan for the upcoming ball in the house—to be hosted by Lord Ashbourne and his aunt—and Rose was deep in the preparation of menus, the hiring of extra temporary maids and footmen, and the cleaning of the old ballroom which had not, apparently, been used in many years.

As the first guests began to arrive for their afternoon at home her mind turned, as it usually did, to the Viscount. Lord Ashbourne had been away a great deal of late—first, to a week-long house party with some of his gentleman friends, then more recently he had been dining more frequently at his club rather than at home. His avoidance of Rose led her to the lowering conclusion that Lady Ashbourne's warning had been justified. *No one with a title.*

Izzy and Anna had both remarked on it, but Lady Ashbourne had depressed their speculation by reminding them all that the Viscount was free to dine where he wished. She had not looked in Rose's direction particularly, yet Rose remained convinced their hostess knew—or at least suspected—that Rose had a partiality for the Viscount.

Partiality? She burned for him. She thought of him constantly. She dreamed of him while asleep and day-dreamed of him while awake. Impossible daydreams. Since that night in the garden Rose had been alone with him on just a few occasions, and then only fleetingly. Each time she had searched for any hint of warmth from him, and found none.

Oh, he was not cold—no, never that. But neither was there any *particular* expression, or moment, or glance that gave Rose any hope that he might see her differently to her sisters. He was polite, correct, and urbane, conversing briefly with them then going on his way. If the memories of their encounter in the darkness had not been viscerally etched on her brain, Rose might have doubted it had even happened.

'How is your search for your mother progressing, my dear?' Lady Renton's tone was neutral, but Rose sensed Lady Mary shuffle uneasily on the settee beside her.

'Quite well, my lady.' Rose gave no hint that she sensed any disdain or judgement behind Lady Renton's comment. 'We made a list of eleven debutantes named Maria for the years in which our mama might have been presented, and we have already eliminated eight of them.'

'Indeed? Only three left?' Lady Renton frowned. 'How can you be sure you have eliminated the others correctly? I mean, are you certain none of them is your mother?'

'Oh, yes!' Rose nodded. 'For example, Miss Maria Craven later married William Molyneux—'

'Lady Sefton! Of course!'

'Precisely. And we do remember our mama before she died. Lady Sefton is alive and well, and here in London, and I assure you, she is not our mother.'

'No indeed! An easy case, no doubt.'

'And then there was Miss Maria Berkeley, who died young, we believe.'

'Maria Berkeley! Yes, she was Lady Kelgrove's granddaughter.' Lady Renton shook her head. 'I do remember hearing of it. The unfortunate girl contracted smallpox while at the family estate and died within a few days. Poor Lady Kelgrove. She has no one now.'

Rose glanced across to where the elderly lady was opining forcefully on some matter, Lady Ashbourne nodding in agreement. Despite Lady Kelgrove's indomitable vigour, Rose had often had the strangest notion that she was lonely. 'No one at all?'

Lady Renton sighed. 'She and Lord Kelgrove had only the one child—their daughter, Judith. Judith married Mr Berkeley of Eardley and had two children—Richard and Maria, but all three of them died before their time. Judith and her husband died in a carriage accident while her son Richard, Lady Kelgrove's grandson, was killed by brigands on Hampstead Heath a few years later. Thankfully the daughter—Maria,

Lady Kelgrove's granddaughter—was not there that day but of course, smallpox got Maria in the end.' She shook her head, gazing thoughtfully at Lady Kelgrove. 'Hard to imagine how one person survives so much tragedy.'

'Indeed.' Rose felt a lump in her throat. There she sat, Lady Kelgrove, her back ramrod straight and fire flashing from her eyes. One would never know to look at her how much she had endured. 'What of Lord Kelgrove?'

'Died in his bed three or four years ago at fourscore and ten!' Lady Renton declared. 'Their children and grandchildren should have lived to a ripe old age, I think, had it not been for accident and incident.'

'That is so sad, Mama!' Lady Mary had a hint of tears in her eyes. 'Poor Lady Kelgrove!'

Lady Renton sent her daughter a sharp look. 'Yes, well, our concern just now is for you, and my duty is to ensure you make the most of the opportunity of your season. Now, let us go and speak to Garvald, for an unmarried earl must not be ignored!'

On that declaration she rose, her daughter following with an apologetic look towards Rose, and a moment later they did indeed corner the Earl of Garvald, who had been in conversation with Anna. With a suppressed smile, Rose reflected that it was no bad thing that the Belles' legitimacy was in question, for no one expected them to marry well. Still it allowed forceful characters like Lady Renton to act with a directness bordering on rudeness at times.

Instead of focusing on Lady Renton, Rose allowed her thoughts to drift to the last three names on their list.

Maria Whitchurch. Maria Carew. Maria Selby.

They had agreed to ask certain of their guests today about the young ladies, to find out if anyone remembered them or knew what had become of them. Unfortunately Lady Renton had upped and left just now before Rose had had the chance to quiz her.

In her mind she reviewed everything she knew about the three young ladies. They had not all made their debut in the same year—Miss Selby being two years ahead of the others. Rose recalled with scholarly accuracy all the information they had gleaned from the Court Circulars, from Debrett's, and from *The Times* newspaper—the lists of young ladies making their debut in those years. All, naturally, had been from *ton* families, and it occurred to Rose that if they did manage to discover which of them was Mama, she and her sisters might suddenly discover relations they had never known about. They might even get answers to some of the most vexing questions about Mama.

Why did she run away while expecting?

The most likely explanation was that she had been rejected by her family for being with child and unmarried, and therefore the Belles appearing nearly twenty-two years later would presumably not meet with a welcome from any remaining relatives. Sighing inwardly, and bracing herself for social conversation,

Rose turned to smile politely at whoever was joining her on the settee.

Her smile faltered.

It is him!

Chapter Fourteen

'Good day, Miss Rose.'

'Good—good day, Lord Ashbourne.' Her voice shook only a little, and hopefully he would not have noticed. 'What brings you here today?' she added brightly.

'I live here. Or had you not noticed?'

Ignoring his dry tone, she retorted instantly, 'Actually, I had not. Not lately, anyway.' She sent him a searing look. 'You have no friends to see today? No horse races to attend?'

'None at all!' he responded coolly. 'And so I am forced to endure an afternoon in my own drawing room.' He raised an eyebrow. 'Was that a snort? Did you just *snort* at me?'

'A lady,' she declared primly, 'does not snort.'

'Sounded like a snort to me,' he muttered before declaring, in quite a different tone, 'Miss Phillips!' He rose, bowing to her. 'How delightful to see you! Please, take a seat.' He indicated the half of the settee he had just vacated, and Miss Phillips sat.

'Thank you, my lord. Good day, Miss Lennox. You are Miss Rose, are you not?'

'I am,' Rose confirmed—for only the dozenth time that week. 'Are you well, Miss Phillips?' She forced herself to smile.

Finally he comes to speak with me, and instantly someone else comes along to interrupt our conversation.

'I am very well, thank you. I just wanted to thank you again for letting me accompany you on your shopping trip.'

Rose waved this away, conscious that the Viscount had remained standing beside the settee and was listening intently. 'Think nothing of it, Miss Phillips. It is all still quite new to me too, you understand.'

'Yes, but you have such...' She paused, as if searching for the right word. 'Such *poise*, Miss Rose. How you know your way about London, when everything is so confusing... And when that odious person tried to—well, you dealt with him with such proficiency, while all the while I was quaking in my boots!'

'What is this about an odious person?' The Viscount's tone was sharp. His gaze pierced Rose, and her heart, predictably, skipped.

She made a face. 'It was nothing, really. Just someone who was rather encroaching.'

'He tried to strike up a conversation with us, and made comments about Miss Lennox being beautiful.'

'He did, eh?' His expression was inscrutable. 'What happened?'

'Oh, Miss Lennox put him firmly in his place. Asked him if his mama had not taught him better manners. He slunk away like a fox!'

Now he was grinning. 'I see. He chose the wrong maiden to encroach upon! I too have felt the sharp side of Miss Rosabella's tongue, and I would not wish it on any man!'

He was clearly jesting, yet his words set off a tumble of memories in Rose's mind, and a fiery blush filled her face with heat. Her tongue…his tongue…there had been no sharpness that night in the darkness. Only sensation, and bliss, and—

Oh, Lord!

Her eyes met his, and in that instant she was convinced he was remembering exactly the same event.

'Yes, well…er… I am glad all ended well.' He bowed. 'Now, if you will excuse me—'

And he was gone, in an instant. *Coward!* she thought, the notion giving her some amusement. Still, after weeks of very little time together, it had not taken very long for both of them to recall what had occurred between them.

Something in her was fiercely glad he was discomfited by the memory too. If he had been cool and distant, it might have suggested that such matters were commonplace for him. Desperately she hoped their kisses had meant something to him too. Even though it was impossible for there to be anything between them in future, naturally. Watching him walk away, a pang of pain knifed through her.

'Are you well, Miss Rose?' Miss Phillips was eyeing her in a concerned manner.

'Quite well, Miss Phillips.' Rose smiled brightly, snapping her attention back to her companion. 'Never better, in fact! Now, shall we plan another excursion? For we did not quite manage to take in the bazaars on our last shopping trip.'

Using every ounce of determination within her, Rose managed to avoid looking in the direction Lord Ashbourne had gone, instead focusing on her conversation with Miss Phillips, and bestowing glittering smiles on a pair of handsome young gentlemen who came to flirt, and jest, and pay extravagant compliments to both young ladies. After they had gone, Rose made sure to warn Miss Phillips against taking anything they had said in earnest. 'One thing I have learned, Miss Phillips, in the very short time I have been in London, is that most young gentlemen are full of artifice. Flirtation is a game to them, I think.'

Miss Phillips's face fell. 'Oh! So when they called us "beautiful", they did not truly mean it? That is sad indeed, for no one has ever called me beautiful before.'

'No one? Now that is shocking, for anyone can see how pretty you are! But let me explain. When they said they thought us beautiful, they meant it, I think. But they did not mean anything *by* it, if you understand my meaning?'

The younger girl's face cleared. 'So, they may admire ladies, but have no serious intentions?'

'Precisely! And once we understand that, then we, too, may play at flirtation, a little.'

'But they are not all like that.' Her gaze flicked to her brother, currently in earnest conversation with Lady Mary. 'Some gentlemen are—are motivated by true regard.'

Rose nodded. 'Your brother, for example. He has more depth and seriousness than many.'

She shrugged. 'We have been raised to be sober, I think. This—' she gestured about, 'this feels alien to me.' She clapped a hand to her mouth. 'I apologise, Miss Rose!'

'For what?'

'For seeming to be critical of the highest-ranking people in society. I did not mean to suggest that—that—'

Rose leaned closer to her ear. 'That this is all a hum?'

'Yes! No! I mean—'

Rose nodded firmly. 'We may respect individuals as much as they deserve, behave with politeness and propriety, yet maintain our own thoughts and opinions, may we not?'

'I suppose. It sounds so reasonable when you put it so. But—' She looked towards her brother and Lady Mary again, and Rose followed her gaze. As they watched, Lady Renton came to claim her daughter, drawing her away with a brief word to Mr Phillips. He bowed politely, his gaze lingering on Lady Mary, and Miss Phillips sighed.

'What if our opinions are not welcome, our preferences not regarded?'

What indeed?

Knowing she was likely not the only person here present unable to follow any preferences she might develop, Rose simply said, 'We must understand, I suppose, what is possible, and what is not.'

Briefly, rage burned within her—rage that she dare not even think of choosing the Viscount, and that he himself was making it crystal clear she should not even consider such foolishness. *It hurts.*

She swallowed, then gave Miss Phillips a sad smile, praying that the young lady thought they were speaking only of her brother and Lady Mary. To her great relief, a footman approached with the news that Lady Kelgrove desired to speak with her. They parted then, Miss Phillips to her brother's side, while Rose drew a chair up beside Lady Kelgrove.

'What is this I hear about you compiling a list of girls with the name Maria?' The elderly lady gave no preamble, and Rose's mouth quirked up a little at this further evidence of Lady Kelgrove's disdain for empty platitudes.

'We know that Maria was our mama's given name, and we know the years when she might have made her debut, so we thought we might apply logic to the riddle of her identity.' Rose grimaced. 'Unfortunately, Maria is a fairly common name.'

Lady Kelgrove sniffed. 'It is a good name. Nothing wrong with it.'

'Oh! I apologise! I was informed that your grand-daughter was called Maria. I did not mean to cause you any distress.'

The old lady squeezed Rose's hand with her wizened one. 'My distress was a long time ago, my dear. She was the last of our family. And she did not live long enough to be anyone's mama, I am sorry to say.'

'Would you like to tell me about her? One of the ways we keep Mama alive in our hearts is to talk about her.'

Lady Kelgrove's eyes widened, then she nodded. 'Yes. Yes, I would like to speak of her.'

And so she did. Of Maria and her brother, Richard. How they had played together as children. How they had been good friends together, providing cover for each other when getting up to mischief, and comforting one another when they were sad. How they had come to live with their grandparents following the untimely death of their parents—Lady Kelgrove's daughter and her husband—in the carriage accident. Maria had been bereft each time Richard went away to school, and delighted to see him at the end of every term.

'Of course, that's when Richard befriended the Fletcher boy,' she mused. 'He became a good young man, despite growing up in—yes, well, the least said about *that*, the better.'

'Fletcher? Like Mrs Thaxby?'

Lady Kelgrove nodded approvingly. 'The very same. George was a few years younger than his sister and they were not particularly close.' Leaning forward, she added with a confidential air, 'He had none of her vanities. George spent most of his summers with us.' She frowned. 'All was…not well…at home. So George, Richard, and Maria became fast friends, playing at battledore and crooky all summer long.' She sighed. 'My life is nearly done, I suppose, but when I look back I can be proud of the warmth my grandchildren and their friend experienced in my home.'

She sent Rose a quick look. '*Warmth* was not a virtue typically encouraged in *ton* families, you know.'

Rose nodded thoughtfully.

That explains much. They marry for expediency, not emotion. Not love.

'Maria and Richard and George were happy with you.'

'Yes. Yes, they were.' She frowned. 'And then everything fell apart. I had thought that losing my daughter, Judith, was the tragedy I would have to bear. I did not think to lose both of my grandchildren too.'

Rose waited. If Lady Kelgrove wanted to say more, she would listen with calmness. It was the least she could do. 'Thank you.' Rose nodded to the footman who had offered her another drink, then waited while Lady Kelgrove was served. Momentarily free from focusing on the elderly lady and her stories, Rose glanced about the room. *There he is!* Watching him converse with the Prince, her heart leapt in the traditional manner, and belatedly she berated herself for seeking him out.

I must stop doing this!

Lady Kelgrove was ready to continue. Deliberately, Rose diverted her attention to her, and away from *him*. 'Richard and George were travelling in the Fletcher coach through Hampstead Heath.' She shuddered. 'That awful place! They were set upon by brigands and were horribly outnumbered. They were both left for dead, but some kind soul came upon the scene soon afterwards.' She sighed. 'Richard was dead, and George sorely wounded.'

'I am so sorry, Lady Kelgrove!' Reaching out, she placed her hand on Lady Kelgrove's.

The old lady shrugged. 'It was a long time ago. Poor George! He felt guilty, I think, that he had lived while Richard died. I made him come to us though, and he spent most of his recuperation with us at Kelgrove Manor.' An expression of disgust flickered across her face. 'His family did not even care enough to object. Poor Maria was devoted to him.' She shook her head. 'I should have insisted she come to town with us, but she insisted on staying with George.'

Rose caught her breath, remembering what Lady Renton had said about Maria's death. 'That was when she got sick?'

Lady Kelgrove nodded grimly. 'Smallpox in the village. She was so devoted to caring for others, she probably visited every family affected. By the time she caught the disease, it was too late. My husband was in our country home with her, while I was visiting friends. By the time I returned home she was already dead and buried.' She shrugged. 'They had to bury her quickly, you see. She was full of disease.' She shook her head sadly. 'At least I remember her how she was, whole and beautiful and perfect.'

Rose shook her head sadly. 'I am so, so sorry for your loss.' A recollection came to her—Mrs Thaxby mentioning that her brother had died. 'Did George catch smallpox, too?'

'Not then, though he died less than a year afterwards, at his home. Some sort of flux, as I recall. Perhaps he was never right after the attack on Hampstead Heath.' She shook her head. 'So much sorrow.' Abruptly her demeanour changed, and she fixed Rose with a piercing glance. 'You know what it is to grieve.'

Rose swallowed against the painful lump in her throat. 'Yes. To lose one's mother…though at least we had one another.' She thought for a moment. 'What you have told me is…is important, and moving. We had a loving family home too. Our mama died when we were ten years old, but already we knew the importance of family, of looking after each other. Of love.'

Lady Kelgrove patted her hand. 'Then, my dear, you are rich beyond measure.' She straightened. 'Tell me, what are the remaining names on your list?'

Rose recited them, and Lady Kelgrove thought for a moment. 'Carew…that sounds…you know, the first time I saw you, I thought you looked familiar. I could not say how, but something about you…'

Rose held her breath.

'Let me think on it. Carew… Ah, my mind is soaked in fog… No. Nothing is coming to me.'

'Lady Renton also said we looked vaguely familiar,' Rose prompted hopefully.

'Lady Renton…she was Miss Dean before her marriage, if I recall correctly… Miss Dean and Miss Carew…yes! Anthony Carew!'

'Anthony Carew?'

Lady Kelgrove's face was alive with animation. 'Miss Carew's papa. He was from Wales, as I recall. Some sort of squire. Magistrate perhaps. His daughter was out in the same season as my Maria, as I recall. Now, he may not be in Debrett's book, but some of the Welsh may know him. There!' She smiled, her eyes dancing. 'I have achieved something this afternoon. Now, I shall require more tea, if you please!'

Damnation!

Certain that after all this time it would be safe to begin engaging with R—with the Belles again, James was now regretting joining his aunt's afternoon party. Having limited his interactions with her to pleasantries at the dinner table, and having stayed away from home as much as he could these past weeks, James had been confident he had put behind him any particular attention he may have been giving to Miss Rose Lennox. Today, he had decided, was the day when he could begin to allow himself an easier discourse with her again, confident it would have no effect on him. How wrong he had been!

How ridiculous—outrageous, indeed—that after more than a month of forcing himself to stay away from her, Rose had unmanned him so spectacularly in less than a minute. Even now he was tempted to recall her unladylike snort, her faux primness, the laughter dancing in her eyes... So much for avoiding her.

Under cover of sipping his tea, he stole a glance at her. She was listening intently to Lady Kelgrove, her expression rapt at whatever the old lady was telling her. With some effort he tore his gaze away.

Should I leave?

He had spoken to most of his favourites—Garvald, the Prince, Robert...

Meeting his friend's eye, he saw that Robert—who was standing with the Chorleys—was looking a little troubled, and signalled with a raised eyebrow and a subtle jerk of the head that he should approach. Taking the hint, Robert bowed to Miss Chorley and her mother, then walked to where James stood.

'Well?' James asked baldly. The turmoil within him helped him see his friend's own disquiet. 'Will you offer for Miss Chorley?'

Robert sighed. 'She is pretty, and her dowry is significant...'

'Yet you do not see her as your wife.'

'I—no. No, I do not.'

'Must you choose a bride this season, Robert? As you know, I myself have decided it would be prudent to wait a few years. Caution, my friend, caution!'

'You and your caution! Yet, somehow I think you

are closer to getting wed than you may know.' He shook his head. 'I have no *need* to marry, I know, and yet I feel…ready. That is it. Ready.'

James frowned. Robert's words were unsettling, somehow.

Ready.

'Think you that Miss Chorley's mama favours your suit?'

'I suspect so.' His shoulders slumped, and James decided to be courageous.

'Another lady is your preferred choice.'

Robert's gaze flew to his. 'I—yes, but—' He frowned. 'Lord, I hope I have not been too plain in showing my affections.'

'I know you well, Robert.' James grimaced. 'My opinion, which you may discard if you wish, is that Lady Renton is determined for her daughter to make a stellar match.'

He nodded grimly. 'She is all politeness, yet takes Lady Mary away from me each time we converse. Her meaning, her *intention*, could not be plainer.'

'And the lady herself?'

'I have not spoken to Lady Mary of my affection, but, yes, I feel hopeful that my regard is matched.' He made a face. 'I cannot know for certain, however.'

James took another sip of his tea. 'My advice? Forget about Lady Renton. We have seen ambitious mamas before, and they tend not to compromise.'

'But Lady Mary herself may wish for me to speak! Must her mother—?'

Seeing the clear distress on his friend's face, James made haste to explain. 'I did not say forget Lady Mary. I said forget her mother.'

'But—' Abruptly, Robert's face cleared. 'Her father!'

'Lord Renton is known to be a man of sense, and he adores his daughter.' James took a breath, knowing that what he was about to say went against all his notions that one should marry only with cool-headed consideration. 'If he knows that you offer her happiness, and—and *love*, that may weigh more than such things as titles.'

As the words came out of his mouth, James was struck by the realisation they were true. The word *love* was ringing yet in his own ears, with part of him in disbelief at his own advice to his friend.

Love?

He shrugged inwardly. This was a very particular situation, where Robert, a perfectly eligible young man, also had a sincere affection for the lady. Why should his friend not highlight this to Lady Mary's father, in the hope it would weigh against his lack of title?

'Says the Viscount!' Robert shot back, grinning, then his expression became thoughtful. 'I shall give some thought to this. Perhaps, if I am eloquent enough, he might consider me.'

'Be bold, Robert! Lady Mary would be lucky to have you.'

'And I her.'

There was a pause. Suddenly uneasy about what his

friend might be about to say, James suggested they leave their now empty cups on a nearby side table. As they did so, Robert muttered, 'I am no fool, James. I can see what is in front of my nose!'

When James did not respond, he sighed. 'I suppose she is unsuitable, given the lack of information about...' He gave a short laugh. 'Look at me, bemoaning my lack of title, whereas you would have more freedom to choose if you were *not* a viscount.'

'Ironic, is it not?' was all James allowed himself to say. He was nowhere near choosing any bride, never mind one who might be deemed unsuitable, and yet Robert's words stirred up the uneasy feelings again. Feelings of might-have-been. Or might-be. Or cannot-be.

His aunt, who had paused behind the gentlemen, her attention caught by their conversation, moved on, a deep frown on her face. Neither gentleman noticed her.

Chapter Fifteen

'Maria Whitchurch cannot be our mama!'

The last guest from their afternoon at home had just departed, and Izzy's announcement drew all eyes.

'Oh, no, Izzy! I had high hopes for her, with people recalling that she was fair-haired, like us!' Anna sounded highly disappointed.

'What is this?' The Viscount looked puzzled, and Rose looked his way.

'We are attempting to discover which of the eleven debutantes called Maria from Mama's time is her.' A hint of accusation came through in Rose's tone.

And if you had spent more time at home recently you would have known it.

'Interesting. A clever approach.' He seemed unperturbed, which irritated Rose further.

How can I wish desperately to see him, then when he is present feel so frustrated?

'It was your aunt's idea,' said Izzy.

'I salute you, Aunt!' he declared with a flourish, making the others smile.

'Tell us, Izzy,' she prompted. 'Why must we strike Miss Whitchurch from the list?'

'She is apparently married and living in Kent with a brood of children and grandchildren. Mrs Anderton knows her well.'

Anna sighed. 'Only two prospects left. I should be pleased, for one of them must be Mama, and yet I constantly worry that we shall eliminate them both as possibilities, and *then* what shall we do?'

'Lady Kelgrove remembered something of Miss Carew,' Rose offered, repeating the elderly lady's words.

'Ooh, now that sounds encouraging!' declared Izzy, her eyes alight with excitement.

'Carew...' Lady Ashbourne's expression was thoughtful. 'Yes, I think I know the family she is speaking of. They do not come to town any more, but—' She frowned 'I am sorry to say that I vaguely recall a woman who might be your mama's age was part of their party. Now, let me think...' She thought for a moment. 'I have it! I shall write to Lady Poole. She is sure to know! Rose, remind me in the morning, please.'

Rose agreed to do so, and saw that the Viscount was looking puzzled. Noticing, Lady Ashbourne explained that 'dear Rose' had been of 'great assistance' to her, and was 'showing a real flair for household management'.

'Indeed?' He sent Rose a keen look, then spread his hands. 'I declare the accomplishments of the Belles never cease to amaze me. Belvedere,' he mused, 'must be a truly excellent school.'

Instantly, as he must have known they would, all three sisters chimed in to assure him that, yes, Belvedere was a wonderful establishment, and provided a great mix of learning, from the practical to the theoretical to the creative.

'And of course,' Lady Ashbourne was at pains to point out, 'the Belvedere teachers are almost all from the vicinity of Elgin itself. A special place, I think.'

'I should like to visit one day.'

His words were uttered in a nonchalant tone, the others responding with vague smiles. For Rose however, the inner response was powerful. As the notion pervaded her mind, Rose found that she was speechless. To imagine him at Belvedere, meeting Mr Marnoch, walking down the street on market day or attending church in the Holy Trinity chapel... Elgin was important to Rose, and James was important to Rose. Too important?

Oh! If only things were different.

'So if Miss Carew is this Welsh lady, that leaves only one name,' Anna said thoughtfully, bringing the conversation back round to Mama. 'Maria Selby.'

One week later

'I require your assistance, my friend.'

James looked up. Robert had entered his library without ceremony, and with a martial light in his eye. Since James had been diligently working his way through a substantial heap of documents presented to him by his steward, he welcomed the interruption. 'Am I to be your second at a duel? For shame, Robert! You might have warned me!'

Robert laughed. 'Thankfully nothing so violent. Simply a walk in the park!'

James eyed him dubiously. 'Have you taken leave of your senses, my friend? A *walk*? In the park?' He checked his pocket watch. 'At this hour?'

'Ha! Yes, the fashionable hour is much later, is it not?' A slight flush appeared on his cheeks. 'But I happen to know that Lady Mary is assigned to walk out to the Green Park with Miss Rose Lennox at eleven o'clock this morning. I imagine they will have left here already.'

'You do, eh? And how came you by this information?'

Inwardly James was aware of two things; that he longed to spend time with Rose, and that he was wary of spending time with Rose. After what had happened in the garden that night he had forced himself to be more absent. Not to show her any particular attention. Not to spend much time in her company.

And *damnation*! It was so difficult to keep it up, day after day, when all he wished to do was to be by her side, to tease her and converse with her and drink in her beauty. Last week when he had attempted that light conversation with her, he had come away highly disturbed and back to sleepless nights once again, tormented by her faux primness, the liveliness in her eyes, and the memory of their kisses in a velvety dark garden.

Yet he must not be drawn in.' The cautious instincts of a lifetime were warning him that his unwished-for *tendre* for the youngest Miss Lennox had the potential to spoil all his carefully laid plans. Not to marry yet. To make an advantageous marriage that would enhance the Ashbourne name, reputation, and, ideally, its fortunes. To choose a bride coolly and objectively, not being led by his loins. Or his heart. Or at least, not solely.

'Lady Mary *may* have mentioned it when we were dancing last night at the Countess de Lieven's soirée…' Suddenly serious, Robert added, 'I have been considering your advice all week, and I have decided to act. I intend to speak to Lady Mary of my regard for her, and ask if I should speak to her father.'

James rose.

At least I may be of assistance to Robert.

'I wish you well, my friend. I discern that my role will be to distract Miss Rose?'

'A task that should cause you no hardship, James!'

Robert's tone was decidedly wry, and James bristled a little. 'Yes, well, my situation is a little more complicated and obscure than your own, I fear. But let us go immediately, for they may not dally long in the park.'

'What a beautiful day!' Lady Mary indicated the idyllic scene around them, lit by the warm sun of early summer. She and Rose were walking unaccompanied apart from Lady Mary's footman who was following at a discreet distance, allowing the young ladies to speak freely. Lady Renton had permitted her daughter to develop a friendship with Rose, which, given the Belles' dubious parentage, was something that had long puzzled Rose.

'Indeed!' Rose took a breath. 'Tell me, has your mother ever spoken of our situation? Mine and my sisters', I mean.' When Lady Mary continued to look confused, she added, bluntly, 'Our parentage.'

Lady Mary's face cleared. 'Oh.' Her brow furrowed. 'Well, yes. Obviously she…that is to say…she is only reflecting what others…oh, dear! I cannot find the right words today!'

'I understand. We are the natural daughters of *someone*, but until it is clear exactly of whom, we are merely to be tolerated.' Rose's tone was flat. It was like pressing a sore place to see if it still hurt.

I should not do it.

And yet, she did. Continually. And each time she discovered that yes, it did still hurt. For Mama's sake. For her sisters' sake. For her own sake.

'But you are not simply tolerated, Rose. I *like* you. Many people like you, and like your sisters. You are certainly not "merely tolerated".'

Rose shrugged. 'It is of no matter. I have been wondering, though, why does Lady Renton permit our friendship?'

'Because I like you! Are you not listening to what I am saying?'

Rose nodded. 'I am glad that some people like us for our own sake. But given our dubious background, does it not surprise you that your mother allows our *particular* friendship? For we are now more than acquaintances.'

'We are, and I am glad of it!' Lady Mary smiled. '*And* I concede that my mama may have another reason.' She grimaced. 'Mama means well, but she is determined to marry me off to the highest-ranking nobleman she can find!'

'But—what is that to do with me?'

Lady Mary raised her eyebrows, then adopted a challenging tone. 'Name for me the highest-ranking bachelors of the season.'

Rose did so, beginning with the Prince, mentioning a couple of the royal dukes, and then listing the earls she could think of, including Garvald. 'I have frequently seen your mama encourage you to speak to Garvald. Does she favour him?'

'She may favour him, but I do not! I mean, he is all that is gentlemanlike, yet I do not think he would be the right husband for me.' She grimaced. 'I find him rather intimidating, to be honest.'

'But he is handsome, and young, and he has a well-formed mind. Is it so unreasonable of her to ask you to consider him?'

'Well, no… I suppose. The truth is I believe he has an affection for—for another lady. But pray continue.'

Ignoring the temptation to question her friend on whom she thought was the target of Garvald's affections, Rose pressed on. 'Very well. Viscounts are next, and—oh!'

'Precisely.'

'Wait. She believes your friendship with me will throw you in the path of the Viscount Ashbourne?' Rose snorted. 'Then she has very little idea of him, or me. Why, we barely see the man!'

'Indeed—' Lady Mary giggled '—but since Mama has not realised that, she allows me to visit you frequently with her blessing, and so I am content.'

'And I!' Rose concurred.

Somehow she knew that the Viscount had no interest in marrying Lady Mary. Or any lady, for that matter. Her fleeting thought that he might be interested in Miss Phillips had not survived ten minutes of watching the polite ennui with which he interacted with his friend's sister. No. The Viscount, so far as she could see, showed no preference for any lady.

Even the strange relationship he had with her—one minute raillery, the next kisses—had vanished like mist during the past month and more.

I have lost him.

She swallowed hard. No, whatever her relationship with him now was, it looked nothing like courtship—inasmuch as she understood these things.

'Now,' she declared briskly, banishing all thoughts of vexing, perplexing viscounts from her mind, 'shall we walk in the direction of the Queen's Basin? It is one of my favourite parts of the park.' Lady Mary agreed and slowly they made their way in the sunshine to the reservoir the Queen had ordered to be constructed, and which now served the entire palace of St James. Lady Mary, Rose noted, seemed uncharacteristically agitated, and kept looking about her.

From there, they meandered through the sward towards the wooded area, where they exclaimed at how noticeably cooler it was under the trees. 'And a good thing too!' declared Lady Mary, retying the ribbons on her bonnet. 'Mama will surely have something to say if I come home sunburnt! I—oh!'

Rose followed her gaze, and almost faltered in her step. There, walking towards them, was the Viscount, along with Mr Phillips.

'Good day, Lady Mary, Miss Lennox.' The Viscount bowed, a glint of humour in his eye, and Rose wondered if he was enjoying her surprise. As they exchanged greetings with him and with Mr Phillips, Rose saw that her friend was flushed with excitement but strangely, did not seem particularly surprised to have encountered the gentlemen. After a few moments of idle pleasantries the gentlemen turned to accompany them through the woods—Mr Phillips offering his arm to Lady Mary, leaving Rose to follow with the Viscount.

Eyeing him warily, she slipped her hand into the crook of his arm and they stepped out in silence. They could clearly hear the conversation between Lady Mary and Mr Phillips—currently he was asking if her parents were well—which felt decidedly awkward.

By mutual consent they slowed their steps a little, allowing the other couple to move a distance ahead.

After a fairly safe exchange about the weather, Rose daringly decided to voice the query that was in her mind. 'My lord, it is too early in the day for fashionable social walking. What brings you to the park before noon?'

He sent her a devilish glance. 'I might have known you would discern it. You are much, much too quick-witted, Miss Lennox!'

'*Too* quick-witted? I had not thought such a thing possible. Or are you one of those gentlemen who prefer ladies to have their heads filled with air?'

He chuckled. 'Not at all. And you being too quick-witted is a problem only when one is trying to be subtle. Will you not allow Mr Phillips and me some subtlety?'

'Not since my curiosity was aroused, no. You might as well tell me the whole.' She nodded towards their friends. 'Although I may have divined it already.'

'It seems that Lady Mary mentioned to Robert last night that she would be here today, at around this time.' He grinned. 'We have spent over a quarter of an hour searching for you! But Robert was insistent. He strongly wished to see Lady Mary today.'

'I see.' This was Mr Phillips's doing, then, not the Viscount's. She could not help but feel a little deflated at this information. 'And you were pressed into accompanying him?'

'Well, yes, although I needed little persuading, for I

was shut up in my library with a heap of papers from my steward when Robert called.'

'I understand.' He had not wished to see her, no. It was Robert's desire to see Mary which had prompted their excursion. 'And your role is to take me away so that he might have some unfettered conversation with her.' Glancing ahead, she saw that Robert and Mary had stopped walking. Robert had taken Lady Mary's hand, and was speaking to her in an earnest fashion.

'An objective that is already being achieved!' Mirroring the other couple, the Viscount slowed, then stopped. He did not, however, take Rose's hand, instead gesturing about him while remarking, in a pleasant tone, 'I am astonished by how deserted this place is at this time of day. Why, we have hardly seen a soul since we arrived—apart from you and Lady Mary, of course.'

Rose managed, between gritted teeth, 'You have no need to make conversation with me for the sake of politeness.' Pointedly she withdrew her hand from his arm. 'They are conversing alone, as Mr Phillips wished, and soon you may return to your library, freed from the necessity of having to exchange pleasantries with me as part of your friend's scheme.'

Hearing the sharpness in her own tone, she could not regret it. He had kissed her at the musicale, then ruthlessly avoided her ever since. While her preoccupation with him had not waned, these days she frequently wavered between anger and longing. At present, having discovered his motives for being here, anger was uppermost. For weeks she had searched for *something* in his demeanour—anything to indicate that he felt something for her, that he had not simply used and discarded her. That their kisses had held meaning for him.

He stiffened, jerking his head back. 'Rose! I would never see spending time with you as a necessity, or an unwanted task. Indeed, were I not here, I would currently be trying to decipher the last quarter's accounts. I assure you, being here in the park with you is much more desirable.'

'Humph!' Lifting her nose in the air to indicate her scepticism, she added tartly, 'A sad comparison. Compared to such dull work you would doubtless prefer the company of—of a butcher's boy!'

He laughed. 'A butcher's boy! Lord, Rose, where do you get such notions?' She eyed him stonily and his smile faded. 'You are in earnest.' He took a breath. 'Rose, believe me when I tell you that I hold you in the highest regard. Conversing with you is always a delight, for we share the same enjoyment of the absurd, I think.' He searched her face. 'I see that you frown. Do you doubt my words?'

'How can I do otherwise, when you have barely spoken to me these past weeks?' Something of her anguish was clearly apparent in her tone. It *hurt* that he had been avoiding her. It really hurt.

'But I have been busy, and I was away—' He broke off, running a hand through his hair. 'No, I cannot dissemble with you.' He took both her hands. 'The truth is, Rose, after what happened in the garden that night I had to place some distance between us. Not because I do not like you, but because I like you too well. I had to be prudent, for both our sakes.'

'And of course, you are for ever prudent.' Yet inwardly her heart was taking in his words, his demeanour. His words hung in the air between them, and thundered in her ears, her mind, and her heart.

'I like you too well.'

Vaguely she was aware that their friends had begun walking again, and from the corner of her eye she could see they were even now disappearing around a bend in the path. For her own part, she could not have walked if her life depended on it. At this moment her entire world was reduced to this man who was holding her hands and looking at her with *such* an expression. Fierceness, and desire, and warmth—all of it was there. All of the emotion she had longed to see. Her eyes were locked with his, and abruptly, her anger was gone, leaving only one emotion. Longing.

'To hell with prudence!' With a muffled curse he gathered her in his arms, and then their mouths were joined, and Rose was lost.

This time she knew what to do, what to expect, and so she matched his kiss measure for measure. They kissed fiercely, passionately, fervently, Rose welcoming the sense of the entire world shrinking even further until the only reality was his arms around her, their tongues dancing, and the *feel* of him pressing against her.

Eventually they surfaced to gasp, and breathe, and smile. 'Ah, Rose, Rose,' he murmured, pressing feathery kisses along her jawline and knocking her bonnet even further askew in the process. She cared not. Only James mattered.

He has come back to me! was the confused notion swimming around her mind.

Stepping back, he waited for her to fix her bonnet back in place, then together they walked on, joy humming between them. While Rose would like nothing more than to dally longer and enjoy a hundred more kisses, she knew that in order to preserve her reputation they must quickly catch up with Lady Mary and Mr Phillips. They must do everything to ensure their friends had no inkling of what had just happened.

He kissed me!

That was the only thing in the world which mattered.

Lady Renton's footman grinned at the sight of the young lady being thoroughly kissed by Lord Ashbourne. Staying in the shadow of the trees, he had no intention of alerting the pair to his presence, for they had clearly forgotten him.

Should I tell Lady Renton of this?

His employer had charged him with keeping her daughter safe, and while he could not currently see Lady Mary and Mr Phillips, he had no doubt that they were doing nothing more than walking and talking, for the other pair were behind, and might come upon them at any moment.

What Miss Lennox did was none of his concern, and yet... Everyone below stairs knew that Lady R was mightily proud, and that she sometimes expressed harsh judgements about the Lennox sisters' dubious background.

Why, they may be of no higher birth than me!

And yet, right in front of him, the fatherless Miss Lennox was blatantly attempting to ensnare a viscount.

As he watched her straighten her bonnet, then prepared himself to follow at a distance when they walked on, abruptly his mind was made up. Lady Renton should know of the dubious morals of the young lady her daughter was befriending. It was no more than his duty to report, after all.

Once they came out from beneath the trees the four walked together for a while on the wide path, then Lady Mary moved to stroll alongside Rose, subtly slowing her steps so that the gentlemen walked a little in front. She clearly wished to speak to Rose privately. Rose's heart lurched.

Does she know what happened back there?

'What is it?' she asked, a little anxiously.

'Mr Phillips has declared himself! Oh, Rose, he loves me!' Her step was light, her eyes sparkling with joy.

Rose embraced her. 'I am so happy for you! And for Mr Phillips. You two are so right for one another!'

'Well, I have known *that* for quite some time,' Lady Mary declared, tossing her head. 'I am simply glad that he knows it too. But Rose, I am not certain that my parents will agree to the match. Mama has never favoured him, and Papa usually follows her lead.'

'Then you must speak to your papa before Mr Phillips does! Surely if he knows your feelings on the matter he will take them into account?'

'Perhaps…but Mama can be forceful when her mind is set on something.'

'And so can you!'

Lady Mary eyed her dubiously. 'Can I though? I have never defied my mama—not once in my entire life.'

Rose laid a hand on her arm. 'I urge you to consider carefully, Lady Mary. This is the most important decision you will likely ever make. You will be tied to your husband for life.'

Lady Mary considered this. 'What you are saying is true…and yet I tremble at the very notion of speaking out!'

Rose nodded sympathetically. Lady Renton was indeed formidable. 'One question, then. How important is it to you that you should have a say in choosing your husband? That you should be able to marry Mr Phillips?'

As her friend wrestled with this, Rose's thoughts drifted briefly to her own situation. If any miracle could be wrought that might allow Rose to be considered a suitable match for a viscount, and if a certain viscount wanted her, she knew she would grab that miracle instantly and wholeheartedly.

Lady Mary nodded thoughtfully, then her little chin jutted out. 'It is more important than anything. And so I must find courage.' She smiled grimly at Rose. 'Thank you, my friend.'

'I can only give my opinion, you know. I cannot decide for you.'

'I know. But you have helped me see what is in my own heart, to understand what I must do, and for that I am grateful.'

'When will Mr Phillips speak to your papa?'

'Later today, for I have told him that Papa has no engagements before this evening's ball at Lady Cowper's. Will you be there tonight?'

'Yes, indeed. I shall look for you there, and hope for good news!'

Chapter Sixteen

Number Four, St James's Square, was in the heart of one of the most prestigious areas of London—between Pall Mall and Piccadilly, and within easy reach of the palace. Lady Cowper's balls and soirées were for many the highlight of the season, for she could be capricious, and to be invited at all was a sign of her favour.

It was strange, Rose reflected, how the Belles could be feted as diamonds and invited to the most exclusive assemblies, yet were not considered marriageable by most members of the *ton*. It was entirely contradictory, yet within the fevered, whimsical world of the *ton*, it must to them make some sort of sense. As she mounted the four shallow steps at the porticoed entrance she was conscious of a feeling of unreality surrounding her. Partly it was that she and her sisters had finally been invited to one of Lady Cowper's exclusive balls, and partly it was that James had kissed her again, this very day.

In honour of this momentous occasion—the kiss, not the ball—she had worn her favourite new gown, a delightful confection of rose-pink silk over a sparkling white underdress. While styling her hair Sally had remarked how pretty Rose looked tonight, but Rose was sure this was due to her happiness, rather than anything to do with the features she had inherited from her parents, whoever they might be. Tonight she would see him, and perhaps dance with him, and all the while the happiest of memories would shine through her.

'I like you too well.'

His words earlier meant everything to her, as did the sentiment behind them. It meant that, had things been different he might choose her, as she would choose him. They were both trapped by society's rules, and so she could not dare to dream of anything real. Tomorrow she would have to remember that they could not choose each other, but tonight, bathed in his regard and in the memory of his mouth on hers, it was enough.

He had been ensconced in his library all afternoon, doubtless finishing the tasks he should have completed earlier in the day, had it not been for Mr Phillips's request for his assistance. He had, however, joined them all for dinner, and Rose had had to consciously prevent her gaze from drifting in his direction too often. Living in his household was both a joy and a frustration, for there he was, close enough to touch yet for ever out of reach.

She had sat beside him in the rear-facing seats just now, allowing Lady Ashbourne and the other Belles the more comfortable front-facing seats, and Rose had been sorely tempted to allow her leg to relax towards his, in the hope of feeling the thrill of his warmth. Thankfully, not yet being lost to all propriety, she had managed to resist, and yet her heart had thrilled at being so close to him on the short journey to St James's Square.

Having been welcomed by their hostess, Rose and the Belles followed Lady Ashbourne to the ballroom, where a throng of people were already chattering gaily. The Viscount, with a bow and a few murmured words to the ladies, had made for the Earl of Garvald—one of his preferred companions, Rose knew—and it was hard not to feel a pang at his departure. The dancing had not yet begun, and immediately the Belles were approached by numerous young men and a few greybeards to request a dance. Thankfully, Lord Ashbourne had earlier requested the Belles each hold a dance for him, and so Rose was able to allocate all of the other dances for this evening with no regrets.

Keeping an eye on the door for the arrival of Lady Mary, Rose was rewarded when—just as the musicians were striking up to call the throng to the floor for the first dance—the Rentons arrived. Swiftly she scanned their faces for any hint of news. Lord Renton was his usual affable self, while Lady Renton's visage was a mask of inscrutability. Lady Mary, however…

Rose caught her breath. Her friend looked uneasy. Where was the glow of happiness she had demonstrated earlier? Had Lord Renton refused Mr Phillips's request?

Wasting no time, Rose excused herself and made her way across the room. Lord Renton greeted her with easy friendliness, while Lady Renton's pleasantries were a little stilted. A few minutes later Rose and Lady Mary moved away from her parents, and Rose finally had the chance to hear about what had occurred.

'Well? What news?' Rose asked in a low voice, eyeing her friend with concern.

'Oh, Rose, Papa has agreed to the marriage!' Her words were reassuring, yet her shoulders drooped and there were tight lines at the corners of her mouth. 'It is not to be announced for a couple of days, in order that Mama may become accustomed to the notion.'

'Oh, dear? Was she *very* upset?'

Lady Mary nodded. 'I have never seen her so angry. Papa says all will be well, but—' She bit her lip, and Rose covered her hand with her own.

'I am so sorry, Lady Mary. This should be the happiest of days!'

She swallowed. 'I am unused to disappointing my mother. It is not a feeling I like.'

Rose nodded sympathetically. Lady Renton's ambitions were for her daughter's sake. It was entirely understandable that she might feel disappointed that her daughter had not made a brilliant match. 'And I, who have no mama, envy you the experience of having a mother who cares enough to be cross!'

Lady Mary's jaw slackened. 'Of course! It is only because she is concerned for my future that she feels so strongly about my marriage. But—' she bit her lip

'—Mr Phillips is perfectly amiable, with a respectable fortune and a *sensible* demeanour. Or so Papa described him!'

Rose could not resist a giggle. 'I should hope that your description would be rather different!'

This earned an answering laugh. 'Indeed! He is... he is wonderful.' A slight colour stained her cheeks and her gaze dropped. 'I wish for nothing more than to be his wife. I need no earls or viscounts!'

Now it was Rose's turn to laugh—although it was, to be fair, a little forced. 'Does any lady? What a lady *actually* needs is a gentleman who loves her, and whom she loves in return. Such a little thing to say, and yet...' Her voice tailed away as she swallowed against a painful lump in her throat.

'And yet our path is fraught with trials. Still, at least Papa said yes.'

'That is true. Your mama will become accustomed to the idea. I am sure of it.' She smiled at her friend. 'Do not look now, but Mr Phillips approaches!'

The Viscount was with him, and Rose's heart stuttered at the sight of him. Why, when she had been in his company until a very short time ago, should her heart still, then race in such a foolish manner? They all stood together conversing in a superficial way as the orchestra tuned their instruments, then Rose's first dance partner came to claim her. Lady Mary too, was claimed by another gentleman, and as Rose and her friend went with their partners to form a set for the dance, she was conscious that the Viscount and Mr

Phillips had remained where they were, standing at the edge of the dance floor.

Neither seemed to be in a hurry to claim a partner and it soon became clear they intended to wait out this particular dance, conversing and watching the dancers. *All* of the dancers, naturally. And yet, Rose *knew*, felt certain that James was watching her particularly. That his friend would be watching Lady Mary particularly. The notion was entirely thrilling. The dance began, and she curtseyed to her partner, but inwardly her attention remained focused on the divinely handsome gentleman at the edge of the dance floor.

Oh, being in love with someone was simply the most wonderful feeling she had ever experienced! Abruptly, she missed a step in the dance. Recovering quickly from her stumble, she frowned, concentrating on her feet while all the time her mind was racing. In *love*? In love with the Viscount?

Yes, and yes.

She loved him. Loved his handsome face, his lively mind, his strong body. His loyalty to family, and his integrity. His grumpiness when crossed. Even his overwhelming caution and prudence, which kept them all safe.

A humorous thought struck her. He had not been very prudent earlier, when he had kissed her in the park! *'To hell with prudence!'* he had declared, before sweeping her into his arms. Even the ferocity of his language had been thrilling. With some effort, Rose responded to a pleasant remark from her dance partner, but all the while she was hugging her new knowledge to herself. She was in love, and this day was one of the happiest in her life.

Lady Renton's eyes narrowed as she watched the dancers. Her beautiful daughter Mary—her beautiful, accomplished, *obedient* daughter—had defied her, and was to marry— Her hand gripped her delicate painted fan so tightly she thought it might break. Mary was about to marry a *nobody* with no title, a modest fortune, and no outstanding qualities. Mr Robert Phillips was the sort of young man, indeed, who was instantly forgettable.

Mary had had every opportunity to make a brilliant match. The Earl of Garvald, perhaps. Or the Viscount Ashbourne. Perhaps not the Prince, as he was rumoured to be expected to marry some Prussian princess.

No, Mary was never destined to be a princess, but she might have been a countess like her mother, or even a viscountess. Instead she would be a Mrs, and nothing more. Oh, she would retain her birth title for life, being referred to as the Lady Mary Phillips after her wedding, but her marriage would inevitably be seen as a step down from her birth.

All of the work invested in her—the music teachers and governesses, dancing and deportment lessons, gowns from the best modistes...all for nought. For strangely, horrifyingly, Mary had attached herself to a young man with only passable looks and figure, and who seemed an afterthought at social gatherings. How was this marriage going to contribute to the Renton family's social standing? And how on earth had all her work crumbled to dust in a single day?

Lady Renton's thoughts drifted to the Countess de Lieven's soirée the night before. During the event Mary had spoken with two earls, a couple of viscounts, and the Prince. She had been doing well too, with many complimenting Lady Renton on her daughter's looks and manners.

She should have caught an earl, at the very least!

And yet, here they were, and Lord Renton had thrown his daughter away on a simple mister.

Lady Renton was furious. Indeed, she could not recall ever being so angry. She was angry with her husband, and with her daughter, and with Mr Phillips. How dare he spoil all her carefully laid plans for Mary's future! This—a successful season for her only daughter—had been her focus for *years*, not the short months since the season had begun. Still reeling from her husband's pronouncement at dinner, Lady Renton had yet to understand how it had come about.

Of course she had been aware that her foolish daughter felt more comfortable in Mr Phillips's company. Well, why should she not? The very reason Mary liked him was because he did not hold the arrogant confidence of those higher than himself in the *ton*.

Lady Renton's mistake had been that she had failed to instruct her daughter explicitly that she must not consider Mr Phillips for a husband. Instead she had tried to be subtle, to carefully and artfully detach Mary from him each time their conversations lasted longer than the minimum necessary for politeness. Now she was angry with herself. Angry at her own failure to see what was under her nose. But then, she had trusted Mary. More fool her.

Her mind returned to the shocking moment at dinner earlier when her husband had informed her of their daughter's betrothal. He had seemed to expect her to be pleased.

Pleased? That Mary's hand had been wasted on such an unpromising young man? No, she most decidedly was *not* pleased.

Once the footmen had left the room Lady Renton had lost no time in making her husband—and her daughter—aware of just how displeased she was. Mary had looked crushed, Lord Renton astounded, and Lady Renton could have cheerfully committed violence upon them both.

In his defence, Lord Renton had praised Mr Phillips's character, fortune, and demeanour, and indicated that Lady Mary herself had pleaded to be allowed to marry the man. Lord Renton, clearly, had allowed himself to be persuaded.

Wait.

When had this pleading occurred? Lady Renton's personal maid had informed her after dinner that Mr Phillips had called once, around four o'clock. Surely there had not been enough time between then and dinner for any *pleading* followed by Lord Renton informing the young man of his agreement? Might the pleading have come *before* Mr Phillips's request for Mary's hand?

She frowned, thinking it through, then realisation dawned. Amid all the turmoil of her daughter's betrothal, she had almost forgotten the information provided just before dinner by one of the footmen.

The encounter in the Green Park!

The footman had informed Lady Renton that the young ladies had taken up with Mr Phillips and Lord Ashbourne while out walking, and the footman stated he had seen the Viscount kiss Miss Rose Lennox. Lady Mary, he had assured her, was not engaged in similar behaviour.

Earlier, Lady Renton had dismissed the servant's report as idle gossip, since no young lady would risk doing such a thing, but now she was beginning to wonder if it might after all be true.

I'll wager that's when Mary and Phillips hatched the plot to get my husband's permission, cutting me out of the conversation.

And what had Miss Lennox's role been? Lady Renton had to wonder. To distract the Viscount, perhaps?

Her gaze swerved to the Misses Lennox, currently dancing as though they had not a care in the world. Her gaze finding the one in the rose-pink gown, her eyes narrowed.

Did you persuade my daughter to go against the wishes of her own mama?

Mary was normally biddable, diffident, obedient. It was out of character for her to act as she had today.

And as for Miss Rose Lennox...well, Lady Renton had been sorely mistaken in the girl's suitability as a friend for Mary, that was certain. Any young woman— she hesitated to say 'lady'—who went around kissing gentlemen in parks was clearly unsuitable company for her own innocent daughter.

The dance ended, and immediately Phillips and the Viscount approached Mary and Miss Lennox, seemingly offering them refreshments. Lady Renton watched them walk to where the punch and ratafia was being served, then scanned around the room until she found Lady Ashbourne, currently standing by a gilded pillar and conversing with Mr and Mrs Thaxby. Knowing that no one could tolerate the Thaxbys for long, Lady Renton made her way across the room. Now was her opportunity. Lady Ashbourne had launched the Lennox triplets into society: it was vital she hear of what had occurred in the park earlier. It was no more than her duty to inform her, after all.

'Punch or ratafia?' the Viscount asked, a decided twinkle in his eye.

'Punch!' Rose tossed her head. The recklessness from earlier was still, it seemed, thrumming in her veins. Glancing sideways, she noted that Lady Mary had opted for the ratafia, which contained less alcohol and was seen as a more appropriate beverage for young ladies. Well, of course she had.

Taking the glass from the Viscount's hand, Rose waited until he had served himself before all four of them raised their glasses together and drank, the action seeming to bond them together in some way.

I like these people.

The potent liquid burnt a trail of fire down Rose's throat and she savoured the sensation. Today was a day for thrilling experiences, after all. They had kissed in the park—daringly, for it had been full daylight, and they were lucky not to have been observed. Now she was drinking punch. And she was in love.

Eyeing him surreptitiously, she briefly sent her attention inwards. Would awareness of her own feelings change anything? It did, it seemed. And it did not. The feelings were just the same—fascination, appreciation of his handsomeness, the thrill of inner agitation at his nearness. Yet now, understanding that she loved him, she saw new meanings in the responses of her body and heart to him. Now her mind gloried in the knowledge that this man was not just the object of an unlooked-for *tendre*, he was the target of her true affections. Tonight it mattered not that they could not marry. Tonight it was enough to know that she loved this man—loved him with a heart full of passion.

'May I wish you happy!' declared the Viscount, smiling at Mr Phillips and Lady Mary.

So he knows! Well naturally he would. No doubt Mr Phillips had been sharing the news with his friend even while Lady Mary had been informing Rose of the happy news.

'I too! I am delighted for you both,' Rose declared, enjoying how Lady Mary and Mr Phillips were wearing almost identical expressions—delight mixed with discomfort at being the focus of attention. The next few moments were spent discussing the impending nuptials, the announcement of which would likely be made within the week. Both Rose and the Viscount reiterated their commitment to maintaining discretion—although Lady Mary agreed Rose could tell her sisters and Lady Ashbourne, so long as they promised not to spread it about.

A couple of minutes later Mr Phillips clapped his hand to his forehead. 'Miss Lennox! I almost forgot! My mama is unable to be present tonight, and so I am squiring my sister, but she charged me to pass on to you some information. Now, let me recall the details, for she was most insistent I relay her message accurately.' He thought for a moment. 'Right. I have it. She said to tell you that she knew Miss Selby— Miss *Maria* Selby—and that she sadly died of a fever more than two years ago. They were friends, it seems, although Miss Selby never went out in society. Now, does that mean something to you?'

Rose's heart sank. 'It does, and I thank you for passing on the information.' So another Maria was now discounted. The fact that poor Miss Selby never went out in society would account for the fact that no one the Belles had spoken to could recall the lady.

And so it will be for me, once I leave this place. Eventually I shall be forgotten. Just like Mama.

That left the Welsh lady—Miss Carew—as the only possibility, and if she was still visiting London occasionally then she could not possibly be Rose's mama.

But there was no time to think on this, for the musicians were striking up for the waltz. This shocking dance, involving prolonged eye-gazing between the gentleman and lady, as well as holds that brought them into direct contact, had made its way to private ballrooms all over England, though was not yet permitted at Almack's. Perhaps Lady Cowper—one of the patronesses of that august establishment—was testing the waters by asking the musicians to play it at her ball. Glancing across, Rose saw Lady Cowper herself taking to the floor with Lord Palmerston, but before she could consider what this might mean, she became aware that James had turned to her.

'My dance, I believe, Miss Lennox?' The Viscount held out his hand.

Her heart skipped as she placed her hand in his and they made their way to the dance floor.

'My *dear* Lady Ashbourne! I simply had to come and greet you, for you look resplendent tonight! That gown is simply divine!' Lady Renton gave Lady Ashbourne a brilliant smile, before turning to the couple who had been conversing with her. 'Good evening, Mrs Thaxby, Mr Thaxby. Do you not agree? Have you ever seen anything like this fabric before?'

Lady Ashbourne was eyeing her dubiously. 'It is silk-satin, pure and simple, Lady Renton.'

'But the hue! What is the name of that colour, for I simply must ask the modiste to make me a gown in a similar shade!'

'Er—blue?' said Lady Ashbourne, a decided crease on her forehead, and Lady Renton laughed gaily.

'Ever the wit, Lady Ashbourne! Now, please excuse us—' this to the Thaxbys '—for there is something I must speak of with Lady Ashbourne!'

After further pleasantries, Lady Renton made haste to reassure Lady Ashbourne of her good intentions. 'The truth is I thought you might need to be rescued, my lady.'

Lady Ashbourne waved this away. 'Not at all. I am perfectly capable of ending an undesired conversation, I assure you.'

'But the Thaxbys…'

'Yes? What of the Thaxbys?'

'Oh, nothing. Nothing at all.' The conversation was not going as Lady Renton had anticipated. 'Lady Cowper is looking very well, is she not?'

Lady Ashbourne smiled, her gaze seeking out their hostess, who was even now whirling around the floor in the arms of Lord Palmerston. 'She is. It is good to see her in such spirits.'

'They say,' Lady Renton murmured confidentially, 'that her latest child looks remarkably like a certain Corsican diplomat.'

'No! Really?' Lady Ashbourne seemed suitably interested. 'Not Palmerston, then?'

'Apparently not. Not her husband's either, of course.'

'Well, no.' Lady Ashbourne made a wry grimace. 'The *next* one may resemble Palmerston, of course.'

They conversed on for a few minutes, while the dancers waltzed and the music played. Lady Renton, judging the moment was right, took a breath.

'Lady Ashbourne—' she began '—forgive me, but there is something I think you ought to know.'

Something in her tone must have alerted Lady Ashbourne, for now the other lady was truly listening, her gaze fixed on Lady Renton, her smile frozen.

'I mean,' Lady Renton continued smoothly, 'if it concerned my *own* dear daughter I would hope that someone might drop a hint in my ear. Even unwelcome news must be borne, when one is sponsoring a debutante. Do you not agree?'

'What is it you mean to say to me, Lady Renton?' Lady Ashbourne's eyes glittered, her expression unreadable. 'You have my attention, I assure you.'

Chapter Seventeen

Supper was served, and Rose found her sisters so they could walk together to the supper room. 'Is this not a delightful evening?' she asked generally, and Anna's eyes narrowed.

'You are in alt tonight, Rose. What is making you so…so *happy*?'

Izzy's penetrating gaze was now turned upon Rose, and she felt herself flushing.

'Indeed she is, Anna. I remarked upon it earlier.' Izzy's tone held a hint of slyness. 'Is there any particular reason, Rose?'

Knowing she could not mention the wonderful kisses she had shared earlier with the Viscount, nor her recent discovery that for the first time in her life she was in love, Rose instead diverted her mind to the other source of her happiness: her friend's news. 'Well, yes. There is something wonderful happening. I knew of it this morning—at least, I *hoped* it would occur, but I did not know for certain until this evening.'

Izzy's jaw dropped. 'Have you had an offer of *marriage*, Rose?'

'Lord, no!' Rose affected a light laugh. It was becoming harder to pretend that it did not matter. 'Have you forgotten that no one will marry us, because of… you know.'

'No one of note,' Izzy pointed out. 'But some of those untitled gentlemen of the *ton* might—anyway, what is your news?'

'Well,' Rose began in a confidential manner, 'I happen to know that Lady Mary has received an offer, with her father's agreement, and has accepted. And I am delighted for her.'

'Garvald?' asked Anna, in a strangled tone.

'Nope. Guess again!'

'Never say her parents have agreed she can wed Mr Phillips!' Izzy's eyes were wide.

'Indeed they have—but the betrothal is not yet to be announced, so you must not say anything.'

'Of course not! Well, I never thought Lady Renton would allow Lady Mary to marry Mr Phillips, I must say!'

'As to that, it was *Lord* Renton who permitted Mr Phillips to pay his addresses.'

'His wife did not agree.' Anna's tone was flat.

Rose grimaced. 'No.'

'They do mean it, when they say the *ton* marries within itself, each to their own level in the hierarchy. Mr Phillips is a gentleman, and well-respected, yet he is clearly not good enough for Lady Renton's daughter simply because he has no title,' Anna mused, her brow furrowed. 'The likes of us could never hope to make a fine match.'

'Why, is there someone you might wish to match with?' The slyness was back in Izzy's tone.

'No, no, of course not,' Anna replied hastily. Her eyes narrowed. 'Why, have you someone in mind yourself, Izzy?'

'Definitely not!' she retorted, tossing her head.

Thankfully they had reached the top of the queue for supper by this point, and so all three turned their attention to the food. Rose had the sense there was much unsaid between them, but as she needed to preserve her own secret, she welcomed it.

We are growing up in a new way, she realised.

At school they had never needed to have secrets from one another. Here, though…it was all too complicated.

Waltzing with the Viscount had been all she hoped for, and the memories made her stomach twist in a delightful way. She eyed her plate dubiously. Never would she be able to eat with a thousand butterflies in her innards.

'Come and sit here, girls!' It was Lady Kelgrove, gesturing imperiously at the empty chairs at her own table. 'Quickly, before the footmen put someone else into these seats!'

They sat hastily, and by the time they had completed the formal pleasantries and the footmen had served them all with drinks, Rose found that she might, after all, manage to eat some supper.

Biting into lobster and asparagus, she noticed that Lady Kelgrove's plates contained only cold meat and a couple of small pastries. 'Have you all you wish to eat, Lady Kelgrove? Shall I fetch you something? Some cakes or sweetmeats perhaps?' Lady Kelgrove, she knew, had quite the sweet tooth.

Lady Kelgrove inspected the Belles' plates. 'I should quite like some of the trifle, if you please, Maria. I do not know how I came to miss it, for trifle is one of my favourite sweets! Oh, and some of the elderflower ice cream, for I understand that Gunter himself has provided the ices.'

'I shall fetch some for you instantly, Lady Kelgrove,' Rose announced, rising. As she made her way back to the serving tables she reflected on Lady Kelgrove's error in calling her Maria.

Her own granddaughter should be here, alive and well, and looking after her. And I must be similar in age now to what her granddaughter would have been when she last saw her.

Older people often mistook names, Rose knew, but there was something poignant, almost heartbreaking in Lady Kelgrove's use of her granddaughter's name. No one should be alone without family in old age.

And yet, did Rose herself not plan to become a teacher once her London adventure had ended? The logical outcome for her own life, therefore, was one of loneliness, was it not?

But no, for if my sisters marry I shall live with one of them, and if they do not we might all live together.

Just now neither prospect seemed pleasing, but she could not say why.

Dawn was breaking as the Belles and Lady Ashbourne made their way home. The summer nights were short, and Lady Cowper's ball had been long. For Rose the highlight, naturally, had been the waltz she had danced with the Viscount. As the carriage pulled up outside Ashbourne House she remained lost in remembering. Most of the time she and the Viscount had maintained the decorous attitude of gripping both hands to one another's elbows, whirling giddily with their gaze fixed upon one another. For the final figure, daringly, they had been asked to adopt the much more immodest German hold—Rose's left arm around the Viscount's waist and his right around hers. How shocking it had been, and how thrilling!

Their hands and arms entwined, his eyes on her… the dance and the kisses in the park were becoming already intertwined in her memory, as it had seemed to her that the dance was a continuation of their kissing somehow. Or perhaps their kisses had been the beginning of the dance…

Following her sisters and their hostess into Ashbourne House, she removed her cloak and shoes, handing them to Sally along with the dancing slippers which she had carried carefully home, as had the others.

In those slippers I danced with the man I love, she thought, almost laughing at herself for being absurdly sentimental.

Tonight she would allow herself to enjoy every second, for tomorrow might never come.

They made their way up the opulent staircase, followed by the maids who would help them undress and take their hair down. Briefly Rose was reminded of that first night in London, and how strange it had been to have a maid attend her. Then she had tiptoed out to the landing, and seen him for the first time.

When shall I see him again?

Along with Mr Phillips, the Viscount had left the ball almost an hour ago, destined for their club. Rose surmised they might not seek their beds until the sun was well risen. Which meant it might be dinnertime before she laid eyes on James again.

I can wait until then, she told herself, hugging close the experiences of the past day.

'Rose!' Lady Ashbourne interrupted her reverie.

'Yes, my lady?' Rose brought her hostess into focus. They had reached the landing, and Rose noted Anna and Izzy currently entering their respective bedrooms followed by their personal maids.

'I wish to speak to you.' Turning to Sally and her own maid, she instructed them to wait outside, then followed Rose into her bedchamber, closing the door firmly.

Abruptly, Rose's senses were on alert. This was highly unusual.

What—?

Her worst fears were realised a moment later. 'I shall speak plainly, Rose. Your reputation—a most delicate thing—might have been compromised today.'

Shock held Rose immobile. There was a roaring in her ears and her heart was beating loud as thunder. 'What?' she managed, her voice weak. 'What?'

'You were seen, today.' Lady Ashbourne's tone was flat. 'Kissing my nephew.'

Lord!

Fearing she might faint, Rose gripped the bed-post. All of her pleasant dreams fell away, leaving only the realisation of her own foolishness. Her recklessness.

What have I done?

'I need not tell you,' Lady Ashbourne continued, 'how serious this is. Should this information spread, it will lead to utter condemnation by the *ton*. And not just for you yourself.'

Rose's free hand went to her mouth. 'My sisters!'

'Indeed.' Lady Ashbourne nodded grimly. 'And me, to some extent—although, given my standing, they will probably say that I was misled, and naive to believe you had been gently reared. I shall be condemned as foolish rather than offensive.'

'Lady Ashbourne, I am so, so, sorry.'

I have destroyed everything, in one moment of madness.

Her stomach felt sick. Not the pleasant flutterings from earlier. This time she felt ill. Horribly, horribly ill. 'When you have been so kind to us, and so generous! I should not have wished to cause you an instant's distress!'

I have been selfish, for it did not even occur to me how my actions might affect others.

Lady Ashbourne shrugged. 'That is as may be, but I am more concerned with how best to handle this.'

Rose's mind was awhirl. 'H-handle it?' The implications were beginning to occur to Rose. Condemnation. Sneering. The worst kind of attention. 'Can it be handled?'

'Perhaps. The...incident...is not known about by most people. Not yet, at least. We must do all we can to prevent this disaster.'

'But—but how?'

Lady Ashbourne nodded grimly. 'There are two options, as I see it. I can either inform James, at which point I shall be pressing him to marry you, or—'

'To *marry* me? Because of one kiss?'

Lady Ashbourne of course was not to know of the other kisses, in the Renton garden, and Rose would never ever tell her of them. But—pressed to marry her? While of course she would like nothing more than to be James's wife, for him to be *forced* to marry her because of a moment's imprudence was unthinkable. Besides, she was an unsuitable candidate for any titled gentleman. They all knew it. Never could she allow James to sully his family name by marrying beneath him. She knew by now how strict the *ton* was on such matters. No, there was only one answer she could give.

'No! I shall never marry him!'

Lady Ashbourne blinked. 'So you do not wish to marry James? I had quite thought there was a *tendre* developing between you.'

Rose felt her cheeks begin to flush. 'Well yes, perhaps. At least, for my part… But—but *no*—I do not wish to be married in this way.'

'He has disrespected you, and me, and his own family name by his actions.' Lady Ashbourne's expression was bleak. 'I had not thought this of him.'

'But he— No one should be compelled to marry because of a—a momentary indiscretion. I came to no harm.'

Lady Ashbourne shook her head. 'It is fairly commonplace, sadly. Even the Thaxbys…which was, no doubt, the only way that sour-faced besom could catch a mate. But I digress. If you are certain—'

'I am!'

'Then that leaves only one other choice.' She took a breath. 'You will have to go away, Rose.'

Rose's knees were suddenly soft, and she sank down onto the bed. 'G-go away?'

Lady Ashbourne's eyes held sadness. 'If your parentage was known, and substantial, we could brazen it out, I think. Dismiss it as gossip and say it is all lies. But as it is…'

'Everyone will be ready to think the worst of me.'

Oh, I can just imagine the glee from certain people!

Lady Ashbourne nodded. 'They will. There are already some jealous of your success.' She grimaced.

'Perhaps the Queen's endorsement was more curse than blessing, after all.'

'And what of my sisters?'

'With you gone, it will be less likely that the story will circulate. With hard work, and a little good fortune, I should be able to manage the situation so that their reputations are not affected.' She thought for a moment. 'I shall perjure my brother, who wrote to me yesterday. I shall declare him to be ill, and say that you have kindly offered to return to Scotland in order to ensure he is receiving good care. That will serve to explain your sudden departure.'

'And I shall not return.' It was not a question.

Leave? Depart from London, never to come back?

'Well, no. Not for a few years at least.' Her mouth twisted with sympathy. 'I am sorry, my dear.'

Rose shook her head. 'You have nothing to be sorry for, my lady. All of this is my doing.' Seeing that Lady Ashbourne was about to repeat her assertion that James was the person responsible, Rose rushed on. 'But will my sisters not be subject to—to scrutiny, or conjecture at the very least?'

She shrugged. 'Perhaps. But James has never shown any interest in your sisters, so those subtle signs will no longer be on display for others to see—if they start looking, based on rumours of an indiscretion.'

'But—you saw something between us?'

'I did. It was why I tried to give you a hint.'

'I know.'

I was right, then.

Lady Ashbourne had meant to warn Rose from developing an affection for the Viscount.

Too late!

The enormity of it all was beginning to register.

I must leave.

She knew if she went now, there would not be any reason to return. And yet she must go. For Lady Ashbourne's sake. And her sisters'. Remembering the cryptic clues Rose had gleaned as to her sisters' preferences among the gentlemen, Rose swallowed. If Anna and Izzy were to have any chance of marrying high-born men, she must remove herself. And even then, there was little chance for them, unless by some miracle they could discover their family background.

If only our parentage was known.

A sudden thought struck her. 'Perhaps Maria Carew from Wales will turn out to be our mama, and we shall have respectability. That would help, surely?'

Lady Ashbourne shook her head. 'I received a letter from Lady Poole late yesterday. Miss Maria Carew married a country squire many years ago and is settled in Pembrokeshire with seven children. She cannot be your mama. I am so sorry, Rose.'

'But—' Rose could scarce take it in. 'She was the last one!'

'She was. I am afraid that your mama's given name may not have been Maria, after all. It was likely one of her middle names—which means it will be impossible for us to find her.'

So that was it, then. The last flame of hope within

her sputtered and died. 'I shall return to Belvedere, if you please.' Rose's voice was small, but she knew what had to be done. She lifted her chin. 'As a teacher, not a student, if they will have me.'

Lady Ashbourne thought for a moment then nodded slowly. 'A wise decision, my dear. There you will have your friends at the school, and my brother will be on hand. I shall write to them both to let them know to expect you. The mail-coach will travel faster than you.'

'When—when should I go?' Lady Ashbourne simply looked at her evenly, and Rose's shoulders slumped. 'Tomorrow. I know it.' She gave a short laugh. 'Later today, that is.' She stood. 'Very well. There is much to be done. A carriage, inns to write to—'

Lady Ashbourne laid a hand on her arm. 'You can do nothing at five in the morning, Rose. Get some sleep, then come to the morning room at ten and we shall make the arrangements together. The sun does not set until well after nine o'clock these days, so even if you set out at noon you can make good progress. Why, you might even make it to Stevenage tomorrow—or Hatfield at the very least. You may take the Ashbourne travelling coach.'

'Thank you. But what if Lord Ashbourne has need of it? Another horse racing meet with his friends, perhaps? He—'

'He will do without, then. Such a small inconvenience for him, while you must leave us entirely.' She shook her head. 'It seems the ladies must always come off the worse.'

'Gentlemen forced to marry against their will may not agree with you, my lady!'

'Then they should not kiss unmarried damsels in the first place! He has six years on you, you know, and has been about the *ton* long enough to know better!' She shook her head. 'Lord, I hope I can manage this thing!'

Another wave of guilt rippled through Rose. 'Lady Ashbourne, you have been so good to me. I am most heartily sorry that I have brought you this trouble.'

'Nonsense. It is no trouble.' She shrugged. 'Well perhaps it is a *little* trouble, but it has been worth it. These past months have been a delight.'

'But I should not…have done what I did.'

Lady Ashbourne snorted. 'As I say, you were not the only person involved.' Her jaw tightened. 'My nephew will be hearing from me, regardless.'

'Oh, no! Pray do not—'

'I have always thought it unjust that the lady is blamed, when the gentleman is equally to blame.' She nodded. 'At *least* equally. As I say, with his age and experience, he should have been the one to be…' Her voice tailed off, as she seemed to search for the right word.

'Prudent? Cautious?' Rose offered. 'But James— Lord Ashbourne—is ever cautious. Prudence is his watchword! He cannot be held to blame.'

She was frowning. 'Yes, he is cautious, usually.

Whatever can have possessed him?' She eyed Rose closely. 'Are you determined not to marry him?'

'I am certain.' Glad that her demeanour showed no trace of her true wishes, Rose held Lady Ashbourne's gaze until she sighed and nodded.

'Very well. I shall wait until you are gone, I think, before speaking with him. But I fully intend him to hear my thoughts on this matter.' She kissed Rose's cheek. 'I am so sorry, my dear. If only we had been able to find your mother's family, everything might have been different.'

Everything might have been different.

Long after she had gone, after Sally had helped Rose prepare for bed, eyeing her concernedly at times, long after Rose had blown out her bedside candle, the words were still reverberating within her. If Rose's origins had been known, and respectable, then perhaps the Viscount would have asked her to marry him, of his own free will.

If, if, if...

If was nothing. This was real. Her disgrace, if she stayed. And so she must go, and be separated from her sisters, and never see him again. She turned on her side, eyes open in the darkness, knowing sleep would not come.

By the time the ladies assembled in the morning room at ten o'clock for breakfast, the arrangements were in place. Rose had been up since before nine, unable to sleep, yet weary beyond measure. Sally was currently packing all of her beautiful clothing into three new trunks, bought especially for the purpose by the second footman at Lady Ashbourne's direction. The staff knew only that the Belles' guardian was apparently unwell, and Miss Rose's pale visage along with Lady Ashbourne's grim demeanour seemed to confirm that whatever ailed Mr Marnoch must be worrisome indeed. Rose had ignored Sally's questioning looks as best she could, but was inwardly fretting with mortification at being at the centre of so much bustle and fuss—particularly as the entire situation was due to her own foolishness.

Anna and Izzy had clearly realised that something was amiss, for they entered the morning room together, murmuring in low voices, and immediately demanded information.

'Rose! Lady Ashbourne! What—?'

Lady Ashbourne raised a hand, stopping Izzy's fervent queries. 'All in good time, my dear. Please, be seated.' She jerked her head meaningfully to the two footmen currently engaged in setting dishes on the sideboard. There was a pause while the men completed their task. 'You may go.'

Once the servants had left the room, Izzy repeated her questioning. 'What is amiss, my lady? The servants are all of a fluster, and there is an air of uneasiness in the house.'

Lady Ashbourne looked directly at Rose, who found her tongue seemed stuck to the floor of her mouth, her mind unable to direct it to utter the truth.

Lady Ashbourne sighed. 'My brother, your guardian, is unwell, and so Rose has kindly—'

'No.' Even as Anna and Izzy began reacting with shock to what they believed to be bad news concerning Mr Marnoch, Rose knew she had to speak. 'Everyone else may hear that tale. My sisters deserve to know the truth.'

Now all eyes were on her. Lady Ashbourne nodded. 'Very well. But you must both swear to repeat this to no one.'

Looking decidedly anxious, Anna and Izzy made their promises.

Rose swallowed. 'Yesterday, I allowed…a gentleman…to—to kiss me. In a public place. And we were seen.'

'What?'

'Rose!'

Reading identical expressions on her sisters' faces—shock, horror, disbelief—Rose nodded grimly. 'If word gets out of this, I am ruined. And unfortunately—' her voice trembled a little '—you would be ruined along with me, for society judges all three of us as one. I am so sorry. I have failed you. Failed you all. Failed Mama. Failed Mr Marnoch.' She buried her face in her hands as the enormity of her error struck her anew.

'Lord, Rose! Last night I thought you seemed—' Izzy broke off before commenting again on Rose's evident happiness the evening before. 'So it was *not* Lady Mary's betrothal, then.'

'Lady Mary is betrothed?' Lady Ashbourne came sharply to attention. 'To whom?'

There was a brief silence, as the Belles tried to respond to her question, taken up as they were by Rose's confession.

'Never say she has managed to catch Garvald!' Lady Ashbourne continued. 'That is to say, Lady Mary is a sweet girl, but she has not the strength of character for the Earl.' She continued, musing thoughtfully. 'Not the Prince either, for his passionate nature would terrify her.' She stopped, an arrested expression in her eyes. 'Mr Phillips?'

Rose nodded. 'He spoke with Lord Renton yesterday.'

'I see.' Lady Ashbourne rubbed her chin. 'And I begin to see so much more…'

'Rose.' Anna's voice was low. 'Who was the gentleman? Will he speak of this among his friends, do you think?'

Rose went cold for a second, as the possibility sent her into brief shock. Then reason reasserted itself. 'No. He will speak of it to no one, I am certain. And I cannot say who he is. Indeed, I—' She turned to Lady Ashbourne, as a new aspect of the situation suddenly occurred to her. 'My lady, who was it who saw…what happened?'

'A good question, Rose. My informant declined to tell me, but instead I have a question for you. I am told that this incident took place in the park. Is that correct?'

'Yes.' Rose dropped her eyes to the table, her hand twisting the napkin in her lap and her face fiery with mortification.

'Who was with you?'

'Lady Mary. And the…the two gentlemen.'

'Did Lady Mary see what happened?'

Rose shook her head. 'Definitely not.'

'And who else was in the vicinity?'

'No one. No one at all. Oh!' Rose clapped a hand to her mouth. 'The footman! I had entirely forgotten about him!'

'Lady Mary's footman. Quite.' Lady Ashbourne thought for a moment. 'I see now why I was told this sordid tale. It is all to do with Mr Phillips stealing Lady Mary out from under the noses of all of the more favoured gentlemen.'

'But Lady Mary *prefers* Mr Phillips—even in the face of her mother's disapproval.' Lady Ashbourne's words made no sense to Rose.

Sordid. That stung. Still, it was no doubt deserved.

'Well naturally she does. A good match, I think. They will deal very well together.'

Rose shared a bewildered glance with her sisters. Anna shrugged slightly. She clearly had no notion of their hostess's meaning either.

Is it because Mr Phillips has no title?

Her thoughts were sluggish, and she had to let it go.

'But, my lady. What is to be done?' Anna had pulled her chair closer to Rose's and took her sister's hand.

'Done?' Lady Ashbourne shook her head. 'I have

already had this conversation with Rose. She must either marry the gentleman in question, or she must go away.'

'And I have decided to go away. That is why we are pretending that dear Mr Marnoch is ill.' Tears started in Rose's eyes. 'So much deceit! And all because of me!'

At this, her sisters made their strong objections known, and more tears were shed by all the ladies—including Lady Ashbourne herself, who declared Rose to be a dear, dear girl, and declared she would miss her deeply.

Rose steadfastly refused to name the gentleman, although she wondered if her sisters already knew of her partiality for the Viscount. It took more than an hour for Izzy and Anna to be reconciled to the notion of Rose's banishment, but in the end they, like Lady Ashbourne and Rose herself, could see no other option—so long as Rose did not choose to force the matter of the gentleman offering for her.

'Oh, Rose! I shall miss you so much!' Izzy hugged her fiercely.

'We have never been apart,' added Anna, wrapping her arms around both sisters. 'How shall we do without you?'

'And I you!' Briefly, her mind spun through a lifetime of memories—years of sharing a bedroom, of brushing each other's hair and helping with buttons, of arguing and crying and laughing together. Izzy and

Anna would have each other, but for the first time in her entire life Rose would be alone.

'Oh, Anna! Izzy!'

How am I to manage without my sisters?

Touching her head to Izzy's and Anna's, she cried bitterly.

Chapter Eighteen

In the end the tears dried, as they must, and a few short hours later—while the Viscount still slept upstairs—Rose left Ashbourne House to begin the long, long journey north.

As she stepped outside into the unfeeling inappropriateness of bright midday sunshine, inwardly Rose was huddled in a storm, being battered by the relentless rain of loss and regret and guilt. She kept her gaze on her sisters, who stood together on the step with Lady Ashbourne, until the coach turned the corner and she saw them no more. Her heart was sick, her head sore, and her mind fuzzy with shock and grief. The people she loved were in that house, and she was leaving them to travel far, far away.

Desperately she stared out of the window at the sights of London, as if to imprint them firmly in her mind.

Who knows if I shall ever be back?

Despite everything, she had come to appreciate the

city, with all its noise and smells and drama. Elgin was going to seem drearily quiet in contrast. Why she had ever thought she might be satisfied with the life of a rural teacher, she could not now understand.

James awoke with a clouded head and a mind in a state of confusion, and it was all the fault of Miss Rose Lennox. The kisses they had shared in the park, how she had looked at him while they danced, even the camaraderie they had shared together with Robert and Lady Mary…all of it was making his head spin and his heart pound, and he did not like it one bit. And yet, some of it he liked very, very much. Oh, it was all too damned perplexing, and inconvenient, and—and *unnecessary*!

Once up and dressed he made his way downstairs, carefully avoiding the drawing room, then went straight out into the afternoon sunshine, making for his club. Today he intended to maintain the company of gentlemen, and stay as far away as possible from beautiful, beguiling maidens who were altogether too…too beautiful, too engaging, and too captivating. He was not in a mood to be captivated. Caution would rule him—yes, caution, and reason, and prudence. Anything else was madness, and he was not mad. No. Never.

Just seven hours later Rose was already heartily sick of travelling. The miles she had journeyed so far had brought back all the memories of the discomforts of her voyage south from Scotland. Then, she and her sisters had been blissfully ignorant of just how long it would take, and how much harder day nine would be than day one. This time, Rose knew.

She knew that the lumbering coach would frequently hit holes in the road, would trundle over countless stones until her teeth rattled, would occasionally fly around bends so quickly that she would have to hold onto the leather strap dangling beside the window, fearing that the vehicle would overturn, or that she would be thrown about its interior. And she knew that the weather would seep through the thin coach body, adding to her discomfort. On the way down during the tail-end of a Scottish winter, the girls had shivered under blankets and struggled to keep their hands, feet, and noses warm. Today, in the heat of an English summer, the coach had felt like an oven at times.

Still, her physical discomforts were a helpful distraction from her other pain. The agony in her heart. The tortuous thoughts in her mind. The sick feeling in her body which had nothing to do with the careening coach and everything to do with regret, and guilt, and the knowledge that never again would she even share his company.

This is my life now. A solitary life without kisses, or warm looks, nor even those moments when he vexed me.

Truly, at this moment she would give anything to have him vex her again.

* * *

Tonight, James could not settle. An evening at his club was normally a relaxed affair, full of good wine, interesting conversations, and the company of his friends. Yet James felt strangely uneasy. Having dined with a few of his intimates he chatted with the Prince and then with Garvald for a while, following this by playing an indifferent game of cards with a bunch of his fellow inmates from university. By the time Robert arrived it was well after three in the morning, and James was beginning to think of preparing for home.

'Robert!' He greeted his friend with a sense almost of relief. 'How do you?'

Robert grinned. 'I am well. Better than well, my friend. This evening the betrothal was announced.'

James had sent his apologies for tonight's soirée at the home of Lord and Lady Sefton, not feeling in the mood for public discourse or display.

'So soon? I thought they intended to wait a few days.'

'As did I.' He shrugged. 'My impression is that Lord Renton is impatient with his lady's resistance, and has forced her hand.' He grimaced. 'My mother-in-law has made her disapproval plain.'

'And yet—' James grinned '—you have won Lady Mary's hand. That is all that matters, surely?'

'I suppose. I just wish her to be happy, and she is worrying about her mother's disapproval.'

'What? Do you think she will cry off?'

'Oh, no. I have no worries on that score. She will

have me, though for the life of me I cannot understand why! I am the luckiest fool in Christendom, James!'

'Do you know, Robert, I think you are right.'

It is true. He is damnably lucky.

'Now tell me, who was there tonight? Any new scandals or *on dits* I should know about?'

The footman brought wine, and they sat in a quiet corner, enjoying the moment.

'Of course, the Belles were not present, nor was your aunt,' Robert offered. 'Lady Mary missed her friend.'

'Oh? Had they another engagement?'

'Not according to Lady Mary, for they had talked of it the night before, and Miss Rose had indicated they would be attending.' He shrugged. 'Perhaps, as you say, they had another engagement that Miss Rose was unaware of.'

'Perhaps.'

Unlikely, for Rose helps my aunt with managing all their invitations and engagements. Perhaps one of them was unwell, he mused.

Or maybe they had just fancied a quiet evening at home for once. The whirl of social engagements could be exhausting, as he well knew. But he must not think of Rose, for that way lay danger. 'And tell me, was Mrs Chorley still trailing after the Prince, her daughter in tow?'

With some determination, he wrenched his thoughts away from Rose, for perhaps the hundredth time that evening.

* * *

Sleep was slow to come, and stayed only a few hours. Rose tossed and turned in the narrow bed, listening to the even breathing of the serving maid in the truckle bed that had been set up near the low window, and wondered for the hundredth time what he was doing now.

How had he reacted to the news that she was gone? She knew him to be a good man, and so he would surely have felt a pang of regret that their kisses had meant she had to leave.

Yes, one had to be realistic. Whatever regrets or momentary sorrow he had experienced, he would surely also have had a sense of relief that he would not be forced into marriage with someone so unsuitable.

Unsuitable.

Another tear rolled down her cheek and onto the pillow. If only morning could come!

Morning came, and James, yawning, simply turned over to sleep again. His valet had clear instructions to rouse him at noon. Yet he slept fitfully, starting at every sound in the house, his mind constantly wondering where Rose was. Was she about yet? Perhaps assisting his aunt with her correspondence? When finally the valet scratched discreetly on his door, James was almost relieved to leave his bed.

'Good morning,' he murmured to the man, rising fluidly into a sitting position. 'Tea, please, cold beef, and rolls. I shall bathe now. And I shall wear the gold waistcoat today.'

'Very well, my lord.'

It took nearly an hour for the water to be heated for his bath, and James almost regretted the impulse. Almost. His clothes stank of pipe smoke and snuff, for the particular group present in the club last night had included a number of aficionados of tobacco in all its forms, and he did not wish to present himself to the ladies in such a condition. By the time he had bathed, shaved, and dressed the clock was striking the half hour, and the ladies—if they were at home—would likely be having nuncheon.

Before leaving he checked his appearance in the mirror—something he was not wont to do. 'Something amiss, my lord?' the valet asked anxiously.

'Amiss? No, nothing. Nothing at all.'

Half past one, and the carriage passed through yet another nameless village. Rose, her mind a haze of grief, stared sightlessly at the houses and shops, the drover driving sheep towards the village square, the woman sitting in the sunshine feeding her infant. The church had a bell tower, and they were ringing out the half hour. All human life was out there, and none of it was hers.

She caught her breath. Just for an instant, as the coach rumbled past, she had espied two young lovers trysting in a narrow laneway. The girl had been leaning against the wall, her young man facing her.

As Rose watched, the girl pulled him in for a kiss—then they were gone as the carriage passed, the tableau frozen for ever in Rose's memory in the instant the young man's lips met his sweetheart's.

Never more.

James!

James walked slowly along the landing towards his chamber, pondering. Somewhere in the house, a clock struck the half hour. Something was definitely wrong. Or...*different*, perhaps. Not necessarily wrong. Yes, something was in the air, but he was unsure what it was.

Since he had returned home so late from his club last night he had of course missed breakfast entirely, and had not seen Rose since the ball two nights ago. He had awoken knowing he *needed* to see her as soon as possible, Lord help him. Anxious to see her, and perhaps know what was real and what was not.

Am I given over to madness?

He needed to figure out what it all meant, and seeing her was vital.

Yes, prudence and caution continued to be his watchwords, and he had been rather proud of how he had steadfastly kept from his home all day yesterday.

See? he had told himself. *I am not yet lost to all reason.*

Good sense, logic, and discretion in all things. That was the way of civilised men. Ruthlessly he ignored the small voice within that murmured wryly that he had been thinking of her most of the day yesterday.

Today, the need to be in her company was stronger than ever.

It is a test, he thought.

A test of his resolve to be rational. Yet despite his inner reasoning, he had been almost *nervous* as he had entered the dining room for nuncheon a little earlier. Such foolishness!

Having braced himself for her company, to his great disappointment Rose had not been there, and he could not figure out why. Her sisters had been present, and his aunt. Thinking it would be too obvious to simply ask—it might suggest that *particularity* which he feared was obvious to everyone, yet must hide, in case he might expose her to unwelcome comments even from her own sisters—he had instead eaten in near silence, feeling her absence at every moment, and excusing himself as soon as the meal had ended.

The others—his aunt, and Rose's sisters—were still downstairs in the dining room, and had he imagined a hint of relief from Anna and Izzy when he had stood to depart? His aunt, come to think of it, had looked as though she might detain him, but just now he had not the capacity for dealing with whatever her query was. His mind was full of Rose and had no space for anyone or anything else. And so, instead of calling for his carriage he had mounted the stairs, needing time alone to *think*.

He checked his pocket watch. Two o'clock. Of

course Rose might simply be visiting with Lady Mary or Miss Phillips, or some other friend. It was mid-afternoon, after all. Yes, she may simply have made plans for today, but *something*…something about Anna's and Izzy's behaviour just now had bothered him.

Yes! That was it! They had been full of animation, and so garrulous that neither he nor his aunt could get a word in, yet their smiles had been brittle, false. He was not used to such falseness from the Belles. Lady Ashbourne, he now realised, had seemed subdued, unlike herself. And they had not attended the soirée last evening.

What on earth is going on?

Might Rose be sick? At the notion, his heart faltered, then raced.

But why would they not tell me if she is sick?

A notion occurred to him. Perhaps it was woman's troubles…

Abruptly realising he had halted outside Rose's bed-chamber door he knocked impulsively, before he could talk himself out of it. No response. He knocked again, a little louder, knowing he should not, yet seemingly unable to control himself. Still nothing.

A maidservant appeared from Lady Ashbourne's chamber, carrying a painted fan. His aunt had sent the girl to fetch it a few moments before, he recalled.

'Sally. Are you Sally?' he asked curtly.

'Yes, my lord.' She bobbed a curtsey.

'Please can you check if Miss Rose is within?'

The girl frowned. 'But, my lord——' She faltered

and abruptly the hairs on the back of his neck stood to attention.

'But what?' Still she hesitated, and so he pressed the matter. 'I require an answer, Sally. Where is Miss Rose?'

The maid exhaled, answering him in a rush. 'She is gone, my lord. Left in the travelling coach yesterday.'

'Gone?' The richly carpeted floor beneath him seemed to sway a little. 'Gone where?'

'I cannot say, my lord. My lady will be able to advise you, I think.'

She continued to look at him, as he felt the blood drain slowly from his face.

Gone? Rose is gone?

'Very well,' he managed. 'You may go.'

By the time she had disappeared down the servants' staircase at the end of the corridor his hand was on the door. Opening it, he entered Rose's bedchamber. It still held the faint scent of her, and he closed his eyes briefly, recalling her smile, the tremble in her voice after they had kissed.

The room was otherwise empty. No personal knick-knacks on the side table. No candle on the nightstand. He strode to the garderobe. Empty. She had taken everything.

The travelling coach.

A long journey, then.

The finality of it struck him. Although he had known from the moment Sally spoke that Rose was truly gone, the sight of her empty garderobe made it clear. This was no overnight excursion with Lady Mary's family, or trip to the country with Miss Phillips. No. She was not coming back.

Spinning on his heel, he made for the dining room. He wanted answers, and he wanted them now.

Chapter Nineteen

'Thank you.'

Accepting the coachman's assistance to climb back into the carriage after a comfort break, Rose steeled herself once again for the hours and miles ahead. On the long journey down to London from Scotland she had had her sisters for company and they had entertained one another in talk, creating riddles, or playing cards, whereas this time she was alone. Checking briefly to ensure her book was still in the pocket in the squabs where she had placed it, Rose left it there, knowing she was in no mood to read.

It was all she could do to sit there and cultivate the detachment required. She would not cry again today. In fact, she refused to do so.

Not crying was surprisingly easy just now, for where her heart should be was a lump of what felt rather like ice. A similar lump now resided in her throat, making swallowing painful at times, but it was an acceptable price to pay for the steeliness in her own demeanour.

No one would know that her polite calmness concealed heartbreak, that raw pain raged within her, for ruthlessly, she had pushed it down, down, deep into the darkest recesses of her heart.

Each time her thoughts tempted to stray where they should not, she brought them back by the simple expedient of distraction. Counting gates as they passed. Conjugating Latin verbs. Listing the names of countries alphabetically. It did not matter what she thought about, so long as she did not think about the forbidden things. The things she had lost. The forbidden person. So long as she did not *feel*.

James flung open the door to the dining room. 'Out!' he waved to the footmen who fled, a hint of alarm in their expressions. Anna and Izzy, startled, gaped at him, while his aunt simply sighed.

'Leave us, girls,' she declared grimly. 'No,' she waved away their protests, 'I should like to speak to my nephew alone.'

Once the door had closed behind them James, carefully banking the rage and shock within, bit out, 'Well?'

'Are you asking about Rose's whereabouts?'

'Yes, I am dam—*dashed* well asking about her whereabouts! I am told she left this house in the travelling coach yesterday. Is that true?'

She nodded. 'It was for the best.'

Leaving this aside for the moment, he focused on

the main thread—the need for information. 'Where has she gone?'

'Back to Belvedere.'

'To become a blasted teacher, no doubt!' Fixing her with an intent gaze, he asked, 'What hand had you in this?'

'James,' she offered, 'you must understand. It had to be done.'

'Why? Why must she leave?' There was desperation in his tone. Why on earth had his aunt done such a thing?

'Because, dear nephew, you were seen.'

'Seen?' For the second time in a few minutes, James heard a roaring in his ears. Oh, he knew *exactly* what his aunt was referring to.

Damnation!

'In the park,' she continued bluntly. 'Kissing Rose. Compromising her. How could you, James?'

Oh, Lord.

'Never mind that. Why on earth did you send her away?'

'Are you not heeding me?' She rose, pacing towards him, agitation clearly writ upon her kindly face. 'You compromised her, James. You were *seen*.'

'And? Surely the correct response in these…*situations* is for the gentleman to marry the lady?'

Her jaw dropped. 'Then—you would marry her?'

James's eyes narrowed. 'Let me attempt to deduce what occurred. You informed her she would not be a suitable bride for me. That her parentage means she should not ever be my viscountess. That by marrying me it would reduce the standing of the Ashbourne name.'

She dropped her gaze. 'Well, I did not say *exactly* that, but Rose was very clear that she did not wish to marry you.' She held up a hand. 'No, let me finish. James, you know how I love all three girls. They are like daughters to me now. And Rose in particular— how I shall manage all my work without her, I do not know. She has been a blessing to me these past weeks. But we have failed to discover the identity of their mother. All of the possibilities have been eliminated. Which means...' Her voice tailed off.

'I know *exactly* what it means, Aunt. It means we are unlikely to ever establish their parentage. It means society will always whisper that they are possibly bastards. You flinch, but that is exactly the word that will be used. And do you know, I care not!'

He straightened, feeling as though a burden had suddenly and unexpectedly been lifted from him. 'As I told Rose many weeks ago, no one in their right mind could ever be careless of their reputation! Which means I have a duty to protect hers. And as I also told her—very recently, in fact—to hell with prudence!'

Striding to the door, he pulled it open. Sure enough, a footman and two serving maids were in the vicinity, probably attempting to eavesdrop. 'You!' He pointed to the footman.

'M-me, my lord?'

'Tell my coachman to prepare the travelling carriage, and my valet to pack a trunk. I leave within the hour!'

'Y-yes, my lord. At least…my lord, the travelling coach is gone, and the coachman with it. I—Miss Rose—'

'Damnation! Very well, we shall have to take the old coach. Has the axle been repaired?'

'I know not, my lord.' At James's fierce expression, he added hastily, 'But I shall find out this instant!'

'See that you do! Yes? What is it?' Infuriatingly, the man was still hesitating.

'Shall I—that is to say, your valet may wish to know for how long you will be from home? And will he be required to accompany you?'

James frowned. 'I shall travel alone. And as to how long I shall be gone, I am uncertain.' Rose was almost two full days ahead of him, and he could not hope to catch her in the old lumbering coach. 'Three weeks at least. Now, call my steward to the library, for I shall need him to cancel my engagements for the foreseeable future!'

All doubts were gone. A lifetime of caution, gone. It had simply vanished, dissolved like mist from a meadow.

The haze of uncertainty in his mind had led to this—to his beloved Rose being sent away to Scotland, and for what? For the crime of loving him? Oh, she loved him. He knew it as well as he knew that he loved her. Even the fact that she had gone away from London—from her sisters, and her friends, and the life she had made here—even that told him of the sacrifice she had made. For him.

All was now patent, and obvious, and he felt a lucidity that had been evading him recently. Now he knew that no one but Rose Lennox must be his viscountess. Never had he been more certain of anything.

Cursing himself for his own abominable uncertainty, for the caution that had caused this, he focused on hoping it was not too late. One thing was certain. The time for caution, for consideration, for careful weighing of the options, was past. Now was the time for deeds, not debates. The time for *action*.

Bowing briefly to his aunt, he strode along the corridor, then took the stairs two at a time.

Blearily, Rose watched as dawn poked rosy fingers over the edge of the world, the golden-pink beauty of the morning sky seeming to mock the dark emptiness within her. Having asked the driver to set off at sunrise each morning, after a week of unrelenting travel she now wished she had chosen a more civilised hour to begin this stage in the journey. Still, leaving early meant more progress, and she wished to cover as many miles as possible before sunset. Only two days to go. Three, at most.

Checking the list in her reticule she reviewed again the names of the inns in the guidebook Lady Ashbourne had provided—inns suitable for a gently-reared maiden travelling alone. Inns where the beds would be clean, the food reasonable, and where a maid would sleep on a truckle bed in her chamber each night to guard her reputation.

My reputation!

She gave a cynical snort. This whole charade was because her reputation might already be ruined. And until a letter came from London to Belvedere she would not know if Lady Ashbourne's plan to protect her sisters had even been effective.

This may all be for naught.

Lady Ashbourne had wanted to send Sally with her, but Rose had declined, knowing Sally had recently started walking out with one of the footmen.

I will never see my love again. I cannot separate Sally from her young man even for a few weeks.

And besides, her brief time as a lady of the *ton* was done. From now on, she would be a simple teacher, and a teacher should not be reliant on having a serving maid.

Her hope was that everything would be better once she reached Scotland, and Belvedere. Such a hope was irrational, she knew, yet it was all she had. As the carriage rolled on through the countryside and the sun rose higher in the sky, she gazed abstractedly at hedgerows and trees, mile after mile of fields, and cattle, and sheep, and villages. Occasionally they would pass through a larger town, and she might find herself momentarily caught up in something in the street—an urchin chasing a cat, two dogs snarling at one another, an old man walking slowly, painfully, with the aid of a stick. Out there was the real world, where people laughed and loved and felt things. Inside the carriage there was nothing. No pain. No tears. Just emptiness.

'Faster, man, faster!'

Leaning out of the window, James urged the coachman to greater effort. As his head coachman had gone ahead with Rose at his aunt's direction, it had fallen to his grooms to take turns to drive the old Ashbourne carriage—a vehicle which must be fifteen years old if it was a day.

His urging was pointless he knew, for the old coach had not the capability or the speed of the new one, and so every hour she was getting further ahead of him. His only hope was that she was travelling at an easy pace, no more than a few hours each day. If like him she was setting out at dawn and travelling until near sunset, then urging the horses to go a little faster would achieve precisely nothing.

Days of travel had not brought doubts—at least, none with respect to his own wishes. Finally he knew his heart, and hoped his instincts were correct and that she shared his regard.

His aunt had been clear though: Miss Rose had been adamant she would not even consider marriage to him. Why? Self-sacrifice? He certainly knew her to be generous enough for it. But what if for her, this had been a mere dalliance, and she remained undaunted in her desire to spend her life as a spinster teacher, nurturing other people's children? He could only hope, as the long days dragged on and the long nights brought agonising half dreams.

Rose had never known exhaustion like it. After ten days of travelling, the beloved chimneys of Belvedere School were finally in view, silhouetted against the gold-tinted sunset sky. Relief surged through her. Here she would be safe. Here she would find solace, and peace. Here she would learn to accept the reality of her true destiny, far away from the brilliancy and splendour of London.

A few moments later she was inside being warmly embraced by Agnes. Having contained her emotions since leaving London, this warmth and kindness from the Belvedere maidservant proved to be her undoing, and she burst into tears.

'Ah, now, now, my love,' Agnes tutted, 'you're home now, and all is well.'

Home. Is this my home?

While the familiarity of Belvedere was comforting, something within Rose ached for her other home. The one where her sisters were. Where Lady Ashbourne was. Where James was.

'They've all retired for the night, but I stayed up a little later in case you should arrive tonight,' Agnes was saying. 'The headmistress only got Lady Ashbourne's letter yesterday, so we were not certain when you might get here. Yes, put them in the green bedchamber, Sandy,' she added to the manservant, who was wanting to know what to do with Miss Rose's trunks. 'Your old room is gone, Miss Rose—there are three younger girls in there now—but you will be right and tight in the green room. Now, do you wish for some supper?'

An hour later, having eaten and washed, Rose lay awake, looking at the moon through her window. Even now the same moon would be rising over London. Would he see it? Might he, even now, be looking at it? As another tear trickled slowly down her cheek, tickling her neck, Rose allowed herself to remember that she might never see him again. She certainly had no intention of ever returning to London, even though she had come to love her life there. Well, why would she? If either of her sisters married and had children, they would be obliged to visit dear Mr Marnoch in Elgin, and would wish to visit her too.

Her mind wandered back to her conversation with Anna and Izzy on the morning she had left. Their shock and concern. Their hope that a way might be found for her to remain in London. Naturally they had tried to persuade her to stay—well of course they would.

In the end it had been Lady Ashbourne's intervention which had persuaded them both to let her go. Once they had heard her assessment of the options, they—like Rose herself—had concluded that the best thing was for Rose to leave. And so they had all cried together, and Anna and Izzy had helped her pack her reticule and choose a book for the journey, and then they had stood on the steps of Ashbourne House to see her off.

Travelling alone, without her sisters, had remained difficult. Oh, the well-sprung travelling coach and the comfortable inns had helped. But never before had Rose spent so much time alone. And yet, on seeing a beautiful view or an interesting castle from the window of her carriage, Rose had imagined speaking of it to James just as often as she had wished to share such sights with Izzy and Anna.

How she missed him! Slowly, slowly, over these past months, he had become part of her. Seeing him so often, waiting for that heady moment when their eyes would meet, sending that thrill through her...

Her mind drifted to the harsh reality. It had been torture, living in the same house as him yet knowing they were doomed to spend their lives apart. She was not a suitable wife for a viscount. And as a viscount, he must marry. That meant he would someday marry another, while she would live out her days here in Belvedere. Her pupils would be her only children, and she would never know what it was to bear a child of her own.

Dashing away her tears, she reached for her handkerchief again, blowing her nose with resolve. It would do no good to dwell on might-have-beens. Travelling back to Elgin meant the beginning of her new life—the life of a teacher. Just months ago she had wanted nothing more, yet now it felt like a poor consolation for the life she might have lived.

Tomorrow she must speak to Miss Logie the head-mistress, then visit dear Mr Marnoch. He would be disappointed they had been unable to find out who dear Mama had been, yet Rose was now at peace with it. Perhaps, as Lady Ashbourne had suggested, Maria had not even been Mama's true name—which meant she had truly intended no one ever to find out the truth.

My troubles are as nothing compared to hers.

In her mind, Rose went over it again. Mama had borne triplets—*triplets!*—probably out of wedlock, and without the support of her family. She had made her way to Elgin when her daughters were five, with little money and without the protection of a husband. Her work clerking for Mr Marnoch had undoubtedly been a godsend, and yet she was doomed to fall ill before her daughters were grown, leaving them mother-less many years before she would have wished to do so. In comparison, Rose's own trials were as nothing. She had a roof over her head, safety, and enough to eat. Wishing for anything more was pointless.

On the long journey north, James had plenty of time for reflection. Too much time, perhaps. Setting a bruising pace, for he needed to see her as soon as possible, he spent his days staring moodily out of the window of his rickety carriage. The certainty with which he had undertaken this impetuous jour-ney was slowly leeching out of him. What if it had been Rose, and not his aunt, who had suggested her return to Scotland?

'Rose was very clear that she did not wish to marry you.'

His aunt's words—which he had instantly dismissed at the time—had now taken on huge significance in his mind.

Yes, Rose had been an enthusiastic participant in their kisses, and they enjoyed friendship, and a shared sense of the ridiculous, and sometimes when their eyes had met he had sensed she was as disturbed as he. But none of that necessarily meant that she loved him as he did her, or that she wished to give up her dream of becoming a teacher. His initial belief that she had left London because she loved him now seemed fantastical, unlikely, illogical.

If only he had not been so caught up in his own determination to resist her, in the name of prudence! If only he had been able to speak with her plainly as soon as he had realised his own heart! He might have a clearer idea of her wishes and her intentions. But *if onlys* were of no use to him.

Recalling again her determination that she would never marry, and her desire to spend her life teaching other people's children, he wondered if he was perhaps reading too much into a few exchanged glances and some—admittedly, wonderful—kisses. Just because he adored her, it did not necessarily follow that she felt the same way, or that she would agree to marry him even if she did love him. Certainly Lady Ashbourne was convinced it would be inappropriate for him to marry a girl with no history, no family background, and where at some point in the future scandalous details of her true parentage might emerge. Rose might well agree.

As another day drew into evening he sighed, foreseeing he might need to use persuasion to reassure her. The problem was, given Rose's firmness of mind, he was not convinced it would be enough. Frowning, he continued to consider the matter. Between longing to see her and worrying that she might not wish to see him, he was, sad to say, suffering from a severe dose of befuddlement.

'Now then, Jane.' Rose's tone was encouraging, for she knew already that little Jane worried when she got things wrong. 'Can you show me where France is?'

The child's face cleared. France was one they all knew. As the other girls watched, she stepped forward with confidence. 'It is here, Miss Lennox,' she declared, pointing to somewhere just south of Paris on the globe.

'Excellent! Now, a city this time. Can you find St Petersburg?'

As she spoke, Rose was distracted by the sound of a carriage drawing up outside Belvedere. The window was ajar as the day was warm, and the sound of multiple hooves plus rolling wheels suggested a four-horse conveyance—an unusual occurrence at Belvedere. Might one of the parents have come on an unannounced visit? Or perhaps a new family was visiting, in order to decide if they should send their daughter here?

Either way, it was a shame that Miss Logie, the headmistress, had gone into town and was not expected back for at least another hour. Glancing out of the window and stepping back before she was seen, she had the impression of a large if shabby equipage—of similar style to those used by the *ton* in London—with four horses. Vaguely, she noted a crest upon the door.

'Girls, please turn to your Latin primer, and learn the words on page twenty-six,' Rose instructed, heading for the door to the corridor. There she met the two other teachers—both fussing and flapping about the unexpected visitor. Sandy, their manservant, was even now opening the front door, and Miss Farquhar gave a muffled squeak.

Miss Mortimer tutted at her colleague's display. 'Rose, will you speak to them? Please?' With a little more presence of mind than Miss Farquhar, Miss Mortimer had clearly concluded that Rose—despite being the youngest by quite three decades—was likely to be the most articulate of the three of them.

'Of course.' Reminding herself that she had spoken with the Queen, a European prince, and multiple peers of the realm during her time in London, Rose did her best to ignore her colleagues' clear anxiety. In the headmistress's absence, she would do her best to represent the school. Having every confidence in

Belvedere, she was quite ready to extol its virtues to whatever parent was even now making his way inside.

Lifting her chin, she stepped forward, a polite smile on her face, then froze, shock rippling through her at the sight of the man before her.

'J-James!'

Chapter Twenty

'J-James!'

Seeing him so unexpectedly had made her utter his given name—the first time she had ever done so in his presence.

'My lord!' Remembering herself, she curtseyed in time with his bow, her eyes never leaving his face. Her mind was awhirl, with no clear thoughts beyond *James is here!* And, *Lord, how I have missed him!*

'Miss Lennox. I hope you are well.' He looked sober, grave even, and her heart lurched as she wondered why he had travelled all the way to Scotland.

Bad news? Has he brought me ill tidings?

'I am, my lord. And you? Are you well?'

He gave a short laugh, then said, tightly, 'I must declare myself to be well, I suppose.'

His lack of clarity was entirely unhelpful, but hinted at bad things. Bracing herself, Rose attempted to ask one of the questions swirling around her brain. 'What—is something wrong, my lord? My sisters—?'

He shook his head. 'I must speak with you.' His eyes flicked to her colleagues. 'Alone.'

This brought them forwards, clucking and fussing. Rose performed the introductions, explaining briefly that Lord Ashbourne was Lady Ashbourne's nephew, and that both he and his aunt had shown Rose and her sisters every kindness.

'Please, come to the parlour.' Rose indicated the door to her right. Their little parlour had none of the grandeur of the drawing room in Ashbourne House, but it had its own simple elegance.

I remember noting the contrast when we were in London.

Their little parlour would no doubt seem modest and plain to him.

Rose followed him inside, her colleagues accompanying them with grim determination.

We are not to be alone, then.

Sandy was dispatched to ask Agnes to procure tea, and they all sat down.

There was a silence.

'You have travelled from London?' It was a foolish question, she knew, but her brain seemed frozen with stupefaction.

He nodded. 'I departed two days after you. In the afternoon.'

'You have made good time. I arrived here just three days ago.' There was another pause. 'Had you been to Scotland before?'

'Only to Edinburgh. This is my first time travelling

this far north. I—there is something most particular I must say to you, Miss Lennox.' He looked to her colleagues, who had been watching their exchange with keen interest.

'Oh, but we could not possibly allow—'

Miss Farquhar had the right of it, Rose knew, for a young lady should never be left alone with a gentleman—even a gentleman whom she knew well. Belvedere's rules on such matters were absolute. To her utter astonishment however, Miss Mortimer overruled her colleague, rising without hesitation and drawing Miss Farquhar with her.

'We shall wait in the hallway, my lord. Come, Mildred!'

Had Miss Mortimer and the Viscount just exchanged a significant look? Rose's head was still reeling, her mind confused at the events of the past few minutes. She had barely understood that James was *here*, *now*, in the flesh. To decipher other people's communication was entirely beyond her right now. An instant later the teachers were gone, Miss Mortimer closing the door in a most decided manner, Miss Farquhar clucking and fussing all the way.

Rose turned back to James, and her heart melted as she took in his beloved features properly for the first time since his arrival.

How handsome he is! And how troubled he looks!

'Tell me what has occurred, my lord. Are my sisters truly well?' She eyed him anxiously.

Something is not right.

He sighed. 'They are all well, I swear it.' He gave a short laugh. 'I last saw them in the dining room at nuncheon on the day I left, and at the table they were full of chatter about their planned engagements, I assure you.'

'I am glad to hear it. And yet, I am concerned, my lord.'

'Why?' His eyes held hers, and there was a wildness in his that she could not understand. She blinked, and it was gone. Now she was seeing hesitation—or uncertainty perhaps.

What on earth is amiss?

'You seem…unwell. Or—or *agitated*, at least.' Lifting a hand, she almost reached out to him, only just preventing herself from doing so. 'I *know* you, my lord, and this—you, today—is troubled Lord Ashbourne!'

'Indeed.' He gave a crooked smile, 'We know one another very well, do we not?'

'We do.'

There was another silence, then he rose from his chair and paced about the room, running a hand through his hair. Rose simply watched him, still in a state of bewilderment.

Why has he travelled all the way to Scotland?

Since she did not dare hope he had come for her, then the only other possible explanation was that he had brought news of ill fortune.

He stopped. 'Are you well, Miss Lennox?'

'You have already asked me that, my lord, not five minutes ago.'

'I have. And yet—are you truly well?'

She shrugged. 'I am as well as might be expected under the circumstances.' She frowned as another possibility occurred to her. 'Has there perhaps been a discovery about my mama's identity?' she asked. 'Or is your aunt unwell?' No, he would not come all the way here for that. Her sisters would simply have written to her if something had befallen dear Lady Ashbourne.

'No. And no.' He sat again—this time on the settee beside her. 'The circumstances being my aunt's insistence that you leave London.'

'Yes.' Her voice was tight.

'Miss Lennox, I have just come from Mr Marnoch's office.'

She frowned. 'Mr Marnoch? But why? You must forgive me, my lord. I am dreadfully slow-witted today. But you see, I never expected—'

'No, of course. And I apologise for my unannounced arrival. But I had to come. You see, I should much rather be in your company than that of a butcher's boy!'

Butcher's boy?

He must be referring to that day in the park.

But to what end? Bewilderment was all she knew. Bewilderment, and hungry joy at the sight of his beloved features.

She swallowed. 'My lord, I do not understand your meaning.'

He stilled, nodded, then took a breath. 'Rose, as your guardian Mr Marnoch has given me permission to pay my addresses to you.' He took her hand. 'Rosabella Lennox, would you do me the very great honour of becoming my wife?'

A sudden coldness flooded through her and her muscles froze in shock as she attempted to take in his meaning.

He is asking me to marry him!

An instant later, she was filled with wonder, with hope, with profound joy. But it lasted only briefly.

'No. I cannot, my lord.' Gently, she withdrew her hand.

'And why not? Because of some nonsense my aunt has put into your head about your parentage?'

She nodded tightly. 'While I appreciate the sense of honour that has made you travel all the way to Elgin, it would not be right to accept your offer. You may look as high as you wish for a bride, my lord.'

'I agree.' He tossed his head in what struck her as a wonderful show of confidence bordering on arrogance. 'Indeed, I am doing so. But tell me, is this your only objection?' He picked up her hand again and this time, helplessly, she allowed it. This was the first touch of his hand to hers without the barrier of her gloves between them. Teachers did not commonly wear gloves in the schoolroom. Foolishly, she allowed herself to feel the thrill of his warm skin on hers, knowing the memory would be one she would savour until the day she died.

'Rose, what does your heart tell you?'

At this she rose, emotion surging within her. It was too much. She needed distance between them. 'It is not fair to ask me of my heart. The *ton* cares nothing for hearts.'

'And I care nothing for the *ton*!' Rising, he strode across to her, taking her in his arms. 'Rose, tell me you do not love me, and I shall leave this place and never see you again!'

Never!

His words pierced her chest with the force of a blade. She had had a taste of never, these past days. While heartbreak might ease a little given time, she supposed, her life since leaving London had been akin to a waking nightmare.

'Tell me!' he demanded, and she shook her head.

'I cannot. But—'

His lips covered hers with a ferocious hunger, and she was lost. Measure for measure she matched his passion, his raw need. *Yes!* The word was less a thought, more a sensation, a letting go of fears. *Yes*, to his kiss, to his warmth, to his passion. *Yes*, to the rising flames within her body. *Yes*, to his proposal. She was done.

'Are you certain?' she murmured, a long time later. They were seated on the settee again, and he was pressing myriad feather-light kisses across her cheek.

Leaning back just enough to meet her gaze, he answered in a low voice. 'I have never been more certain of anything in my life.' He shook his head, giving a wry grin. 'And I am not a man much given to certainty—at least, not in matters relating to important decisions likely to affect the course of my life. It is actually astounding how certain I am. I love you, Rose.'

He loves me!

Of course, it was there in his kiss, in his gaze, in the fact he had followed her all the way to northern Scotland. Hearing the words, though, made it real. They gazed at one another, a slow smile growing on both their faces, then Rose took a breath.

'I love you too.'

With a muffled exclamation he pulled her close again, and their kisses this time were soft, reverent, full of meaning. In between, they talked of love, and fear, and uncertainty. Of relief, and joy, and anticipation.

Eventually they came to speak of his aunt's well-meaning meddling. 'She adores you, you know,' he murmured. 'But with my uncle gone, she tries to carry the weight of the family reputation for all of us.'

'And will marrying me diminish your standing?' she asked, hearing the anxiety in her own voice.

'I have had a long time to consider these matters—all the way up the Great North Road and beyond. My answer is this. Lady Kelgrove will likely welcome our marriage, and Mrs Thaxby disapprove. Now, whose opinion matters more to you?'

She gave an unladylike snort, making him grin. 'Lady Kelgrove, naturally. Indeed, earning Mrs Thaxby's disapproval will feel like earning a medal of honour!'

'But you are a darling!' he declared, kissing her again.

They were interrupted, finally, by a discreet scratching at the door, which then slowly opened. Miss Mortimer peeped around the door, a broad smile growing across her face as she saw them seated together, both her hands held in both of his, for one hand was not enough.

'How lovely!' she declared. 'I can be the first to wish you happy! My dear, dear Rose!'

'Oh, Miss Mortimer, I can scarce believe it!' Rose went to her, and they embraced. 'Truly, it is like a fairy tale!'

Miss Farquhar joined them, and Rose then sent for Agnes, who expressed her delight in the strongest of terms, departing to find a bottle of wine for, she stated, it was not every day a viscount came to their own parlour with an offer of marriage for one of the Belvedere girls. No, no, she declared, the tea was decidedly cancelled, for it was most definitely inadequate for the situation!

Chapter Twenty-One

The Viscount had indeed visited Mr Marnoch on his way to Belvedere, and Rose's guardian had given his blessing to the union—subject to Rose's agreement. Naturally, he invited his sister's nephew to stay at his neat mansion during his stay, while Rose would remain in Belvedere for now.

Dinner that evening was magical, or so it seemed. Sitting quietly while Mr Marnoch and the Viscount became better acquainted, Rose hugged to herself the knowledge of her unexpected good fortune. Never had she anticipated such happiness would be hers!

They spoke again of Maria Lennox, and the Belles' failure to discover her true identity in London, and Mr Marnoch was full of understanding. 'She must have been determined not to be found, I think. I have often wondered who or what she feared. It had to have been something more than—er—the usual.'

Knowing 'the usual' referred to the likely reality that the triplets were conceived out of wedlock, Rose sighed. 'It seems unfair that she should have suffered such hardship, and yet I should have found such happiness.'

Mr Marnoch shook his head. 'She would not agree with you, you know. Everything she did from the day she arrived in Elgin was for you three.'

'It sounds as though she was a special lady.' The Viscount's voice was low, his expression sober.

Mr Marnoch beamed at him. 'Indeed she was!' He glanced out of the long windows. 'The sun is setting, Rose. Shall I call for the carriage?'

'Or I can walk you back to Belvedere?' the Viscount offered. 'For it is not far. Would you prefer to walk?'

Rose accepted with alacrity. 'Oh, yes, for the evening is mild.' She thought for a moment. 'And there is a place I should like to show you, on our way.'

Dusk was falling as she led him into the small churchyard at Holy Trinity, making her way unerringly to a particular gravestone.

Maria Lennox, it read. *Died 1801.*

The grave was unremarkable, simple, understated. Nothing to suggest how wonderful Mama had been, how much her daughters had loved her, how missed she had been when her illness finally defeated her.

'Mama,' Rose murmured, just as though her mother could hear her. 'Here is James, who is to be my husband.'

He squeezed her hand. 'You have raised a fine daughter, Mrs Lennox. Three of them, in fact. I am honoured that Rose has agreed to be my wife.'

'If only you could be here for my wedding, Mama. I still miss you.'

With his free hand he fished for a clean linen handkerchief, and gently wiped her tears. She clung to him, safe in the ability to express her true feelings. Afterwards she tried to explain. 'The grief is always there, and always just as strong. But it only appears on occasion now, unlike when we first lost her.'

'I know,' he said. 'It is the same for me, when I think of those I have lost.'

'Your parents?'

He nodded. 'And my uncle. I shall tell you of them, tomorrow. Grief lives in me, as it does in you. But we have one another now, and you will never be alone again, my love.'

'It is true. How lucky we are. Oh!' She pointed to the horizon. 'Look!'

All across the sky, the heavens were dancing. Purplish-red and green waves of light waltzed across the sky, as if Rose's mama wished to express her delight at their betrothal.

'What is it?' he breathed. 'I have never heard of anything so wondrous.'

'Mama used to call them the merry dancers,' Rose replied softly. 'They are usually easier to see in winter, not summer, so we are fortunate indeed to see them tonight.'

'And have scientists explained it?'

'They cannot. They speak of water vapour, and earth gases, and magnets, but they do not know for sure. Until they do, I shall continue to believe that when the northern lights shine, it means they are dancing in heaven.'

'If so, then tonight your mama is surely celebrating your betrothal.'

'And your parents and your uncle along with her perhaps?'

'I like that notion.'

They turned then, and walked on, Rose feeling close to Mama in a way she had not done for many years. How blessed she was, and how fortunate! And she was not even married yet!

Together with Rose and James, Mr Marnoch had decided a special licence was required, for they must be married before their return to London. No one wanted to wait the month it would have taken to write to Lady Ashbourne and the other Belles and invite them to Scotland.

And so, on a sunny morning in June, Miss Rosabella Hemera Lennox married James Arthur Henry Drummond, the Viscount Ashbourne, in the Holy Trinity chapel in the centre of Elgin. The Reverend Hugh Buchan conducted the ceremony, and the Viscount subsequently made a substantial donation to his church building programme. The silk gown worn by the bride was said to have been designed and made in London, and the townspeople fortunate enough to glimpse the wedding party all commented on how beautiful she was, and how handsome her aristocratic groom.

After the wedding breakfast, hosted by Mr Marnoch in his elegant home and attended by all the local gentry, along with the bride's former teachers and other Belvedere staff, including Agnes, who wept with joy throughout, as well as all of the older Belvedere girls, the Viscount and his new Viscountess withdrew to a private room with Mr Marnoch, where her former guardian handed Rose a package.

'It has been a privilege being your guardian, Rose. Never having married and with no children of my own, I worried about my ability to care for you all properly. But your mother was insistent, and so I agreed.' Taking out a handkerchief, he dabbed the corner of his eye. 'You and your sisters make me proud every day, and I hope your mother would not be too unhappy with my guardianship.' He nodded to the package in her hands. 'I believe I mentioned this before. I have been looking after it since your mother died. It was to be given to the first of you to leave my guardianship.'

Carefully, Rose opened the package, exchanging a quick glance with her husband.

My husband!

Disbelief warred with pure joy within her at the sight of his handsome face, his eyes alight with love for her. Sternly, she turned her gaze to the parcel in her hands. Reaching into the small parcel she felt a curious swirling sensation in her gut. Here might be more clues to her mama's identity.

'A letter! And something else...' Carefully, she opened the small wooden box. 'Earrings!'

'*Diamond* earrings,' James highlighted, taking one and holding it up to the light. 'And of substantial value, I'd wager.'

Rose was studying its twin. 'The cut is unusual…it has been made to look like a flower. Beautiful!'

'They are distinctive indeed,' Mr Marnoch offered. 'Perhaps even recognisable to someone who had seen them before.'

'After more than twenty years?' Rose shook her head. 'I should love to think so, but I doubt it very much.'

Handing the second earring to the Viscount, Rose broke the seal on the letter, a pang going through her on seeing her mama's beautiful flowing script. In a voice that trembled only a little, she began reading aloud.

'My darling daughters, if you are reading this then I am gone, and you are no longer children. Oh, how I wish I could know you as young ladies! Your father loved me very much, as I loved him. There were people who wished him harm, and so he sent me away for my own safety, for fear they would harm me too. I wish I could share with you my true name, and his, but I cannot assume you are safe, even now.

'My Belles,' she continued, 'my beautiful Belles. Annabelle Georgina. Isobel Judith. Rosabella Hemera. By these names you will be known.'

Rose paused, swallowing hard. *Mama.*

'Look after one another, and try to make the world a little better, as I too have tried. I hate to leave you now, but I know you are safe with Mr Marnoch—one of the kindest people I have ever known.

'Others have been kind to us too, like the Lady we lived with for the first five years of your lives. You may not remember her, but I do, and I can assure you she is as good-hearted and as generous a person as I have ever encountered. It was hard to leave that place of safety, that haven, that sanctuary, but the old danger had returned, and so I had no choice but to flee once again.

'Please thank Mr Marnoch on my behalf, for I know that what I have requested of him—taking on the guardianship of three children—is no little task. Despite all the evil, all the harm that has been done by wicked, wicked creatures, I know there are still good people in this world.

'I love you all, my wonderful girls. Be happy.
'Mama.'

Rose's voice faded to silence as emotions boiled within her. Thankfully James was there, his strong arm holding her and words of comfort strengthening her. Mr Marnoch too, was emotional, and needed to make use of his handkerchief again. In the midst of the happiest day of her life, Rose was almost overcome. Love, loss, memory, joy…all of it was here.

'She would be happy, my dear, to know you have married such a good man.' Mr Marnoch blew his nose. 'I know you miss her, today of all days, but I am certain she would be delighted for you.'

'And, my love, you will never be alone again,' James reminded her, squeezing her hand.

Rose nodded, her eyes shining with tears. 'She is dancing again today. I know it.'

'Now,' James declared in a brisk tone. 'I believe it is time for us to go, for we need to reach Edinburgh by evening.'

'Where will you stay?' asked Mr Marnoch.

'I have reserved a suite of rooms in Dumbreck's Hotel in St Andrew Square,' James informed him, and Mr Marnoch's eyes widened.

'Dumbreck's? Luxury indeed!'

Embracing Rose, then shaking James's hand, he bade them both a safe journey, and exhorted them to visit him as soon as they may. Twenty minutes later they set off in James's well-sprung carriage—the old one having already been dispatched—with Rose's trunks attached to the back. Alone for the first time as husband and wife, they kissed and kissed again, looking forward to the privacy of their suite.

A new life awaited, and Rose could not have been happier.

Chapter Twenty-Two

Three weeks later

'Well, and what do you mean by it? Marrying in Scotland, without so much as a by-your-leave?'

Rose's heart sank. Lady Kelgrove sounded cross. Extremely cross. Since their return to London yesterday, Rose and James had spent their time at home with Anna, Izzy, and Lady Ashbourne, all of whom had expressed their delight at their marriage. Lady Ashbourne in particular had been rueful about how matters had turned out.

'I was trying to do what was right,' she had confessed, 'even though in my heart I always wished for James to wed you.'

'I understand completely, my lady,' Rose had replied. 'I agreed with you, if you recall. I knew it was best for me to leave. But James had other ideas.'

'I certainly did,' he had affirmed.

It had been his notion to call upon Lady Kelgrove

first today, as he believed she might favourably influence some of the other leaders in society.

Perhaps that was a mistake, Rose thought now, looking at the elderly lady's frowning expression.

'Lady Kelgrove!' he declared, entirely ignoring her question. 'It is a delight to see you again. Are you well, my lady?'

She sniffed. 'As well as can be expected I suppose.' There was a pause then, with seeming reluctance, she echoed his enquiry.

'My wife and I are both well,' he replied, taking Rose's hand.

At this, she gave a bark of laughter. 'Incorrigible!' She sighed. 'Very well. Please be seated.' She waved a hand towards the settee to her right. 'Brooks, ring for tea please.'

'Yes, my lady.' The butler did so, and having sent the housemaid on her way he took up his post again, standing impassively to the right of the fireplace.

'I am told…' Lady Kelgrove remained stiff, 'that this was no elopement.'

'Indeed, no!' Rose found her voice. 'I left to visit my guardian in Scotland—'

James made a sound that was suspiciously like a snort. 'Yes, because my aunt told you to forget me!'

'And I agreed with her!' Turning to Lady Kelgrove, Rose decided to be direct. 'My lady, you must know I believed myself to be an unsuitable wife for J—for Lord Ashbourne, given the uncertainty about my—my family.'

'Nonsense!' James, as ever, was unequivocal.

'Of course it is nonsense!' Lady Kelgrove's tone matched the Viscount's. 'As I told you many weeks ago Rose, the Gunning sisters! Remember the Gunnings!'

'Then—you do not mind that Lord Ashbourne married me?'

'Not in the slightest! I mind only that I was not privy to your plans. You should have talked to me my dear, before running away. I would have instantly put such foolish notions out of your head.'

'I do suspect that others will not agree with you,' James replied wryly.

She banged her stick on the floor. 'Let 'em! What care I for the opinions of such people? I counsel you to develop a thick hide and ride it out. There will be some other scandal for them to exclaim at before long.'

The tea arrived then, and there was a pause in the conversation as the butler presented the tray, and Lady Kelgrove poured.

'Here you are, my dear,' she said, holding out a delicate cup and saucer to Rose. Relieved at the thawing in Lady Kelgrove's tone Rose went to take it, but strangely, the elderly lady did not let go. Instead she sat frozen, a stricken look upon her face.

'Lady Kelgrove?' Rose spoke softly, but Lady Kelgrove seemed not to hear. Exchanging a troubled glance with her husband, Rose gently placed her other hand on Lady Kelgrove's arm, taking the teacup and placing it on the side table beside the settee. Still Lady

Kelgrove said nothing, just stared at Rose as if in severe shock.

Is she unwell? Is this apoplexy?

Rose had never actually seen anyone experiencing a stroke, and so was unsure what to do. Thankfully the butler was approaching, his lined face creased with concern. 'My lady?' he asked softly. 'Are you unwell?'

At this her gaze snapped to him, and—thankfully—awareness had returned to her expression. 'Brooks, regard Lady Ashbourne's earrings.'

My earrings? Mama's earrings!

Rose caught her breath.

Does she recognise them?

Clearly puzzled, Brooks swivelled his gaze to Rose, and he blanched.

'Quite.' Lady Kelgrove's tone was clipped. 'Now explain to me, Brooks, how these earrings come to be worn by Lady Ashbourne, when you and my dear departed husband assured me many years ago that my granddaughter had been buried in them, on my husband's insistence?'

Her granddaughter? Maria Berkeley, who was said to have died of smallpox?

Rose's heart began to race. Beside her, James stiffened, then his hand reached out for Rose's.

Brooks visibly crumpled, if such a thing were possible. 'Oh, my lady!' He took a breath. 'I heartily apologise. Lord Kelgrove insisted. He said it was for the best.'

Lady Kelgrove, pale as paper, but with a grim determination in her expression, did not miss a single heartbeat. 'What was for the best? *What*, Brooks?'

'He said you would be heartbroken if you knew the truth. Told me to shut the house up because of the smallpox. All the staff were dismissed, and we put it about that Miss Maria had died. I bought a headstone and everything.'

'She did not die of smallpox.'

'No. No, my lady, she did not.'

'The truth?'

'She ran away. Lord Kelgrove threw her note in the fire, so I never knew what it said. "She is dead to me now." That was what he said. I am so sorry, my lady. He made me promise never to even hint of anything.'

'He could be quite the autocrat at times...' Lady Kelgrove's gaze turned to Rose. 'Where did you get the earrings?'

'My guardian had them in safekeeping until such time as one of us wed or left his guardianship. They belonged to Mama.'

'Maria Lennox.'

'Yes.' Rose fished in her reticule. 'There was also a letter.'

Taking it, Lady Kelgrove reached for her quizzing glass. 'Oh! It is her handwriting!' Her hand gripped the quizzing glass so tightly that the knuckles showed white. There was a tight silence as she read the letter and Rose allowed herself to understand that Mama had been Lady Kelgrove's granddaughter.

Which means—

'Well!' Lady Kelgrove's throat was working, but no further words emerged. 'Well.' She took a breath, exhaling through her teeth. 'It seems, my dear, that you do have a family after all. Me!'

'I—I do not know what to say. This does not seem real!'

'Oh, it is real, my dear. It is wonderfully real. Now come here!'

Lady Kelgrove opened her arms, and Rose gladly went to her.

My great-grandmother!

Their embrace finally released the emotion that had been building within them both, and both ladies had a little cry, while the men in the room respectfully pretended not to notice.

'She ran away,' Lady Kelgrove echoed, dabbing her eyes. 'But why? And what danger was she in?' She thought for a moment. 'The dates do not make sense.' She shook her head. 'She had you when she was about seven months along, I think you said? So she could not have been in the family way when she left. That would only have happened a month or two later, I think. Which means she did not run away because she was with child.' She pursed her lips. 'What was it, Maria? What was so terrible you could not even tell me of it?'

Rose was holding her breath. It all seemed too fantastical to be happening.

'We may never know,' said James softly. 'Today, though, you have found each other. And—if I may be so bold—may I suggest we send for my wife's sisters?'

'A capital suggestion! Brooks, can you—'

'With pleasure, my lady.'

'I have not forgiven you, Brooks. Indeed I may never forgive you.'

'Of course, my lady.'

'Now go and send a messenger to Grafton Street. I wish to see my other great-granddaughters! And tell Cook we shall have guests for dinner!'

And so they came, and James's aunt along with them, and together they spent a long happy evening, the first of many. Anna and Izzy were ecstatic that Mama's true identity had been discovered, while the dowager Lady Ashbourne kept exclaiming in wonder, then giggling at the notion of all the girls' detractors finding out they were of the Kelgrove line.

Later, much later, Rose lay in her husband's arms in their large and comfortable bed in Ashbourne House. Having succumbed twice already to mutual passion, Rose was now in a state of delightful stupor. James was on his side, gazing at his wife in the candlelight, and her eyes roved his magnificent form. 'So…' she murmured.

His fingers trailed down her arm, from shoulder to hand, and their fingers entwined. A rush of love went through her, like warm sunshine rippling through a meadow.

'So…?' he prompted, and for a moment she could not remember what she had intended to say.

It came to her then. 'It seems I may turn out to be a suitable viscountess after all.'

'Oh,' he teased, 'I am not so certain. There is still nothing to suggest that Maria was ever married.'

'Save her surname!' Rose retorted, stung on Mama's behalf. 'Lennox was not her family name. Maria's birth name was Berkeley.'

'Of course,' he replied, now serious. 'I only meant to tease you. But there is something you must remember.'

'And what is that?' Lifting a hand, she traced his beloved face. His nose, cheekbone, jaw…

'That you were always destined to be my viscountess. And that we married *before* your mother's true name was known.'

'We did. I will be eternally grateful to know you risked your reputation for me.'

'Pah! Reputation! No one in their right mind could ever care too much for reputation!' He smiled, reminding her of a time, a long time ago, when he had been of the opposite opinion.

'Indeed? Then if the Thaxbys sneer at me—'

He growled deep in his throat. 'Let them dare!' he muttered, bending his head to kiss her.

* * * * *

COMING SOON!

We really hope you enjoyed reading this book. If you're looking for more romance be sure to head to the shops when new books are available on

Thursday 23rd November

To see which titles are coming soon, please visit
millsandboon.co.uk/nextmonth

MILLS & BOON

MILLS & BOON®

Coming next month

MISS ROSE AND THE VEXING VISCOUNT
Catherine Tinley

'You really ought not to be falling asleep with a candle alight, Miss Lennox. Particularly—' he gestured at the floor-to-ceiling bookshelves '—in a library.'

Rubbing a hand over her face, she shook her head. There was a silence, as James found himself rooted to the spot. She, adorably bemused. He, hoping his own bewilderment was not evident in his expression.

Lord, she is like a goddess!

Their eyes met, and instantly the atmosphere was charged with possibility—as tense as the air before a thunderstorm. The urge to kiss her was almost overwhelming... There was puzzlement in her gaze, as well as—Lord save him—desire. She desired him!

But no. She had likely never even been kissed, and might have no notion what she was feeling. Focusing on her clear confusion, he reminded himself sternly that she was his aunt's guest, and he the master of the house.

I am a viscount, not some green boy free to dally with a chambermaid.

And she was no courtesan or merry widow, but a young lady of quality.

Breaking her gaze, he brushed an imaginary speck from his right sleeve, then pretended to stifle a yawn.

'It is late. I was surprised to see a light in here.'

...something like relief, he was conscious of disappointment.

...se. I apologise, my lord.'

...d, then briefly, daringly, he allowed his gaze to sweep ...e over her form, delightfully hinted at through the thin ... As he watched, transfixed, she tied the belt on her sheer ...gnoir—a garment trimmed, he noted, in rosebud pink.

'I could not sleep, you see,' she continued, 'and so I came downstairs to choose a book…' Confusion briefly flashed across her face and she looked about, bending to pick the book up from the floor.

'Oh, dear! I do hope I have not damaged it!'

Rising, she inspected the small tome, turning towards the candle on the table to see better. Unfortunately, this gave him an unhindered view of her delectable rear, glorious golden curls cascading down her back, her shapely legs outlined through two layers of thin, candlelit fabric. Stifling a groan, he turned away. 'I shall bid you goodnight, Miss Lennox,' he threw the comment over his shoulder as he made for the door. 'Do try not to burn my house down, I beseech you.'

On that note he left the room, marching briskly to the staircase that would take him to the sanctuary of his own chamber. Lord, he had expected his quiet life to be disturbed by his aunt's debutantes. Just—never had he expected the disturbance to be quite so…personal.

Continue reading
MISS ROSE AND THE VEXING VISCOUNT
Catherine Tinley

Available next month
www.millsandboon.co.uk